THE DOMINO CHILDREN

ESMAE SHEPARD

Contents

I dedicate this book to everyone who sees it. You see me. I see you, in turn.

PROLOGUE

CORONATION SPEECH WRITTEN FOR THE WOLF QUEEN: STATE OF AFFAIRS AND PLANS FOR THE COUNTRY

I AM ADDRESSING YOU all today due to a tragedy that struck those dearest to me, so forgive me if I am less composed than I should be. As the world knows, my husband, Viktor Astran and the crown prince of Shka, and his parents, the king and queen of Shka, were killed by bandits when their carriage driver drove them down the wrong path. My advisors are dedicating every resource to finding out what caused this unspeakable tragedy. I cannot emphasize how well and truly devastated I am.

But we, as a country, as a people, and as leaders, cannot allow our devastation to detract from what needs to be done. We must continue going about our lives. We must continue to be productive, as people, and as a country. I am no exception to this rule. First and foremost, in my new standing as your queen, I would like to address a few things.

As many of you know, there were royal advisors of the Astrans who believed I should not be queen. They vied for the position of leader. They were so blinded by hunger for power that they dared to challenge the very laws that *govern our fine country. It is common knowledge that I was born a commoner. I was brought to the royal court at thirteen to paint portraits of the royal family. I was taken directly from the streets of Rowak, the city of crime, and handed a new life on a silver platter. Viktor, against his parents' wishes, married me. Though at first the king and queen didn't agree with the choice, they quickly grew to appreciate Viktor's decision, as I had a talent for all things politics and policies. I was taken under the queen's wing and became like a daughter to her, and she like a mother to me.*

There are those who say I did not earn my right to be queen. That I simply married well and got lucky. Let them spread their rumors, but in truth I have worked incredibly hard behind the scenes in order to acquire the knowledge it takes to run a country. And now, I will be doing it alone. It is a fact I can hardly bear to face, but I will face it. I will face every issue head on and tackle every problem with my full attention. I will not waver in my responsibilities as your queen.

Which brings me to my next point. There have been concerns about foreign affairs, the economy, and rising crime rates in our nation. I will address these problems, and implement solutions to solving them. Shka has been slipping in terms of world power. I intend to stop that.

Shka will prove its might to the world. We shall not be meek any longer. I intend to defend Shka's presence in Omari. Omari has long since been a country with good foreign relations with Shka, and after my predecessor made them a colony, we have maintained a mutually beneficial relationship in terms of economy. However, Omari has recently been fighting for independence from our arrangement; many rebels have been attacking the soldiers and diplomats stationed there. Rest assured, I will stamp this out.

I intend to make Sunan a colony as well. I do not wish for a war, but I will resort to that if I must. Sunan and Shka can assist each other with the trade and natural resources of each country. Sunan has been a threat for a while, and they are an economic powerhouse. There has even been talk of strengthening their meager military. They are governed primarily by their own citizens, who know nothing of running a country. Shka's support will allow Sunan to prosper like never before.

I have also begun to improve foreign trade with several other countries, such as Duskra. Duskra has agreed to a free trade agreement, which is being drawn up now. In recent meetings, Talir has refused to cooperate, but I am sure that they will see reason soon enough. We will continue our shaky trading with Taahua. Although the Taahuan ambassadors have been unresponsive, I will not let trade relations between our two nations fall.

As far as crime rates go, I have employed personal attendants of mine at every major police station in large cities. The police have been authorized to use deadly force when necessary for several years now, but tightening security even more will ultimately lead to a decrease in crime rates.

I know that Shka is a good country, filled with good people. However, I want Shka to be a great country, filled with great people, and for that, you need a great leader. I am that leader. I will continue to be that leader. I swear my full love and attention to this country: I shall never again marry. I am sacredly bound by my dedication to this position and Shka itself. As your queen and as a fellow citizen, I will never fail you. While I am only seventeen years old, I am wise beyond my years, and this *country is my top priority. I have bled for this country, I have cried for this country, and, when the time comes, I will die for this country.*

As you all know, it is customary to have a new crown fashioned from the crown jewels of the previous one. The previous crown is buried with the ruler it belonged to. I have begun construction on my crown, and I would like to share with you all my reasoning behind it.

I have decided to make a wolf skull out of metal that will cover the top half of my face. The jewels will be set in various places along the crown, but that is not what is important. I have chosen a wolf skull because I am your wolf. Wolves are pack animals. They are vicious creatures, but they are loyal to their very core. They are ruthless fighters, but loving caretakers. I will be that for my people. I will be strong, fearless, and loyal.

I ask that I be addressed as the Wolf Queen from here on out. I am not Atina Parev. Forget you ever heard that name. I am your Wolf Queen, only and forever. Many rulers in the past have had monikers such as this. I have assumed a new identity as your ruler, and the country comes first, before myself. The girl I was is no longer.

And lastly, I would like to end on a hopeful note. I love this country. I love the people of this country. And I know, in my heart, that the people of this country will love me. I will become the ruler you all need. I will lead by following the examples set by you all. The everyday citizen has so much heart and strength, and I will emulate this in my ruling. You have all inspired me, and now, it is my turn to inspire you. You can be great, and you will aspire to greatness. Hard work will help you climb any mountain. Perseverance will let you cross any border. So, my dear citizens, I implore you, be the wolves I know you are. Be strong, and cunning, and caring. Fight relentlessly for what you believe in, and care tenderly for what you love.

Be the great people I know you are. Be the fighters I know you can be. And, together, we will get through this together, and come out the other side better for it. My citizens, I am loyal to you, so please, in turn, be loyal to me.

Thank you very much for your time and attention. I will serve you with the dedication you all deserve.

PART ONE: WICKED AND WRETCHED

CHAPTER ONE

SALEM

SALEM RATTLES NAMES OFF under her breath as she waits. She lists them again and again. It's pointless, really; they're already burned into her mind. These are the names that will save her. She wouldn't dare forget them.

Today is the day she leaves. Today is the day she snuffs out fire with ice.

Salem has been gathering intel from the queen's army as a loyal soldier for four years. Today, she will be free.

No. She will set herself free. She learned long ago that one has to fashion their own freedom. It is not a thing that can be handed to them.

She has never been more ready for anything in her life. She would shudder with anticipation, if not for the weight on her mind for all the people she is about to kill.

She knows it will be worth it. It is either her, or them.

Footsteps ring in her ears, and then she hears thoughts, which she quickly shuts out. Slinging her bag over her shoulder, Salem lets all the weight drag her back to earth. She lets herself breathe in the finality of this. This first and last step she is about to take.

A man steps into her assigned army barrack. Salem does not know him, and she does not care. She knows why he's here; she made sure to spread the rumor of her rebellion weeks ago. Now, he's come to investigate.

"A coup? Really, *dog*? You think you can pull it off?" he snarls at her, taking in her backpack and twin daggers. He draws his sword.

"I really do." She doesn't move. She's an excellent chess player, and she plays for black.

Let him move first, she reminds herself and allows his thoughts to flood into her mind.

It's chaos, but Salem sorts through thoughts until she has what she needs.

He lunges. She sidesteps. He swings. She ducks.

This dance continues for roughly a minute. *Enough*, Salem thinks, *don't make his death more difficult.* She knocks his sword easily out of his hand with the flat of her blade. He steps back and draws a revolver. When it fires, she's already out of the way.

She steps into his reach and delivers a swift blow to his neck with her dagger's hilt. He crumples to the ground and scrambles for his sword. Salem has already picked it up, and she stabs it through his hand and into the floor.

For a fleeting moment, she can hear his pain reverberate through her own thoughts.

He tries to move his impaled hand but fails. He attempts to knock her off her feet with his free hand, but she grinds her boot into his forearm before he gets the chance.

Salem hears his fear.

And then he speaks. "Please! Please. I have a family! I —"

He's cut off by a dagger plunging into his neck with a horrible noise. She's far too inured to killing.

Memories flash through Salem's skull, and they are her own. A screaming infant, smoldering flesh, pleas and cries and locked doors.

Fire and death and *end* all around.

Rage, so visceral she can taste it, rises in her throat. Her anger numbs her mind and turns her blood to ice. Her eyes narrow as she drags her dagger out of the stranger's neck.

"So did I," she replies, calmly: frigid, like frost.

Salem knows, by now, that to quench the fire she must burn like ice. Hot to the touch and frozen to her core.

She burns through the army barracks and the palace courtyard and out the gates into the forest. She freezes the life around her, until she has freed herself from the place that has been her prison for four years. In her wake there is nothing.

A rippling white banner of a silver wolf hangs in front of the courtyard. She had been in the queen's personal army. One of the best of the best, stationed at the palace itself. The one who wiped out over three-fourths of the queen's personally selected forces.

Salem bites back a smile at the thought. She was chosen by the queen herself. Atina chose her undoing. She wove her fate with the threads of her own future. This is just the finishing knot, the pattern of needlework to make things whole.

And now, Salem's leaving. It is up to her to decide the manner in which she will conclude Atina Parev's tale.

Looking up at the banner, she dips a finger in the blood of one of her victims, and writes her message in brilliant red for all the nobles to see.

NOT A COUP
A REVOLUTION.
She doesn't look back.

♣

It's winter in Shka. But it's nearly always winter in Shka. Luckily, Salem brought warm clothes, and the walk to Rowak is a mere two days. She sets up camp when night falls, using meager tinder and flint to light a small fire that she stays too far away from to reap any benefits.

She falls asleep in the cold, and forgets her dreams when she wakes. The cold is bitter as she packs up her camp and then moves on her way, kicking snow over the ash from the night before.

Having traveled half the distance to Rowak, she's so utterly lost in thought that she doesn't notice the dog sled approaching until it sprays snow into her face.

"Need a ride?" comes a taunting voice from behind.

Salem ducks her head and keeps walking.

The girl driving the dog sled thinks: *Doesn't this kid have any manners?* before Salem manages to tune her out.

"Hey! I asked you a question!"

"And I didn't respond. I thought that was obvious."

The girl drives the dogs forward until she's right beside Salem, who tugs her hood further over her face and makes sure her scarf is pulled up. Salem doesn't bother glancing over. "A snarky one, are you? No one in Rowak matches me for wit. Maybe I should rescind my ride offer. Don't want competition, after all."

For a moment, Salem wonders how she figured out her destination—and then remembers that Rowak is the only end to this road, unless one were to head back towards Maciek.

Salem keeps walking.

"Tell you what, if you can beat me in a fight, I'll drive you to any destination in Rowak. Free of charge."

Salem falters for a moment, pausing in her tracks, still not looking back at the girl. "That's an interesting wager."

"Let's call it my own personal code."

"So do you challenge all your potential customers to duels?"

"Only the interesting ones."

A smile creeps under her scarf. This should be *interesting* indeed.

"Okay." Salem turns around to face the girl, examining her opponent, who is removing the thick clothing she's wearing in preparation for the fight.

She has dark brown skin, tightly coiled brown hair that turns blood red halfway through, and light brown eyes that seem to be dancing. She's taller than Salem, by a lot.

The most eye-catching thing, however, is the thin scar that goes from her cheek to her jugular.

"Fascinating scar, right?" She grins playfully.

Tugging off her own hood with one hand and scarf with the other, Salem leaves her full face on display.

She can see the girl take a mental step backwards. People generally do.

The entire right side of Salem's face is marred by burn scars. Her right eye, naturally black, is burned and blind, leaving it mottled and white. Her right ear is practically melted off. The right side absorbed the brunt of the damage. Half of her body is ragged with the burns. The other half, while scarred, is still recognizable as skin.

"I think I got you beat," Salem says coolly.

The girl whistles appreciatively. "What'd you do? Get into a bar fight with a forest fire?"

"House fire, actually." The girl winces guiltily. Salem doesn't really care about the careless remarks, she's used to them. "You should see the other guy."

The girl laughs warmly at her joke. "I'll bet."

Unsheathing the matching daggers from their place on either side of her hips, Salem twirls them around her fingers, showing off for some unfathomable reason. "What are the rules?"

"Whoever's on the ground first loses."

Salem's lip twitches as she forces down the words *should be easy enough.* If the girl backs out, there's no ride.

Waving the dogs off to the side, the girl removes her thick parka, and pulls a long wooden pole from her back.

"Where's your accent from?"

"Taahua." And then the girl lunges, twisting the pole so that a blade flicks out from either end, swiping one end towards Salem's feet. Already springing backwards, snow sprays from where Salem was just standing.

She's fast. The girl charges at her again, spinning the pole around and slicing towards Salem's midriff, but she steps out of the way with ease.

Blinking, shocked, the girl brings the pole down in an arc towards her shoulder. She rolls neatly into reach and away from the impact, but the girl takes a hold of the staff with both hands and shoves it like a bar towards Salem, who blocks it with one dagger and tucks the other one on the other side.

Salem grips the staff tightly with her daggers and twists it abruptly, so that the girl has no choice but to drop it. Immediately, Salem steps closer and punches the girl lightly in the stomach, and then kicks her shin for good measure.

She falls to the snow. Salem reaches down, offers her a hand and pulls her up. She brushes the snow off her legs. There's a moment before laughing starts: loud and bold.

"What the hell just happened?" Her voice is incredulous. Her eyes are bright.

"So how about that ride?"

⚑

The girl blinks, startled when Salem says she wants to go to the Poisoned Drink, but takes her there anyway.

The Poisoned Drink has a battered and beaten outside, but its interior is decorated nicely and the atmosphere is pleasant, despite the multiple illegal activities that are undoubtedly taking place.

As Salem steps inside, she expects the girl to leave, but she just follows her in. "I have some business to attend to," she explains. Salem shrugs and makes a beeline for the elderly bartender.

This bar is supposedly owned by Kioh Taa, who Salem needs to speak to. She's allegedly the best thief in Rowak - good enough to have a devoted following of fellow swindlers.

Most of the gangs in Rowak deal in violent, bloody affairs. Kioh Taa has more money than all of them, and has built her empire silently.

The thing Salem knows, that others don't, is that Kioh is more than she seems.

She shuffles up to the bar and glances around while she waits for the bartender. She finally comes over with a glass and asks, "What can I get for you?"

"I'm looking for Kioh Taa."

The woman gives her a quizzical look, and then laughs heartily.

"Kioh!" she calls to someone behind Salem. "You really ought to start introducing yourself."

"She's here?" Salem asks.

The old woman laughs again. "You walked in with her, kid." She stalks off towards someone who is waving her down, just as Salem whirls around and grabs Kioh's staff mid-swing. This time its blades aren't out.

"How do you *do* that?" Kioh asks, awed.

"I have very good reaction time," she lies, voice flat.

Kioh arches an eyebrow, not quite believing her response. "What business do you have with me?"

"I have a job offer."

"I'm assuming it's of an illicit kind."

Salem's lip twitches, barely. "Why would you assume that?"

"One doesn't come to the number one crime lord in the so-called 'city of crime' unless one wants to commit crimes."

Salem tries to suppress a smile but it's difficult. More difficult than it should be. "I suppose you're correct."

Kioh laughs. "Sorry, but my answer is no."

"I haven't even told you how much money you'll be getting."

She grins sympathetically, seeming sorry that she's denying the request. "Answer's still no."

Salem tilts her head as her own expression goes frigid. "I haven't even blackmailed you yet."

The smiling face across from her drops. "Now what sort of dirt could you have on *me*?" Kioh asks, looking down her nose at Salem.

"You have a *very* big secret, Miss Taa. A secret I think you'd prefer me to keep."

Salem can tell that she's nervous now, however, Kioh retains her composure. "What's your name?" Kioh asks.

"You don't need to know that."

"If we're working together I'd like to know your name."

"I'll tell you if you agree."

"This is me agreeing," she bites, her calm and friendly personality fraying from Salem's words.

"My name is Salem Oto." She lets her shoulders relax and her glare die down. "And we're going to rob and kill the queen of Shka."

Kioh takes Salem to her quarters above the bar so the two can talk privately.

The ceilings are high and lofty, with wide windows mostly covered by burlap stapled to the edges. All the furniture and decorations are lavish, but the apartment itself is simple: a neatly made bed shoved into the corner of the room. The apartment is sparse, with the exception of the cluttered kitchen. It surprises Salem, she expected one of the richest gang bosses in Rowak to have a bit more to show for it. However, with the exception of some truly splendid paintings (likely stolen), and the luxurious decorations; it's extremely plain.

Kioh sits down on a plush white sofa with red pillows, and gestures for Salem to take one of the red cushioned chairs across from it. She notices the chess board sitting on the dark, glass-top table.

"You play?"

"A little." Her eyes tell Salem it's more than a little. "Would you like a game?"

"Sure."

She straightens her back and slides a drawer out from the side of the board, and begins placing chess pieces on their respective squares. "Do you want white?"

Salem shakes her head. "I always play black."

She snorts. "Of course you do," she mutters. Salem scoffs at her jab, and begins sifting through Kioh's thoughts as she moves her first piece.

Immediately, Salem makes her move as soon as Kioh's hand is off her pawn and she looks at Salem, startled. "I play fast," Salem says with a wolfish smirk.

She moves again. "So do I."

Within ten moves Salem has Kioh beat. She's surprised she held out for so long. Salem leans back in her chair once the game is done, "Now, then, to business?"

Kioh glares, as though hoping to smite her with a look. "You're good at just about everything, aren't you?"

"I think you'd probably have me beat on the swimming front," Salem says, and Kioh's mouth parts in shock.

Faster than any other opponent Salem's ever faced, Kioh's blade is pointed at her. Without even sitting up, Salem knocks it aside with the flat of her dagger. "Don't play with me," she snarls up at Kioh.

"Who *are* you?" Her rage crackles quietly around her like the flames Salem so despises.

She shoots a glare up at Kioh. "I am a deserter of the queen's army. I am currently one of the most wanted people in the country. I am the child of Xian and Zhengli Aotuo, renamed Oto. I am a skilled fighter and chess player, as you know. I am a criminal of many facets. I am many things, all of which you do *not* want to trifle with."

Kioh rolls her eyes and sets her staff aside. "Got it, no fighting. Don't be dramatic. Allow me to rephrase. Where did you come from? I'd say Zhidi, but you don't have the accent."

"Omari. My parents were from Zhidi. I walked from the queen's castle up north to where you found me in the forest."

It takes a moment, but her eyes widen in realization. "Wait a minute. *You* were the one who killed all those soldiers? You're who the Wolf Queen is paying that massive bounty for?"

"Don't call her that. Her name is Atina Parev and I suggest you treat her more like a dog than a wolf, at least in my presence."

Kioh raises her hands in mock surrender. "Got it. You and the queen are on bad terms. How do you know her *name*? She buried it years ago."

"I do my research. Any other questions?"

"I mean, many, but I don't think you'd answer them. So really, just one." She looks down from where she's standing, and Salem looks up at her expectantly. "When do we start?"

CHAPTER TWO

KIOH

THIS GIRL MUST BE *insane*, Kioh thinks. However, she still agrees. Salem's eyes glint and she sheathes her dagger, which she somehow had out before Kioh even pointed her staff at her. "Today."

Salem opens her pack and takes out a bundle of tied papers, filled with rapid, scratchy handwriting. She unties the string holding them together, and begins spreading them out across Kioh's small table. There's four wanted posters in the bundle, two of them with portraits. Kioh scans them for the names.

RIOZ TAMEN: *wanted for the murder of the nobleman Jance Way. Reward: 6000 metlins.*

The girl in the picture has dark, straight hair cropped around the middle of her ears. She also has blunt, choppy bangs that frame her pointy face and brown eyes. Her skin is smooth and bronze, and her face filled with various piercings; she must be Talirian.

KIOH TAA: *wanted for petty theft, grand theft, grifting, blackmailing, pickpocketing, and various other crimes. Reward: 3000 metlins.*

There is no picture of Kioh. She feels a sense of pride at that. Although she's definitely worth more than three-thousand *metlins*.

JAZ WESTFEN: *wanted for murder. Reward:* 700 *metlins.*

The boy in this picture has wild black hair and ice blue, nearly white eyes. His face is gaunt and thin. The artist really captured the *murderous* look.

The fourth wanted poster has no picture either, and is written in a language Kioh can't read. The reward number is small, but then she realizes it's in *haics.* Haics are the currency for Sunan, and she's traded in them before. She does a quick calculation, and quickly realizes the bounty on this person is *enormous.*

Kioh turns to Salem, incredulous. "Twenty *thousand metlins?*"

She nods. "Kabet Oreh is a wanted insurgent in the country. Besides, it's not like Sunan can't afford it."

"How are you getting all these people here?"

Her lips twitch, almost indiscernible. Kioh is quickly realizing that's akin to a grin for her. "Mister Oreh is on a ship here right now. He'll arrive in three hours. The Tamen family lives approximately twenty miles from here. Jaz Westfen is a tad out of the way. And, well, I already found you."

Kioh nods, absorbing the information quickly. "I can take you twenty miles in about two hours."

"Rioz Tamen it is, then."

❦

Kioh is delighted to find that Salem enjoys speeding as much as she does, and her dogs spend the two hours running at a wild pace while she cheers and shouts into the wind.

Salem, of course, sits impassive and expressionless, but Kioh sees her eyes glint with something like joy when her sled rattles around a sharp corner at breakneck pace.

"Turn here," Salem directs Kioh as she glances at a hand drawn map from her stack of papers. Kioh snaps the reins hard, making her dogs swerve and snow spray from the back of her sled. Her cargo (including Salem) leans, before falling back into place.

They continue on with only the wind as conversation for a while longer. *Man, she sure doesn't talk much,* Kioh thinks as the silence starts to choke. As she glances backwards at Salem, she finds she's already glaring at her.

She rolls her eyes. "We officially met about an hour ago. Forgive me if I'm not *chatty.*"

Vaguely, Kioh wonders how she knew what she was thinking about, but dismisses this and turns her eyes back to the road ahead of her. "You're the one who had extensive documents about me. I'm pretty sure I saw copies of my birth papers in that stack. If anyone is overly friendly it's *you.*"

Salem makes a noise of stifled anger, but says nothing. There's another awful, stretching silence. *That conversation accomplished nothing,* Kioh thinks bitterly.

"Oh," Salem says suddenly.

"What?"

"We're here."

Kioh guides her dogs to a stop and then hops off the sled to look over Salem's shoulder at the map. Salem shoots her an unimpressed look, and passes it to her.

"Looks like we've got another three miles."

"No," her voice is quiet. "We're here." She stands up and walks straight to the left. Kioh scoffs at her chilly demeanor, then follows after.

After about two minutes of walking seemingly aimlessly after her, they reach a clearing with a house. Kioh's surprised by the accuracy of Salem's guess.

"So... do we go up?"

She thinks for a minute. "No. She's not in there."

"How the hell do you know?" Kioh is starting to get tired of her cryptic words.

Salem sighs, as though she's annoyed with her stupidity. "Trust me, she's not in there."

Kioh's biting back a sharp retort when, suddenly, she feels something warm trickling down her neck and jaw. No later than this realization, Salem reaches out and touches her ear. When Salem's fingers pull away, they're coated in blood.

Her eyes focus and her body language grows even colder. She stands there for a few seconds, intently staring off into the distance.

"She's that way," Salem says quickly, pointing in the direction of Kioh's sled, then takes off running.

Without even thinking, Kioh runs off after her.

There's a pounding in her head now, and she can feel blood flowing from her other ear, as well as her nose. It hurts, but not as bad as certain pains that she's felt in her life of crime. So, she keeps running.

The two of them run past Kioh's sled, and Salem bolts into the trees, leaping over fallen logs and debris like a deer. They reach a creek, and she jumps nimbly over it, tackling an unsuspecting figure with ease. She's mid-scream when Salem begins to grapple with her.

"GIVE HIM BACK," the figure screams. Salem flies backwards, far too quickly and with far too much force to have been shoved. She leaps forward again, silently, with daggers drawn. The girl whirls and screams, and Kioh's stomach lurches painfully as soon as she does. Salem drops her daggers and falls to the ground.

Kioh can feel herself starting to die. It's unfamiliar in the sense that little pain is accompanying it, but familiar in the sense that she's felt it before. She grits her teeth and decides to deal with the consequences later, as she's always done.

Water erupts from the creek and starts to drown the figure. As she falls Kioh recognizes her face, and it takes her a moment to realize this is Rioz Tamen, from the wanted poster. She opens her mouth in a silent scream as Kioh forces water to fill her lungs.

Salem jumps up and snatches her daggers from the ground, before nodding at Kioh. She releases Rioz and draws her staff.

Rioz's eyes flit between Kioh and Salem, she keeps them trained on the weapons. "I will *kill* you."

"We didn't take him," Kioh says, remembering her words from earlier.

"I don't know that, now do I?"

"Bran." Salem blurts out. "Bran Fehner. We didn't take him."

"Then how do you know his *name*?" Rioz snarls.

Kioh's mind races. "Because we know where he is!" she exclaims, desperately trying to keep herself from dying.

"No we don't." Salem says. Kioh glares at her. *What the hell are you doing?* She continues talking. "We don't know where he is, but you do. He left you a note, didn't he? He went to find his parents."

Rioz tenses. "You wouldn't know that unless you wrote the note!" she shouts and Kioh feels that horrible sense of dying again.

"Think of a number between one and ten." Salem says, pained and panicked.

A confused look crosses Rioz's face, and Salem looks as though she's in immeasurable pain, but says: "Seven." She coughs thickly. "Between one and twelve. Three."

Her breath rattles on the inhale, and Kioh realizes that Rioz is growling. "Now think of any number. Ninety-seven. Any number. Thirty-six."

"How are you doing that?" Rioz bites viciously, lunging towards Salem, but Salem is already out of the way. She's clutching her stomach and stumbling, but out of the way nonetheless.

"I'm a mind reader."

Rioz's eyes widen, and Kioh thinks that if she were in less pain, hers would as well. "Impossible."

And Salem actually laughs. Kioh sees a look of determination cross her face, and she straightens, standing to her full, unimposing height. Pain flares on her face, but her eyes crackle with a cold fury. She draws her daggers. "You can die here, with my knife in your throat, or you can die later, with me as your ally. Choose carefully."

Rioz glances between the two of them, and then she opens her mouth.

Kioh lets water rise behind them and snow melts to join her horde. She twists her hand and a wave crashes over Rioz and she slams to the ground. Salem pounces on top of her. One knife slides into the ground by her hand and the other gets pressed against her throat. Rioz opens her mouth and Salem lets go of the dagger in the ground and covers her mouth.

"I said, choose carefully." Salem moves her hand away.

Rioz is silent for a long moment, eyes focused and fierce. "You cannot have something without giving in return."

"I never said I wasn't giving."

"What will you give me? What will I give you? You cannot make baseless propositions."

Salem considers for a moment. She then stands up and turns to Kioh. "Do you know how much the queen of Shka is said to have in her personal vault?"

She doesn't even need to think. "Of course. Twelve million *metlins*."

Rioz sits up and her eyes widen. She winces from her pummeling as she does so. She doesn't stand. "Twelve million *metlins* between the three of us?"

"More than twelve. Between five." Salem amends. "And you will be free from your crimes and protected by me for the rest of your life."

"How does this work?"

"We head back to Rowak, for one. I will share what information you need with you along the journey. First, you have to agree."

Rioz considers this for a moment before standing up. "It's a two hour ride back to Rowak. I expect everything explained by then, or I will not help you. And I have two conditions."

"Tell me."

"You help me find Bran. And he stays with us."

Salem considers. "Done," she says, after a beat.

Rioz nods. "You have my interest. Lead the way."

Chapter Three

BRAN

△

BRAN IS UTTERLY, HOPELESSLY lost. His wallet was stolen about two hours ago. The ports of Rowak seem like they were made confusing on purpose, and now he doesn't have money. At this point he's considering going back home. The only thing deterring him is that he would not be able to look the Tamens in the eyes.

I know I took the kindness you offered me, and shoved it right back in your face, but would you mind housing and feeding me while I work out a new strategy to find my real parents?

Not to mention Rioz would beat him senseless for making her worry.

Someone bumps into him, and briefly he wonders what other valuables he has that could be stolen, already resigned to his fate. He then realizes that the person who bumped into him is speaking in a foreign language.

"What's that? I can't understand you."

The person frowns. "What is your name?"

A strange question, from a foreign stranger, but the Tamens taught Bran to be polite. "Bran Fehner. And yours?"

"Kabet Oreh." He pauses, face twisting in concentration. "Can you show me to The Poisoned

Drink?"

Bran should probably go home, anyway, and it's on the way. Sighing, he says, "Yeah, come with me." He gestures for Kabet to follow, and the two of them start off towards the famous bar.

"So what brings you to Shka?" He doesn't recognize Kabet's accent, but after all he *has* lived in a secluded home in the woods for most of his life.

"Umm... I received a letter." Kabet takes out a piece of paper and hands it to him. Bran briefly skims over it, but he hasn't slept in almost a day, so the words blur together and lose meaning. Kabet almost seems to recognize this and says. "I am... excuse me, it is easier in my home language. I am a rebel leader in Sunan. This person with the letter promises to help me with my efforts. They will give me money if I help them with my abilities."

"What abilities?"

He considers for a moment. "Do you have something you do not mind parting with?"

Bran feels around in his coat pockets before grasping the paper with his parents' names on it. He has them memorized, so he passes it to Kabet.

Kabet holds the paper in the palm of his hand, and Bran watches as it shifts before his eyes into a crinkled yellow rabbit. He then folds his hand around it, and closes his eyes, and when he opens it, the rabbit moves of its own accord.

Bran nearly crushes the creature as he shoves Kabet's hands towards his chest, and whispers, "Maybe don't do that for other people."

Kabet waves his hands dismissively. "It matters not. I am wanted in every country, they all know what I do."

"Why are you out in the *open*?" Bran hisses, pulling him towards the shadowed part of the street.

He gives Bran a wicked grin that resonates in every language. "They would have to catch me."

Bran is starting to realize that Kabet's somber tone is coincidental to his accent. He's starting to realize that this boy is everything he's not: proud, reckless, and unafraid.

Rolling his eyes and deciding not to focus on his own issues too much, he grabs Kabet's hand and drags him towards The Poisoned Drink.

Δ

They arrive at their destination, and the tables have been pushed to the sides, making a sort of arena. There's a scarred Zhidish girl and a hulking man circling each other in the center. People are slapping down money and placing bets, and all of the *metlins* are swiftly passed down a chain of command to a dark girl with red hair that's too bright to be natural.

Kabet watches, enraptured. He turns to Bran with a wide smile. "I enjoy this place," he says.

"Of course you do," Bran mutters bitterly as another figure jostles him as they pass by.

An elderly bartender whistles from somewhere in the crowd, and the huge man lunges after the tiny girl.

Bran turns his head, not quite willing to witness a murder today. However, the Zhidish girl does not go down. She sidesteps, and the man's arms crash over empty air. He swings a meaty fist towards her, and she takes the punch, but he sees her tense seconds beforehand.

Bran's sparred with Rioz enough to know when someone is letting someone land hits.

"*Don't give me pity points!*" He would always yell, and Rioz would always laugh.

He misses her dearly, but he refocuses on the fight.

The girl allows her opponent to land a few more hits, feigning pain. Each time, Bran sees her brace before the blow lands.

He notices she keeps glancing to the left, and he follows her eyes to where the red haired girl is standing. She makes a sudden hand signal, and the shift in the fight is almost palpable.

The Zhidish girl swings out, *fast*. Her hand makes an audible crack as it connects with the side of the man's face. As he stumbles back, she swings her leg up in a way that should be impossible, driving her boot straight into his chin. He cries out, and as his mouth opens Bran sees something tumble out.

Teeth, he realizes with a shudder.

Kabet is delighted beside him. "Holy shit!" he exclaims, with his formal, scholarly accent. He reminds Bran of Rioz, a bit.

He blinks and the man is on the ground. He attempts to stand back up, but she stamps on his knee and Bran hears a crack resonate through the bar.

The red haired girl coughs, and Bran sees her mouth something to the fighter.

Tone it down.

He almost laughs as he watches the team rake in the money as disgruntled patrons demand a rematch. He wonders how quickly this bar would devolve into chaos if they knew how they were being cheated.

"Hello," Kabet stops a passerby as Bran's mind drifts aimlessly. "Do you know where Kioh Taa... resides?"

"Who's asking?"

That voice snaps Bran back to earth, and he whips his head around to see his sister standing there, bemused but guarded look on her face. She notices him as soon as he notices her. She moves faster than Bran can think and punches him in the jaw before he can even get a word out.

"You piece of shit!" she exclaims, enraged and joyful, before wrapping him in a bone crushing hug.

Kabet looks at the two of them, confused. Behind Rioz, Bran sees the two girls from earlier striding over.

"Look, we found him!" the red haired one boasts.

"You didn't do anything." Rioz releases Bran and then shoves him angrily. "Ass," she says, glaring.

"Do you know Kioh Taa?" Kabet asks the red-haired girl.

"I guess you could say that, yeah."

The fighter from earlier elbows her. "Kabet Oreh, a pleasure. I'm Salem Oto, this is Kioh Taa, and I wrote that letter. Excuse my peers, they aren't aware of who you are."

"Everyone is not um... aware?"

"I'm afraid most Kendrens don't know your face or name," Salem gestures around the bar at everyone continuing about their business.

He smiles. "Not my true name."

Salem nods and says, "Of course, allow me to introduce you. Everyone, this is Kabet Oreh, leader of the insurgents in Sunan, and one of the most wanted people in the world. He is professionally known as The Hare King."

Kioh's jaw drops for a split second, but she quickly recovers. "For his luscious locks, I presume?"

Salem scoffs and Kabet looks quizzical. "I am not familiar with this expression," he says.

Rioz covers a laugh with a cough. "Because of your hair." Kabet opens his mouth to inquire further, when Rioz interrupts. "Wait like *The* Hare King?"

Bran elbows her for an explanation but she ignores him. Resigned to looking foolish, he asks: "Who's The Hare King?"

"Me."

"No, yeah, I got that. What'd you do?"

"Not much."

Rioz scoffs. "This guy single handedly dismantled the Sunani king's entire military force."

"I had a far smaller hand in that than the media was led to believe." Kioh laughs at this and he practically preens.

"Would you care to explain why they call you The Hare King?" Salem asks in a way that makes Bran think she already knows.

"Ah. In Sunan, rabbits are cunning. I have read they are not like this here. However, in Sunan they are so clever they are thought to be the spirits of keen children, their lives cut short." He pauses, seeming sad. "The king only recently came to power, before we were run by my people. After Shka, the king was installed. He is not from my country, he does not care for my people. A plague has been ravaging my country. We had it controlled, before he decided to remove the provisions put in place to protect us. Thousands of children died because of him. My—" Kabet falters. "I am called the Hare King because I am cunning, and because I seek revenge for dead children."

There's a beat of painful silence before Kabet roots around in his pockets and pulls out the little rabbit from earlier. "And they are cute, yes?" And the room feels like it has air again.

Kabet wordlessly hands the rabbit to Bran, and Bran gives him a quizzical look. He smiles kindly and says, "He was yours from the beginning, no?"

The paper rabbit dances in Bran's palm.

Δ

The five of them go upstairs to Kioh's broken-down, but still lavishly decorated, apartment. She and Salem play chess for a while, and Rioz catches Bran up on the plan that Salem concocted. Plan is a generous word.

He's stunned by the insanity of it all. "*Rob* and *murder* The Wolf Queen? Do you really think she can pull it off?"

Rioz considers this for a moment. "I don't know." A pause. "What I do know is that she fought me, and, as you can see, is still alive."

"You fought her seriously?"

"As seriously as I dare."

Rioz can kill with nothing but a well spoken word, Bran can't fathom how Salem could possibly have an edge. "How did she—"

"Wait a second!" Kioh shouts, enraged.

Salem grins, the first genuine smile seen from her. "Finally sank in, did it?"

"You *bastard*. Here I was thinking you're some sort of chess prodigy when you're just a *cheat*."

Kabet looks up from his borrowed book. "I do not understand." He stares intently at the chess board. "How can one cheat at chess?"

Kioh opens her mouth and Salem clamps a hand over it. "Do you want to play chess with me, Kabet?"

Kioh manages to pry Salem's fingers off. "Don't fall for it. You won't win."

"It's not my fault you didn't realize what I can do until now."

"What *can* you do?" Bran asks, growing increasingly confused.

Salem's smile is faint. "Kabet, think of a number."

"This again," Kioh remarks, throwing her hands in the air. She turns to Salem. "How hard is it to say you're a mind reader?"

"Generally, people like proof when presented with the impossible," Salem snarks.

Kioh rolls her eyes. "Not having proof didn't stop you from blackmailing me, oh, four hours ago."

Bran is taken aback. "Wait, you guys met four hours ago?" They act like they've known each other for their entire lives.

"Yep. Miss Oto here accosted me in my bar and forced me into this hare-brained scheme of hers."

"If I'm remembering correctly, you accosted me."

Rioz's eyes sharpen and a shudder runs down Bran's spine. He knows how she gets when she looks like that. "What did she blackmail you with?" she asks. There's a palpable shift in the atmosphere, and everyone seems to tense, ready to fight.

Kioh freezes. "Oh, various crimes and that." Bran can tell she's forcing nonchalance.

"I don't believe that."

Kioh's hand twitches ever so slightly. "The more people who know a secret the less of a secret it becomes." Her eyes glow like twin suns.

"I think we have a right to know," Rioz pushes, and Bran has a bad feeling about what's about to happen.

Without warning, water begins to pour quickly out of the sink in the kitchen. It rushes towards Kioh, and swirls like a shield around her. She charges Bran's sister.

Rioz yells, and the water morphs away from the sound, but Kioh continues surging forward like a force of nature.

I have to do something. So he does.

Fire surges around Bran, roaring in his ears and coating his arms. He hears a scream of terror from somewhere in front of him, but can't see who it was through the fire all around. He throws a wave of fire towards Kioh, but the water morphs and parts around it until it reaches him, and then forces itself into his throat and lungs.

"I've been doing this a lot longer than you, petulant fool." Her words hiss in Bran's ears along with steaming water.

"That's enough. Let him go." Rioz sighs, tired and dejected. Her anger burns bright and fast, but after a while her common sense kicks in.

The water is extracted from his lungs and he collapses to the ground. "Looks like I'm not the only one keeping secrets," Kioh says.

There's a long stretching silence as a breeze flows in through the window.

That's when everyone seems to realize that Salem is gone.

CHAPTER FOUR

SALEM

☗

A WALL OF FIRE lights up around Bran, and before Salem processes it, she's screaming in fear. Instinctively, she lunges towards the window and throws herself against it until she's tumbling out the side of the building.

She regains her senses just before she hits the ground, and rolls into a neat ball, landing precariously on her feet with a grunt.

The cold smog that passes as air in Rowak fills her lungs, and she starts running.

The past swarms the edges of her mind, and her vision swims until she collapses in an alley, lost.

☗

Fire dances around her. Beams of her beautiful house collapse. Paint peels from the heat, and the floor burns the pads of her feet as she runs towards her parents' room. She shakes the door, the metal handle burning her hands beyond recognition, but at this moment she is composed of fear and not flesh. The door pops open, and she goes flying backwards with a wave of heat, her back colliding with a burning wall, and she screams in pain. Her parents' dead faces stare back at her as she writhes helplessly on the ground. Blank eyes shrivel and pop as fire consumes the bodies of the only people who ever loved her. Her baby brother lays somewhere in the wreckage, but she feels in her soul that he is dead as well. Laying amidst the flames, she elects to let herself die.

Some unforgiving deity has other ideas.

It urges her to get up. And she does, stiffly, coldly, she stands and walks through the fire towards the door.

It urges her to get out. So she tries. And fails.

It urges her to try again. So she does. And fails.

This process repeats and repeats. Until whatever force forcing her to stay alive has her smashing the right side of her body against the door. She collides and burns. The door shudders. She collides and burns again. The door shudders. This process repeats and repeats.

Finally, the door creaks open, quietly, and she stumbles out towards the cold snow. She collapses into it, and finally, finally she is given reprieve from consciousness.

And that is how her life begins and ends when she is eleven years old.

ψ

Kioh finds Salem shuddering in an alley, covered in grime from snow and scrapes from falling. She doesn't know how far she ran. She asks. Kioh tells her. She doesn't know how far she ran.

After walking about an hour in silence back towards the Poisoned Drink, Kioh finally asks.

"How old were you?" her voice crackles with something unseen.

Salem tries not to respond. She tries to force down the pain and keep quiet. But it's clawing at her throat to get out. "Eleven."

"What happened?"

She succeeds in forcing it down, this time, and says nothing.

Kioh doesn't say anything else, and they walk upstairs to her quarters in silence. Bran opens his mouth to say something, then takes in Salem's appearance and promptly clamps it shut.

Rioz, of course, has no such reservations. "Tough girl can't handle a little fire," she scoffs.

Cold rage surges inside Salem, and it feels familiar and comfortable. She draws a knife and hurls it quickly towards her. It embeds itself in the wall next to her.

Rioz screams in indignant anger as Salem surges her way towards her. Salem feels blood flowing from her nose. She wipes it away easily, and flicks it in Rioz's face, walking towards her. She snarls, and Salem barely feels the pain that comes with it.

"I suggest, Rioz, that you learn to control that temper of yours. Because I am not a very nice person, and I have few reservations about ending you, should you step on my toes again."

Rioz growls as Salem wrenches the knife out of the wall next to her. "The difference between you and me," she continues, "is that you are all bark." She presses the hilt of her knife into Rioz's shoulder and twists, hard. Rioz howls and glass shatters about the apartment. Salem stares coldly at her. "And I am *only* bite."

Her renegade team watches in horror as she removes the hilt from Rioz's shoulder, and presses the tip of the knife to her chest. She removes the knife after a moment and looks calmly around the group of people.

The words Salem speaks seem to freeze the room over. "When I was eleven years old my parents and brother were killed by Atina Parev, the Queen of Shka. I had taken up using my abilities to perform street tricks for money. My family, while far better off than most in

Omari, was still desperately poor. I raked in thousands of worthless currency, barely lifting a finger. The price I had to pay for such tricks was my family, my life, and, as you can see, my body."

Something akin to guilt flashes over Rioz's face. Salem's sure she's incapable of feeling guilty, but she appreciates the sentiment.

"Atina Parev will die by my hand. But before she can die, she will feel what I felt. That woman will suffer and cower like a dog before I allow her to die." Pausing, she glances around the room at the criminals she has recruited. "I need you to help me with that. I will not lie and say that you are not strong, are not fearsome each in your own right. But in order for all of you to receive your money, and in order for you to receive my allyship, you *cannot* kill each other.

"Each of us are degenerates. Each of us are filth that a good, upstanding citizen wouldn't bother saving. Whether we are crimelords or renegades, we are all criminals in our own special way. And that's precisely why I chose you."

"People with nothing to lose have everything to gain," Kioh says for her.

Salem nods. "Each of you will fight tooth and nail for yourself and your personal interests. You're getting staggering amounts of money out of this job, so make sure you fight the right people."

"So you're calling us selfish?" Rioz asks.

"I'm calling you smart. But smart and selfish are members of the same family. People who do not care for themselves get killed." She pauses. "I only have a few rules for you. Stay alive. Don't kill each other. Do your job, and lastly—" she takes a long, slow look around the room "—fight like an animal, and think like a god."

Everyone is silent for a long while, considering her words. Kioh rolls her eyes and makes her way slowly to the kitchen. Glass clanks together as she sweeps up the bottles Rioz shattered. Salem hears her take down a few mugs, spared from the carnage. She then walks back into the living room, an unlabeled bottle of alcohol in one hand, and five mugs in the other. She slides down the wall with her back, until she folds into a sitting position on the floor. With a fluid motion of a pickpocket, she spreads out all the mugs into a neat line, and begins to dole out the alcohol.

Rioz is the first to walk over, and Bran quickly follows her lead. Kabet hums thoughtfully, and then sits down next to Kioh. She passes him a plain brown mug.

Salem stands there stubbornly, not wanting to move. Not wanting to give in to whatever Kioh is asking her to.

"You gonna drink, birdie?" She says, waving the cup around; the liquid sloshing within. She says it like a challenge.

Salem crosses the distance between the two of them, and it feels like she's both won and lost something. *It's just Kioh being foolish*, she reminds herself, taking the cup she passes up to her. She takes a sip of the strong alcohol and the warmth that shoots through her is unfamiliar and uncomfortable.

Kioh seems to sense this. "'Fight like an animal and think like a god,' huh? That's something I can drink to," she says, taking a swig.

"It's a Zhidish principle. My mother taught it to me." Salem's voice comes out as a whisper.

Kioh stares intently at Salem, and for the first time in a long time her blind eye is throwing her off balance. Kioh's eyes meeting hers sends an angry prickle along her skin. "Can you tell us some others?" she asks, quietly.

Salem shifts her gaze to stare intently at the bottom of the cup, feeling as though she's on the precipice of something. "I don't know," she admits. "She never taught me."

There's a silence that falls across the room. Salem knows, somehow, that everyone is thinking about what they've lost. What they now don't have left to lose.

Kioh stands up, slow and languid, like a cat. Her eyes cut sharply around the room and she grins a grin of unadultured mischief. She holds her cup out, and says, with the tongue of a born liar: "Well then, I think we ought to drink. So here's to our wicked, wretched selves." Kabet stands as she says this, and as the cups clink together it feels like a nail in her coffin.

CHAPTER FIVE

JAZ

Ø

JAZ'S EYES OPEN AT the first slant of sun that creeps in from the curtainless window. He is not stuck in a half-sleep state, as soon as his eyes open, he is awake. With the way his life is, he has to be on edge.

His life is not allowed to consist of, or even contain, in-betweens. Everyone here must always be on guard, him in particular. The only time he is granted reprieve from this awful, haunting awareness is when he sleeps, which is not often.

The first to rise and the last to fall. He must sleep half as much as the other orphans here.

There's a period of time between the time he wakes and the time the orphanage heads wake. He relishes in laying on his designated spot on the floor and staring at the door.

He is lonely. For a while, he struggled with this, but the truth of the matter is that he has been isolated for his entire life, which tends to do things to one's mind. So he has long since accepted this fact. He stares at the door for a while and thinks about the immense hole inside his chest that will one day consume him.

Eventually, the door opens. His eyes are wide open, but Lee lunges for him anyway, attempting to get the drop on him. He rolls easily to his feet and sidesteps.

Arloch comes in. He's banging a broken metal pot with a wooden spoon, waking everyone in the vicinity. He smacks them with the spoon if they are not quick enough to duck.

Jaz realized long ago that these people are evil, that *most* people are evil. He can't be sure if he's one of them yet.

Lee shoves Jaz to the ground. He sees it coming, but doesn't really care. One of his wings snaps out as he falls. Lee grabs it and starts shaking him by it. Jaz's lip curls indiscernibly, but he stays silent. She yanks his wing, and he doesn't try to shove her off. He no longer attempts to do anything.

"Stupid mutant boy can't even fight." This line is old and recycled. Most of her tricks are. It no longer stings.

Arloch kicks Jaz in the stomach, and he grunts; grabs him by the ear and hauls him up, only to club him in the eye socket with a gloved fist. Jaz falls to the ground again.

"Get to breakfast, wicked one." He kicks him again.

Jaz feels that rage bubbling inside him. The hot anger that he is so quick to embrace snarls through his core. He lets out a melodic scream. Everyone in the room falls into a trance. Jaz watches as Alroch snaps the wooden spoon and brings the point to his neck. He doesn't tremble, doesn't hesitate, as he rears back to plunge it into his neck. Jaz, however, does hesitate. Dropping his harmony, he hurries down to breakfast before anyone realizes what happened. Not that they ever do.

Jaz quickly makes his way down the stairs and sits at the table. They're not going to give him breakfast. The only food he ever gets is what he steals when he's barely able to stand. As he sits at the table, the other orphans are given food. Some of them are skipped over for yesterday's crimes. Some of them do not eat, most likely too miserable to even bring the forks to their mouths.

As the twelve other people around him either sit quietly or dig in, there's a knock at the door. A young boy, Isacar, Jaz remembers, stands up to go get it. Lee strikes him on the head with her slender fist.

"We're not expecting anyone," Arloch snarls as his red nose wrinkles in distaste at his food, which is still far better than what the orphans are eating.

The knock comes again, and Jaz gives himself a moment to appreciate it. It is bright and cold. It reminds him of ice.

Everyone continues eating in silence. Whoever it is, they will go away.

There's a cracking noise as the door splinters open. Five people step in, one right after the other. A short, slender Zhidish girl takes a split second to throw a dagger into Arloch's thigh. It embeds itself up to the hilt, and blood gushes from around the knife. He howls in pain. A Taahuan girl with bright red hair starts to smash the walls with a staff, knocking whatever valuable possessions Lee and Arloch Tish own to the ground.

She twists her wrist as Lee lunges for her, and Lee stops short with a knife pointed in her face. The blade tucks away neatly and the staff behind it bashes Lee's nose in with a loud crunching noise. She screams and scrambles away.

"Everyone out!" the Zhidish girl commands, and for a moment, nobody moves. Everyone evaluates their fears —these five strangers versus these two abusers. A few people move: about five people rush out of the house.

The Taahuan girl brings her staff down onto Lee's knee, and Jaz can practically feel the snap reverberate about the room. She points to the Zhidish girl. "She's going to kill these two and burn the house down. So, kindly, get out."

This gets people moving. All around Jaz, people stand, now more afraid of this very real threat than whatever Lee and Arloch can muster up while mortally wounded. He stands to leave as well, almost in a trance. The fog that has clouded his mind is far from lifting, but its source is about to be murdered in front of him.

Just like you murdered Prolok, a voice too reminiscent of his own reminds him.

Jaz is following his peers out of the house when a tall girl, so tall she looks down at him, stops him. Her face is full of metal and her eyes are as sharp as knives.

"Not you," she says, eyes trained forward, not looking at Jaz. He follows her gaze to where the Zhidish girl brandishes her knife against Arloch's throat.

"Please. Please don't kill me, please, I—" The girl doesn't hesitate for a moment as she slides her knife across his neck with inhuman speed.

Her face doesn't even twitch. She glides across the room to Lee, who pulls herself to her feet and screams a furious scream. She lunges at the girl, and Jaz backs instinctively away.

The girl kills her handily. It's over within seconds.

She wipes the blood from her daggers onto the yellowed curtains of the Tish home. "Jaz Westfen, a pleasure." The intonation of her voice says it's not a pleasure at all. "I am Salem Oto, and these are my compatriots. Kioh Taa, Rioz Tamen, Bran Fehner, Kabet Oreh." She pauses after gesturing to each person and fixes Jaz with an icy stare. "And you, Jaz Westfen, are the last."

Ø

Salem does not explain further. She takes Jaz outside of the building, and he sees that everyone he shared this house with is gone. There's a village about three miles down the road. That is likely where they're headed. Salem looks at Bran, nods tersely, and then continues walking down the hill, Kioh trailing after her.

Jaz decides to hang back. Salem doesn't seem much like the kind of person who will talk much. Standing out of place next to Kabet, he watches as Bran produces a flame in his palm, which then extends all the way up his arm. He walks into the house, returning a moment later. Jaz can see flames licking across the walls.

Jaz glances over his shoulder and sees Kioh and Salem halfway down the hill. Kioh is watching the building go up in flames, while Salem sits in the snow, head in her hands and back turned to the fire.

Rioz answers the question he didn't ask. "Salem has a thing about fire." She pauses. "She doesn't like it much."

Jaz nods, silent, and glances over his shoulder again, where Salem sits drawing something in the snow with a small branch. The house is crumbling and falling, and he flinches as it begins to shudder to the ground, throwing heat off in thick, stifling waves. As everyone stands in uncomfortable silence while it burns, Jaz attempts to connect the pieces that led him here. He discovers there is no rhyme or reason to most of his life.

Once it's been razed to just the bones, Kioh appears before the house, and Jaz watches as the snow around melts into pillars of water and rises upward as Kioh lifts both her palms skyward. The fire is quickly doused and the house is crushed beneath the weight of the water. He feels nothing as he gazes at the charred remains of his long term prison.

Everyone stares at the remains of the orphanage for a moment. Jaz turns away, still not processing what has happened.

He walks down and stands next to Salem as she draws something in the muddy snow. She's writing quickly, slanting words and symbols together in one messy line. The others gather around and attempt to read what she's scrawling. She scrapes a toe through it before they can make it out.

"Alright," she says. "Here's the plan." There's a beat of silence as she confirms everyone is listening. "From here on out, we are known as The Domino Children. From here on out, we exist only for ourselves and our interests. No more bindings by the rules of society, we do what we want and we take what we need. Recklessly, ruthlessly, mercilessly."

She continues. "We need to make a name for ourselves. I do not want Atina Parev to die by a nobody's hand. I want us to be the worst of the worst and the best at what we do. Fortunately, this entire undertaking has massive amounts of practice included. But before I tell you our first step, we leave our names. Kabet has already abandoned his name, professionally, and we *are* professionals, or we will be." She swipes a finger at all of them as she says this.

"I am The Hare King, of course." It is the first time Jaz has heard Kabet speak, and his Kendrak is clipped and short, each word enunciated perfectly. Language learned from books. Jaz's Kendrak slurs together with Duskran. His words will never sound like that.

Kioh considers Salem's proposal and taps her foot. "The Grifter's got a nice ring to it."

"This seems a bit silly, doesn't it?" Rioz asks, glancing at Salem.

"I don't plan to live past this endeavor," Salem says. "But if the rest of you want to have lives afterward, I suggest you keep your names out of it." Kioh looks at her worriedly, and Rioz shrugs, accepting this answer.

"I guess you can call me Howl," Rioz grins and Jaz can see Bran stifling a laugh.

"Really? Our code names from when we were five?" Rioz elbows him and glares down her long slanted nose. He laughs and says, "I'll be Dragon, I suppose." He glances nervously at Salem, whose face is impassive as ever.

Salem shifts her gaze to Jaz. He's starting to realize that the numbness reeling through his body is from the shock of his life changing so abruptly. He stares blankly at her. "The Empty One," he says, because it's how he feels. It's how he's always felt.

Her lip twitches in what looks like a repressed smile. She takes all of them in and her eyes glint with ice. "I," she pauses, "am Truth. And this plan comes in four parts."

"Can the first part be us getting out of these backwater woods?" Kioh asks.

Salem shoots her a glare and says, "Not yet." She begins to scrawl in the dirt.

CHAPTER SIX

RIOZ

RIOZ IS STILL REELING from how quickly this all happened. One minute, she's screaming in the woods for her lost brother, the next, she's involved in a plot to con and kill the Wolf Queen herself. Rioz thinks she will be alright, however, with Bran by her side.

It was a three-day trek through the woods and into the outskirts of Duskra. Three days for all of them to reach Jaz. After Salem's speech (and the five of them drinking illegally pilfered alcohol), Salem told them to get their affairs in order. Kabet replied that he had no affairs, but Rioz and Bran took the night to pack their things and say goodbye.

They didn't actually *say* goodbye. Bran left a neatly written two-page letter, and the two of them slipped into the night, for presumably a long time.

It doesn't feel right to leave her parents like that, even though she knows she was a burden to them. It can't be easy to harbor a wanted murderer.

Now, she has changed into what seems to be a natural fit. She has morphed into a criminal, a degenerate, a born killer. It feels wrong, but at the same time, it is far too easy for something that she has never done before.

Perhaps she was made for this, after all.

After Salem has retrieved the sixth and final member of their party, she finally lays out her plan. Or, at least what she's willing to share of it.

"Step one," she says, "control the narrative."

"What does that mean?" Kabet asks.

"It means that we need to take control of the story. We make Atina Parev seem weak. We break her kingdom at its knees, highlight its greatest flaws, and generally make the queen seem incompetent. If she doesn't have her subjects' loyalty, she can't cushion the blow we deal next."

Kioh's eyes light. "Which brings us to step two."

Salem nods. "Run the con. The next part is to trick the queen, the same way we trick the country."

"There's no way in hell any of us can get close enough to manipulate her," Rioz points out the obvious.

"Of course not," Salem says. "But we can do other things. Like terrify her."

"And how do we do that?" Rioz challenges.

Salem's eyes flit to her. "I killed half of her personally selected army."

Kioh seems a tad confused as well now. "So?"

Salem's eyes narrow. Rioz thinks she might be laughing at them internally. "So the queen's personal bodyguards have been broken in half. The queen has several living quarters dotted throughout Shka, and some other countries, for situations like this. We go to where she is, which is far easier to infiltrate, and we terrify her. Manipulate what she sees. She's a very paranoid person; her power was gained through being ruthless and cautious. So…" Salem looks around at all of them.

"Let me guess," Rioz deadpans. "We rob her."

Salem nods. "We rob her of *everything*. By the time we're done with her, she will have lost even her very will to live."

"And then we kill her," Kioh finishes.

"So where do we go from here?" Bran asks. Rioz is glad that everyone other than Kioh and Salem seem to be confused.

"As I said, the queen has safe houses littered throughout the country. But I waged an all-out attack as a single person and dismantled half her personal forces, it's going to be more drastic than just moving from one palace to another."

"This means what?"

Jaz, for the first time, speaks up. "It means our journey doesn't start in Shka."

Salem's eyes glint coldly. "It starts in the heart of Duskra."

#

Rioz remembers sitting at the table with Bran, their parents cooking dinner at the stove, frying traditional food in a hot skillet, and the smell of marinated meat permeating the air.

"Do you think it's weird?" she whispers. "That we're both like this?" The two of them make quite a pair. Bran with his pale, warm skin, numerous freckles, and red-brown curls. And Rioz, brown as both her parents, with her thick dark hair and her piercing dark eyes. Her face, filled with metal bars and studs and loops, only serves to further elaborate their differences.

Yet the two of them are siblings, through and through. Everyone can see how she protects him as though her life depends on it. Everyone can see that, even through the bickering and teasing, he aspires to be like her. They are bound to each other, not by blood, but by bone. They are each other's support. They live inside one another.

He taps his foot and gazes at their parents as they cook. "I don't think it's strange," he says carefully. "I think there must be a reason, we just don't know it yet. Besides," a pause, "it's fun." Flames lick around his slender fingers.

Later that night, their parents tell them both about a Talirian belief. Bran is not Talirian, far from it, and their parents never attempted to pretend he was, so it's a tad odd.

(Rioz will realize when she is older that they must've been listening to their conversation.)

The story, if they can call it that, is told like this.

"In Talir, long ago, there were gods," their mother says. Rioz likes how she tells stories: straightforward and direct. It's unlike their father, who adds unnecessary details.

She continues, "These gods were kind but strict. They showered their followers in love and prosperity, but they had rules. One of these rules was this: do not go into the mountains, or you will never find peace. One day, a girl went into the mountains. She was the first, but certainly not the last. The gods did not curse her, for they were far too benevolent, but they did not save her."

"What happened?" Bran whispers, eyes wide.

"The girl was both cursed and blessed with power. She, who had gone into the mountains seeking fertility treatment, could conjure children now from anything. A beautiful boy could be born from flint and stone, or a daring girl carved from nothing but the howling wind. It was a blessing. She could have children, as many as she wanted to love. But there was an addendum.

"The children she created were not fully human, as they had power over whatever they were born of. See, a child conjured from a lightning storm, had a lightning storm within."

Rioz shudders. She feels incredibly attached to these mythical children. "What happened to them?"

Their mother smiles sweetly. "They spread out across the world and had many descendants. You see, even despite their powers, they were human at their core. So they lived their lives the best they could. However that may be."

"Why did the gods tell people not to go into the mountains? It didn't end badly, after all." Bran was always trying to find morality behind their parents' stories. There was rarely any to be found.

"Ah. Well you see, in Talir, we believe that you must trade for anything. Nothing given is ever free. Perhaps you give someone a gift, they give you their love. Nothing comes without a trade. This mountain granted wishes. It was against nature. So the burden the woman bore from her power, that was the trade she made. Not a bad one, no, but trades are usually equal."

"But shouldn't she have been punished?" Rioz asks. "For breaking the rules?"

Their mother frowns, and says, "There are far worse sins than desiring something, my children. The woman didn't hurt people, so why should she be hurt?" She kisses each of their foreheads and strides silently out of the room.

♯

Rioz is reminded of that night now, as the six of them make their trek towards the capital of Duskra. A four-week journey by foot, according to Salem and Jaz.

"It's odd," she remarks, bored of the silence enclosing them, "that we all have powers."

"It is by design," Salem says. "Each of you has a skill that could save our lives, at some point." She pauses. "Just like all of you have been trained to fight, just like all of you are criminals, all of you have abilities that level the playing ground against Parev."

"Why do you think that we're like this?" Bran asks, clearly thinking the same as Rioz.

Kioh speaks. "I was born in a coastal city. My parents said I was blessed by the sea."

Salem, surprisingly, responds as well. "My mother said that I inherited my grandfather's spirit. That I had his powers because he lived inside me."

"Why would your grandfather have powers, though?" Rioz points out.

She smiles, just barely. "Some things just are. Zhidish culture doesn't try to reason its way into existence, some things just happen. It is better to focus on your family and yourself than try to work out why the clouds get dark when it rains."

Rioz notices Jaz glaring intently at the ground, kicking his shoddy shoes through mud and snow as he goes. His wings hang limply by his side.

Kabet says nothing either, and the conversation ends there.

♯

The six of them walk for about an hour more before reaching a small village. The buildings in this town are old and dilapidated, with shabby roofs lined with snow and mud. Only a few people bustle in the street, giving the whole place a ghostly, ominous feeling. Jaz's eyes flicker sadly about the town, then Salem spies a supplies shop, hands him a fistful of *metlins*, and tells him to go buy some necessities. He leaves the five of them, and they find a small outside stall where Rioz sits and shivers in the cold.

It starts to snow, and then it starts to storm. The five of them are barely sheltered from the harsh elements. Kioh stands up, determined, and begins to make her way about the nearly desolate streets. She disappears from view and Rioz turns to Bran.

"What do you think she's doing?"

He smiles. "Leaving, if she has any sense."

"Are you saying we don't?"

"Well, yes. But I'm also fairly sure she's the only one Salem wouldn't murder if she bailed." He's laughing and she drinks in the familiarity of family.

Rioz and Bran have been talking quietly, but Salem shoots them both a good-natured glare. *Oh, right. Mind reader*, she thinks.

Kioh comes back, and as she approaches their bench, she shakes several wallets and pouches out of her thick parka.

"There's a tavern right next door." She begins to remove meager amounts of *metlins* from the stolen items. There are a few *drunes* mixed in with them, but not nearly as many as one would expect, for being in Duskra.

"Why don't they have their own currency?" Rioz asks as Kioh begins to split the money.

"We're not over the mountains yet." Rioz stares expectantly. Kioh sighs and continues. "These little border towns are closer to Shka than most of Duskra, so the traders they come in contact with trade in *metlins*, and generally have Kendren goods. The culture here is more of a melting pot of poor people fleeing

Shka's brutality, and has its own special rules and terms." She pauses. "Border towns are my *favorite*."

Jaz practically apparates from inside the growing snowstorm. "We should find lodging, this one's looking nasty." He pulls a scarf around his head and face, then tugs up the hood of his coat so only his eyes are visible. It seems excessive to Rioz, but then she sees Salem and Kabet do the same.

"You should probably cover your face," Jaz tells her. "I've seen your poster about, and bounty hunters make a killing off of these towns." He hands her a thick, green, woolen scarf.

She wraps the scarf around her mouth, and tugs her hood over her face. The six of them make their way to a tavern, and Salem pays the bare minimum for a small empty room, with space for bedrolls. With the money Kioh stole, she instructs everyone to buy food for themselves. Rioz is practically starving, so she heads down before anyone else, and purchases a large bowl of soup.

She's not really thinking when she tugs the scarf off of her face to eat.

Unfortunately, she only recognizes her mistake about a minute later, after she notices a burly man with scars eyeing her suspiciously. She stands up to leave, taking the half-empty bowl with her, and he stands as well. Rioz sets the bowl down and bolts for their room upstairs, just as Bran, Jaz, and Kabet are making their way down.

"We're blown," she hisses. Jaz and Kabet seem to recognize what happened and immediately swivel to run up the stairs. Bran hesitates. "What happened?"

"I'm stupid is what happened." She shoves him up the stairs, but it costs them precious seconds.

The bounty hunter hauls her up by the back of her coat like a limp, dead animal. She doesn't want to use her voice. Yet. So she uses her momentum to swing around to face him. Taking advantage of his large stature, she crashes her leg into the side of his neck. She plants her other leg on the other side of his neck, smashes her fist into the hand holding her, and twists her body violently as he lets go. They both tumble to the floor, but Rioz lands in a handstand, flipping herself onto her feet and back out of harm's way.

Rioz's party is standing at the top of the stairs. Salem is grinning at her, which feels natural, somehow. She says, "You'll have to teach me how to do that." She hands Rioz her pack as the six of them take off running out the door.

#

It is freezing outside. Wind swirls in violent, howling bursts, and snow burns the exposed parts of Rioz's face. The six of them walk until they reach a thick grove of trees, somewhat protected from the howling storm, and they all decide to stop for the night.

Salem seems to be born for this kind of thing. She clambers up tall trees and tears down branches thick with evergreen needles, dropping them softly onto the snow below. She then weaves them together into a dense cover and slants one end against a large boulder by a tree.

"Get this snow out of here, will you?" She asks Kioh.

Kioh begins to kick snow out of the way. "Where'd you learn to do this?" she asks.

"Jen Van Otto." She explains no further.

Salem somehow starts a tiny fire in the middle of a brutal storm. Bran didn't even think to do it. She then cleans off some other branches to prop the shelter up more to fit everyone inside. They all roll their bedrolls out at odd angles in order to squeeze into the shelter.

Rioz is watching the fire slowly die when Jaz asks nonchalantly, "So, was the soup worth it?" He tucks his wing around his side and looks at her intently.

She has a good cackle for the first time in what seems like months. She hums noncommittally. "It was *delicious* soup," she replies, after a beat.

The two of them devolve into laughter as the wind screams joyfully through the trees.

CHAPTER SEVEN

KIOH

IT'S A TWO DAY trek to the next town over. Salem then explains, very thoroughly, that it's the only town for another four days. Kioh thinks she's worried about rehashing the Rioz incident. (Jaz and Kabet had come hurtling into the room, wordlessly, and packed up their stuff. Salem's face had twitched in annoyance. Just barely. But Kioh saw it.)

This town is far more prosperous than the previous one, and large enough to have a name. It's called Tellek, and Kioh remarks on the name as soon as she learns it. "See, Duskra is *much* better than Shka. The *names* just roll right off the tongue. Not a mouthful like Shka." She mangles the pronunciation of a country she has lived in for years.

Everyone rolls their eyes at her, which she considers a smashing success.

She spends her day in the town pickpocketing well-off looking folks and snagging small items from the street vendors under the perfect cover of light snow. Stealing a few pieces of old fruit (the kind that has been juggled around in the back of a cart from warmer climates), she skips around the streets of town and eats her stolen goods. She continues nabbing various items and wallets as she goes.

Eventually she spots Salem, standing at a weapons stand, inspecting a few items. Kioh jaunts over towards her, and Salem's eyes twitch in what she hopes is a smile. Her face is still covered by her hood and impossibly blue scarf. She throws something towards Kioh as she approaches, and she snatches it out of the air easily. It's preposterously heavy.

Kioh inspects what Salem has tossed her, and she quickly realizes that it's a cane. It's made of metal, and it's the alluring blue of high quality steel. The head is a cluster of delicate flowers. The steel they are made of has been turned into a glinting pink that fades seamlessly into the blue. She shoots Salem a questioning look.

"You favor your left leg," she says flatly. "That's more helpful than the staff." She nods to the staff in Kioh's hand which is resting firmly on the ground.

"I'm rather attached to my staff." Kioh quirks an eyebrow, and weighs the cane in her hand. "But I will admit, this is *very* nice."

"Does your staff have a name?" Salem asks. Kioh shakes her head. "Then you're not that attached." Her eyes are alight with what Kioh thinks is akin to mischief. She considers this, and then straps her staff to her back, shifting her weight to the left as she plants the cane into the ground.

"Well, what would I name this one?" she taunts, immediately attached to the cane.

Salem shrugs. "Anything you want." She hesitates, then unstraps something from her waist and tosses it to Kioh. She catches it with her free hand. It's the holster for Salem's daggers. "The hilts," she says simply. Kioh cannot read the words written on the butt of each hilt.

"*Mao*," she points to the left one. "*Yao*," she points to the right. "They were my father's."

"What do they mean?"

"Rage and Wish," Salem replies as Kioh unsheathes the twin daggers, which, she's starting to realize, are not as identical as she thought. They are the same in shape and size, but the weight and heft of them are completely different.

Mao is a mottled dark grey, with no uniformity to the pattern, and it seems chaotic. The handle is a marbled blue and white, too light to be stone.

Yao is completely reflective. Kioh can see her brown eyes staring up distorted at her. The handle is a plain red wood.

Kioh hands the belt back to Salem and she wraps it around her waist, fastening the ornate clasp in the shape of a wide, sharp leaf. She begins walking away.

Kioh smiles to herself. "For someone so straightforward you really enjoy the beautiful things in life."

Salem sighs. It seems forlorn. "I didn't always look like this." The words hit Kioh like a punch to the gut. "I have lost so much," she continues. "Maybe I'm trying to get some of it back."

Salem stares at her. Kioh realizes she's waiting for her to say something. She shrugs at her, sets her staff down on the weapons counter she was standing at. She places her hand around the leather grip of the new cane, and walks towards her.

"Hey, did you pay for this?" Kioh asks as she walks away, realizing no one is manning the stand and that the cane looks very expensive.

Salem laughs, almost incredulous. "What do you think?"

"Here," Kioh tells her, digging around in her pockets. Once she finds what she's looking for, she flips the small ring off her thumb like a coin towards Salem. "Stolen good for stolen good. It ought to fit your child's fingers."

Salem glares at her and inspects the ring. It's small: too small for anyone without Salem's long, skinny fingers. The band is a few ornate ropes of silver that twist together, small leaves embossed on them, giving the appearance of vines. Embedded on the front is a massive, bright ruby.

Salem seems shocked, or as close as she gets. "This is nice," she remarks.

"Sure is, birdie," Kioh says, walking away.

❦

The six of them are discovered on the day they're leaving town, which is fortunate. This time, Kabet is recognized by a trader, and the rest spirals from there. Kioh supposes he had gotten too secure, let his guard down. She doesn't mind; they were leaving anyway.

The meager law enforcement of the small town chases after them as they make their way down the main drag: a road that cuts right through the heart of town. Salem grabs Kioh's hand suddenly, and drags her into an alley. Kabet, Bran, and Rioz all make their escape as well, darting past the two of them and turning into a winding street. Jaz, however, is not fast enough and gets a police baton smashed into his back. He crumples to the ground. Salem is moving before it even happens, daggers drawn. Kioh's behind her, swinging her new cane as she exits the alley.

Salem flicks towards an officer, but what the police lack in finesse and skill, they make up for with brute strength. Salem dodges each blow, but his reckless, rapid attacks leave few openings. The other two are turned towards Kioh, guns still stored neatly in their leather holsters.

She has a distaste for the police. It stems from both the fact that she's a criminal by trade and that the police in general tend to be rather horrible.

"Well, boys," Kioh grins, eyes daring and full of malice, "any day now." They both charge at her.

Kioh swings her cane out with one hand towards one's leg. The force behind it shocks her. The man cries out as she hears the wet crunch of his bone snapping inside his body. The other cop rushes straight at her. She shifts her weight to the other side, bracing her feet against the ground in a firm stance. She grips the cane with two hands, rears it back over her shoulder, and swings it forward in a perfect arc. The blow lands squarely on the other man's chest. Once again Kioh feels bones fracture as she drives it forward.

Salem has dispatched the final one as Kioh turns around. Jaz is standing up from the ground and clutching his shoulder where the baton struck.

"Anything broken?" she asks him. He shakes his head and rolls his shoulder, wings shuffling slightly under his cloak. Said cloak starts to slip, and he hurriedly tugs it back up.

"Good, because it's time to dash." The cop who Kioh struck in the ribs starts to attempt to stand back up. She brings the bottom of her weighted cane into his kneecap, and he wails as it shatters.

Kioh sees Rioz hanging back as she waves them forward, urging them to get out of here. Kioh takes off, coiled red hair flying behind her as she runs. Salem pulls even with her and Jaz lags slightly behind.

"I've gotta say, I am loving this cane," Kioh tells Salem. She says nothing but Kioh sees her eyes crinkle through the edges of her hood. As they reach the edge of the forest, their group starts to slow.

Ψ

Later, all of them are sitting in the forest around a fire. Salem stays a good distance away from it, and after Kioh has finished unpacking her things, she drops her pack next to her and sits on it.

"I know what to name my fancy new weapon."

Her face morphs into a smile for a second before dropping back to it's cold facade. "More like your new weapon of mass destruction." She turns to Kioh. "I saw what you did to those cops. Don't even try to pretend it's not."

Kioh laughs and tosses remnants of her meal into the fire, wondering if there's any gods out there to heed her sacrifice. "*Kahiji*," she says after a beat. "Taaish for pride."

The fire glints on one side of Salem's face. "Why Pride?"

"Because," she pauses. "It holds me up. If I didn't have my pride, I wouldn't have anything left."

Salem casts her eyes towards the fire. They have gone dark and cold once again. She removes *Mao* from its sheath, staring at it. After a moment she turns to face Kioh again. "*Mao* means rage." She twirls the dagger around her hand, like she did when they first met. "Keep that in mind."

It takes Kioh a moment to realize what she's saying. A flash of anger rushes through her. She takes a deep, steadying breath. "I don't think it's the same," she says. "Because I wear my pride well." A pause. "Confidence is money, in my profession. But, Salem, your rage looks a lot like fear."

Salem's eyes dim, growing darker than the night around them. She turns to Kioh just as a wind blows through the trees, leaving them shuddering from the cold. "I forgot how to be afraid, Kioh. So don't accuse me of that again."

Salem's demeanor is telling her not to press. Everything about the situation is telling Kioh not to push her infinite patience further than it normally goes. But searing anger rushes through her, and she cuts her eyes towards hers. "Accuse you of what? Being human? Because trust me, I would *never*."

Kioh expects her to do a lot of things, but she doesn't expect her to laugh. She tilts her head back and cackles. This full blown laughter is far more frigid and far more emotionless than the minute smiles Kioh sometimes gets from her. Salem turns towards her and her eyes are manic; crackling with cold ire. "It's *adorable* that you think I ever claimed to be." She tilts her head and Kioh swears she feels a force knock the wind from her. Salem turns to the rest of their compatriots with that furious grin, her eyes dance in the firelight: nothing behind them. "I am not like you. After this is done, I have nothing. There is nothing for me to go back to, nothing for me to chase. I am a tool to execute my family's revenge. Nothing more."

She swivels that horrible gaze back towards Kioh, and points to her daggers. Everyone stares in horror as she increasingly becomes unhinged and unrecognizable. "*Mao* and *Yao*. Rage and Wish. I want you to understand that I am made of rage. Not flesh. Rage. And my wishes," she opens her mouth and a grating, terrifying cackle comes out. Kioh opens her mouth to interrupt, maybe to apologize. Maybe to argue. She doesn't give her the chance. "My wishes. Well, those burned up a long time ago."

Salem stands up and rolls her bedroll out. She turns back towards Kioh with a grin so cold it could kill. "You're right!" she says. Her eyes are screaming at her. "We're not the same!"

Kioh feels a horrible sense of distress at those words: those words feel like a frozen fist around her heart.

Chapter Eight

KABET

KABET THREADS HIS LONG hair into a braid, twining his fingers at a ruthless pace as he rushes to prepare. The five people he has grown accustomed to bustle about the room. They pack up objects and fistfuls of money, grabbing everything the six of them had strewn about the room over the past three days. He ties his braid off with a piece of yellow woolen yarn. He then pulls on his thin brown cloak. He flips the hood up and pulls the yellow bandana he wears around his neck over his mouth.

He contemplates the piece of steel in his backpack, and takes it out. Holding it in his hands feels strange. He's never been a weapons kind of person, but Salem had given this to him and told him to make his own. He focuses his energy into the piece of steel, and changes it into a chain. He wraps the thin steel chain around his arm, up to the elbow.

Kabet will figure out what to do with it later.

Bran pulls on his brown parka and looks at the chain wrapped around Kabet's arm. "What're you going to do with that? Intimidate people to death?" He's joking, but Kabet rolls his eyes and morphs the chain into a dagger to prove a point. Bran smiles as he changes it back. He then pauses for a moment and says: "We're heading into the mountains now, so you're gonna need something warmer than that." He nods to Kabet's thin, yellow cloak.

"What would you suggest I do?" he asks, standing up. Bran tilts his head to look up at him. Kabet practically towers over him.

"Rioz packed an old parka. Might fit you." He eyes Kabet, almost judgmentally. "I'd give you one of mine if you weren't so tall."

Rioz walks behind him and ruffles his hair. "Don't volunteer to give my stuff to strangers, pipsqueak." He kicks her in the shin and she yelps.

"Don't *call* me that. And Kabet's hardly a stranger. We've been on the road for, what? Eight days now?"

"Nine," Rioz corrects. "I'm practically married to this lot," she grins at Bran, "with how close the sleeping quarters are."

He laughs, and Kabet feels a pleasant warmth watching them interact. They're nothing like his own siblings, who were always cold and removed towards him.

He supposes they weren't really his siblings, in many senses.

Salem slings her backpack over her shoulders, and everyone stands to attention. Somehow, this deranged, cold girl has become their unofficial leader.

"We're about to cross over the Duskran mountain range. We won't be progressing from the north, so the journey will be survivable. However," she reaches into her coat pocket and pulls out a folded paper with print on it, "I found this last night." She passes the paper to Kioh, who reads the headline aloud.

"'*Wolf Queen Devotes Personal Forces to Finding a Group of Six Criminals*'."

"What's that mean?" Jaz asks.

Salem sighs. "It means that the full force of the queen's personal attendants will be hounding us. And, let me tell you, it's a nasty place to be in." A pause. "The queen's personal attendants consist mostly of other mutants. People who've trained relentlessly to hone their powers for use in battle. People who have the exact skillset to deal with people like us."

Rioz sighs. "So we're dead in the water?"

Salem smiles, barely. "Well, you might be, but I'll be fine." She glances around the room, almost nervously. "If you want to keep your lives, you'll have to train. Some of your fighting skills are up to par, but if we want to pull this off, they has to be perfect."

"So, basically, fight like you." Kioh teases.

Salem smiles, and Kioh's face lights up as she does so. "No one fights like me." She tugs something from off her back and spreads it out on the ground. It's a bundle of various weapons. She looks towards Jaz and Bran. "Pick one, and name it. That goes for all your weapons. If it doesn't have a name, it can't fight for you." Jaz gives her a quizzical look. She shrugs. "Call it superstition."

Almost without hesitation, Jaz picks up a garrote with a thick silver wire and black handles. The handles slide apart and he tugs it experimentally.

"*Nynem.*" Kabet recognizes it as Duskran, but not the word itself. "Void," he says.

Bran considers the weapons laid before him for a moment. He then carefully picks up a short (but wicked looking) sickle. He twirls it experimentally, doing so perfectly. Salem looks at him in shock.

"Where'd you learn to do that?" She asks.

Bran shrugs. "I didn't." He considers for a long moment before groaning in frustration. "I don't know what to name it."

Salem shrugs noncommittally. "Figure it out later, we have to get on the road." She rolls the stack of weapons back up, and tucks it into her pack once again.

She then looks towards Kabet. "The naming goes for you, as well."

"I have named it, already."

"What is it?"

"*Amalhe.*" He hesitates, working out his next words. "It means the devil on your shoulder. The opposite of a guardian angel. I thought it might be fitting."

Kioh grins at him. "Fitting indeed." Everyone else nods thoughtfully, and that is all the endorsement he needs.

♂

"You're not mine," Kabet's mother snarls as he calmly packs his things. "A witch put you inside me. This is why you are wicked. You were never mine, never natural." He slings his small bag over his chest and shoulder, standing to leave.

"I am well aware, Rema." Kabet strides towards the door, feeling empty.

"You bring shame to us. To your family. You with your reckless ways. Is that head of yours empty as well as your soul?"

He opens the door, and turns back to look at his mother, who he still loves. He will always love her. But she will never be his. "You said it yourself, Rema. You're not my family."

He takes in Rema's strong face glowing in the moonlight. She seems proud. She seems sad. And in that moment she stops being his mother, and just becomes a mother. A generic face of his past, who he loved, and who he left. "May the gods protect you and yours. May the family prosper. May hope live on." These are his favorite prayers she gave him, and he is giving them back to her. He lets go of the love she gave him. He gives her back her effort, so it may be redirected.

Whatever pain was in her face melts into peaceful oblivion. She is no longer Kabet's mother. He is no longer her child. She nods at his words. "Do them proud."

"Who?"

"Your family, when you meet them. We're not yours, but someone is."

He remembers Adena. Remembers her cold, young face: dead as dead gets. She was his family, but she's been gone for years. He wonders if that was the only chance he'll get. Rema notices his face twisting, and while she is not Kabet's mother anymore, she still knows him.

"You will find your family. And you will love them with everything inside the earth. And they will love you with everything under the sky. I am sorry we could not give this to you, but you will find it, Kabet. I promise."

He nods, then bows slightly in thanks. Then he walks out the door and lets it close behind him.

♂

Salem makes a camp in a clearing right at the base of where the hike through the mountain begins. There is a wide road that leads up to it. Kioh says that there are a few towns littered in the lower parts of the mountains, but the colder it gets the less life there is. They set up in a sheltered clearing a mile or so out for the road.

"It's too dangerous to stay in towns or out in the open," Salem tells Rioz when she complains about trudging through the deep snow. Rioz sighs and kicks at the snow, annoyed.

They all sleep in the shelter Salem constructs. Everyone lays down at odd angles to fit. Bran conjures a small fire and touches it to a pile of wood that sits just beyond the border of his shelter. Kabet lays as close to it as possible; he's not a fan of this all-consuming cold. Bran laughs as he scoots closer to the dying fire.

"You're gonna set yourself on fire if you get any closer."

"At least then I would be warm," Kabet grumbles. Bran grins and points a finger towards the dying fire, which is then renewed by the bolt of flame that shoots from his fingertip.

"Marvelous," he says in wonder, staring at the flame. He glances behind them to see if Salem is uncomfortable by this display, but she is fast asleep.

Even asleep she looks angry, he realizes. He turns back to Bran. "Do it again."

He rolls his eyes but a flame appears in the palm of his hand. He rolls it over his knuckles and between his fingers; like how a magician might with a coin.

"Can you do that with a coin?" Kabet asks.

Bran tilts his head back and laughs. "Oh, absolutely not." He closes his palm over the flame and extinguishes it.

The two of them sit in silence for a while. Rioz and Bran chat in tones Kabet cannot hear, but eventually Rioz falls asleep, leaving only him and Bran awake.

"Why are you doing this?" Kabet asks suddenly. He's never had much couth.

Bran looks at him, quizzical. "What do you mean?"

"You are not—well. You are not a criminal like us. You have other options."

Bran casts his eyes down. He seems to deflate at Kabet's question. He's mentally berating himself when Bran responds. "I've been lonely," he says simply. "It's not the kind of loneliness that comes from being alone or isolated. Not like Jaz, though he'll never admit it. I just—" He cuts himself off abruptly. "I know I'm not as quick or clever or ruthless as you guys. I know I don't really belong here; Salem didn't even know about me until Rioz insisted I come."

He pauses for a long time and Kabet is about to say something when Bran speaks again. "I think the cure to my loneliness is to learn about people, and have people learn about me. And, trust me, I love Rioz to death, but just having one person, well, it gets a little boring." He laughs, then casts his gaze beyond the shelter and to the slit of stars visible just above the treeline. "I want to be known. I want to be loved."

Kabet is reminded so viciously of Rema's words that it knocks the breath from him. He swallows thickly, remembering the family that was never his. He realizes Bran is waiting for him to respond. "I think that is all any person wants. To love and be loved in return. To choose and be chosen the same."

"Do you think love is a choice?"

Kabet remembers when his family stopped being his, when he stopped being theirs. "What else would love be?"

Kabet falls asleep with that thought in his mind, and Bran's green eyes locked curiously on his.

He wakes up to darkness and Salem staring down at him. "Get up," she says, tossing his shoes at him. Kabet climbs out of his bedroll with all the grace of someone who's just been rudely awoken while the sky is still dark. He starts pulling his boots on.

"What for?" His voice comes out as a croak.

"Training." She ties off her second shoe and stands up. "You're up first." She turns and walks away.

Kabet huffs and pulls his other shoe on. He trudges on after her until they reach a small area clear of trees. As soon as he steps near her Salem whirls on him and brings a dagger towards him in a savage arc. He doesn't have time to dodge and feels her blade pierce into him.

Except it doesn't. Salem pulls her arm back, and he sees leather caps over her blades. He also realizes these are not her usual daggers.

"Lesson one," she says, "do not wait for a signal. Well trained fighters will not give the barest hint that they are about to attack, they just will. Don't wait for something that's never going to come." Faster than he can think, she drops down and swings her leg towards his shins. She hits him squarely, and he falls backwards into the snow.

"Lesson two: don't get distracted by anything." She walks over and hauls Kabet up by his hands. "Combat is won in moments, and the moment is everything that matters when you're battling." She pauses. "Feel the toe of my boot." He does as she instructs, beneath the leather he feels steel.

"I am guessing that is lesson three?"

Salem smiles. "Yep. Lesson three: be aware that anything can be dangerous. If you get tricked or trapped, that's the game." She points to his chain. "Now we start for real. I suggest you use that."

Salem beats Kabet. Many times, successively, and within seconds. Not once does he get the upper hand. She thoroughly bests him, and he is exhausted by the time the sky starts to glow with light.

"Send Bran to me, when you recover." He's doubled over, breathing heavy and clutching the arm that Salem smashed her foot into seconds previously. Kabet hadn't landed a single hit, and she barely seems phased from their training. He takes that as his excuse to leave, and takes off back towards the camp to find Bran.

He's still asleep when he gets back, but everyone else seems to be awake. Rioz is actually sparring with Jaz, who doesn't seem to be faring too well. His wings are bulky and he doesn't do well with them. He's the least experienced fighter of all of them.

Kioh gives Kabet a friendly wave, but she, too, seems to be just waking up.

Kabet kneels on Bran's bedroll and carefully prods him awake. He rolls over onto his back as he wakes and gives him a half-hearted smile. "Morning," he says, sitting up. "What's going on?"

"Salem decided to train us today and I am afraid it is now your turn."

Bran grimaces. "How badly did you get beat?"

"Quite."

He laughs and grabs his tall boots from behind him. He seems a bit worried. Kabet elbows him in concern, giving him a questioning look. He hesitates. "Is she going to be alright? Fighting me?"

He laughs. "I doubt you will be able to touch her."

"No, I meant like, mentally." Bran sighs.

"It would be like taking a hammer to sand."

This doesn't appear to bring him any comfort, but he laughs anyway. "I suppose you're right. As always."

Kabet laughs louder than he has in a while. "Believe me, I am almost always wrong."

Bran smiles at him, and he feels warmth in this frozen wasteland.

CHAPTER NINE

JAZ

Ø

THE DAYS DREDGE ON as Jaz travels with this rag-tag group of fellow criminals and outcasts. Most of the time, he keeps to himself. He eats in silence, pretends to sleep until everyone else is, and generally just pretends everyone doesn't exist.

After a while, they start making it hard to do so.

He starts making quips. He starts voicing the thoughts that constantly swim in his head while he remains silent.

"Aw, Rioz, he's making the face again," Bran laughs as Jaz glowers at his jerky. It is midday and they have all stopped for a brief rest.

"What face?" Jaz asks.

Bran laughs. "The 'I'm brooding and mysterious but still ridiculously attractive even though I look like I'm plotting your death' look."

He stares flatly at Bran. "That's a rather long name, isn't it?" Jaz pauses. "And I am."

Rioz finally chimes in. "You're what?"

"Plotting his death."

"What's the plot?"

Jaz cracks a smirk at her. "I'm thinking strangulation and then burying him in some snow."

Rioz clicks her tongue. "I think throwing him off the mountain would work better."

Jaz immediately tenses at her words, just barely. Not enough for anyone to notice. Anyone but Rioz. She quirks an eyebrow. He gives a halfhearted shrug.

"Oh, that's right," she mock-whispers. "You did actually kill someone." Bran laughs and Jaz feels like he's left out of a joke.

"Join the club, mystery man. Bran's probably the only one here who's not responsible for a death."

It's not a shock, but it's not something he expected either. "Who'd you kill?"

She shrugs. "Jance Way," she says, and faintly Jaz recognizes the name. "You?"

My best friend. He doesn't say. *It was an accident.* He doesn't say. Instead he just shrugs, not wanting to talk about it.

Rioz seems to sense his discomfort. She cracks a smile that feels nice to look at. "Keep your secrets, then."

Bran shakes his head and nods over to where Kabet, Kioh, and Salem are standing. "Either way, they've got you both beat in terms of crime."

"About fifty times over."

Jaz whispers in the same way Rioz did. "A notorious thief, a rebel insurgent, and worst of all," he pauses for dramatic effect, "Salem. We never stood a chance."

Rioz and Bran devolve into laughter so loud that Kabet looks towards them. Jaz sees a knowing smile flash across Salem's face, and he wonders what it's like to know everything like she does.

Later that day Jaz is training with Salem. It's not the first time he's done so, but it's the first time he decides to try to use his power. Before she can get into a fighting position, he begins to sing.

Instantly an uncomfortable prickle crawls across his neck as everything inside him screams at him not to sing, not after *that* time. He pushes forwards.

Salem turns to Jaz, looking confused. "You have a very lovely singing voice?" She's smiling a bit at his unexpected display.

Jaz drops his voice and stares at her, scanning her for signs of what has happened every single time without fail. There are none. He stares at her in confusion.

Realization flashes across her eyes as the pieces seem to click together in her mind. "Wait. Is this it?"

Jaz nods, still dumbstruck. "It always works," he says quietly.

"How does it work? Is this how you killed Prolok Vinsky?" The name sends a horrible jolt through him and he is hurled back into the moment of watching his best friend's body shatter on the rocks in the canyon below him. Salem looks at Jaz expectantly.

"I sing, and people do what I want them to do," Jaz says, voice thick and slow.

"Come back to camp and show me," she says. "It won't work on me, but I bet it—"

He cuts her off. "No. I—No."

Salem stares at him for a long moment. "Who was Prolok Vinsky?"

"He—" Anger starts to choke him. "No." He turns on his heel and walks past Salem, back towards the camp.

Ø

Rioz talks to Jaz. Rioz sees the unspoken things that he omits from his mind, and ignores them with him. She provides a distraction; when he talks to her he forgets that dull emptiness. He wishes she would stop talking to him. He doesn't want her to stop.

Whenever Jaz freezes up, or flinches, or trails off, Rioz just shrugs at him and says, "Keep your secrets, mystery boy."

"Where did you get your scars?" Kabet asks one day. Jaz glares at him, lip curling in anger, but not at Kabet. He forces his rage down, stamping it out. He says nothing. Kabet raises his hands in surrender, a habit picked up from Kioh.

Rioz looks at Jaz intently. "I am curious, though." She tears a piece of jerky and pops it in her mouth. "Where'd you get them?"

He casts his gaze downwards and shocks himself by speaking. "One of the people who ran the orphanage." Jaz looks up to see everyone staring at him. "She had this ring that had a spike on the outside. She'd slap me, and it was designed to leave gouges, as you can see."

Jaz hesitates before saying the next part. "One day, I forced her to swallow it." His voice is quiet.

Everyone is silent for a moment. Rioz shrugs. "Sounds like she deserved it," she chirps cheerily, before biting off more jerky.

He feels as though an immense weight has been taken from his shoulders with those words.

Ø

They all eventually tire of eating jerky. It's become the main staple in their diets. Salem doesn't seem to mind, but everyone else is used to eating actual food, disgusting though it may be. Kioh convinces Salem to stop in one of the last towns leading up the mountains to stock up on supplies.

"Okay," she says after five rounds of pestering. "We can stop, but hurry up. And don't get things that will rot."

Kioh lets out a victorious whoop and grins at Salem. "No more jerky!"

"No more jerky," Salem agrees.

Jaz splits off with Rioz and Bran to go get items off a list that Salem had rattled off. He's fairly sure no one remembers what was on it. They mostly get cured meats, bread, and a few jars of various pickled items.

Rioz keeps eyeing the fresh fruits and vegetables. Jaz elbows her. "Salem said nothing that will rot."

"I have an idea," she says.

He scoffs. "Well that's never good."

She glowers at him and darts off. He doesn't see her again for the rest of their supplies trip.

Bran comes back with an armful of small jars full of various powders. "What are those?" Jaz asks.

"Spices?" Bran's looking at him in amusement. "They make food taste good?"

"Orphanage, remember?"

He laughs. "Ah, that explains it."

They join up with the rest of their group after about two hours. Salem is carrying a brown bag full of potatoes, while Kioh has dried fruits and seeds. Kabet is also carrying spices as well as a few mystery jars. Rioz is nowhere in sight and Jaz starts to feel anxiety prickle at the back of his mind.

"If any of you lot want to get something else, Kioh robbed the entire town," Salem says with a faint smile. Kioh begins to dole out fistfuls of various currencies.

Kabet glances around and then looks towards Jaz. "Where is Rioz?"

Jaz shrugs, pocketing the money Kioh gave him. He then stalks off in a sulk, worry prickling at the back of his mind.

He's mid panic when he hears a vendor yell: "Talirian Jewelry! Authentic from Talir!" His head snaps up and Jaz glances around for Rioz, but she's nowhere to be found. He looks towards the Talirian merchant, speaking in accented Duskran. He walks over.

"Have you seen a Talirian girl come by here?"

He gives Jaz a confused look. "No. No one here is Taliran. Mostly strange Duskran folk interested in my culture." He pauses. "It would be nice to see a friendly face, but I didn't see her. Take a look at my wares, while you're here."

Jaz gives a polite glance over the piercings, rings, and other various items of jewelry laid out over the table. Then something catches his eye.

It's a necklace cut in the shape of a vulture. The design isn't detailed, but it's well done so he can clearly tell what the animal is only with a few interconnected lines. It's shaped like a view from the bottom, wings spread, beak pointing upwards. Suspended by chains in the empty center is an intricate, tiny mold of a skull.

Jaz remembers that vultures are respected immensely in Talirian culture.

"Why is that?" he asks as Rioz aims another blow at his side. He dodges.

"They do the job no one else wants." She strikes towards his face. "That is a big responsibility to bear."

Jaz picks up the necklace and shows it to the vendor. "How much is this?"

He seems to brighten when Jaz shows it to him. "Thirty-five *metlins*." He pauses while Jaz digs out the appropriate amount. "Vultures are respected in my culture. Do you know why?"

"They do the job no one else wants," he repeats, handing over the money. He beams at his words. He pockets the necklace, and walks towards where he sees Kioh standing.

Jaz gets thirty feet towards her when he feels someone watching him with a prickle across his neck. He whirls around and sees a figure standing in the shadows in the alley. The only light that's being cast is across the tip of their hood and what is showing of their face. Jaz cannot see their eyes.

He sees a sadistic grin flash across the pale, cracked lips beneath the hood. They look familiar. He blinks, and the figure fades into the shadows.

Kioh walks up to him. "You okay there? You look like you've seen a ghost."

I *might have*, Jaz thinks. "Fine. Let's go," he says.

Ø

They're within feet of the camp when Jaz smells food. Everyone seems to. They all pause for a split second, and then keep walking. Rioz still hasn't appeared, and there's a nervous tension strung about the group.

Jaz sees Rioz as soon as he gets to the clearing, and a sigh of relief seems to hit everyone. She's standing over a fire, holding a large skillet and wooden spoon. She's stirring the mixture with care and she grins when she sees the group.

"Thank the gods. Someone come hold this, my arm is dying." Kioh laughs and walks over, taking the skillet from her.

"We thought you died," Bran says, clearly relieved. "Shame, I was really hoping to have my own room."

Rioz laughs and Jaz remembers the necklace in his pocket. He takes it out, and holds it for a few seconds, before yelling, "Catch!" He chucks the necklace towards her like a ball. She drops the wooden spoon to catch it.

"Ass!" she yells as her spoon falls into the snow and her fist closes around the necklace. She opens her palm, and Jaz sees her grin. She silently puts it around her neck with ease.

Salem walks over towards where Kioh is holding the skillet, and then looks towards Rioz. "Can we please stop delaying food, now?" Rioz laughs.

"Yeah." She takes the skillet from Kioh and sets it down on a large rock by the fire. "Last hurrah before we're confined to preserved foods, once again." She pauses. "Well, first hurrah for Salem, I suppose."

Kioh bursts out laughing and Salem glares at her, but her eyes lack their normal ice.

Jaz walks over to join them, as Rioz doles out food into their portable bowls. It's a mixture of fried greens and fruit, with chunks of meat, all in what looks to be a creamy, bright red broth. She also had a few spices with her, which she put into the food.

It's the best thing he's ever eaten, though he supposes there wasn't much competition.

Later, when they are all sitting around the fire, jovial and full of good food, Rioz whispers to Jaz. "Do you still think it was a bad idea?"

He laughs. "All your ideas are bad." He remembers the worry that fell over the five of them. "We really were worried. What were you thinking?"

She shrugs. "Just doing the job no one wanted."

Jaz smiles at her, and even though it stretches facial muscles that have been out of use for seventeen years, it feels familiar.

Chapter Ten

BRAN

Δ

SALEM'S EYES GO COLD whenever she looks at Bran for too long. He tries not to take it personally. It's not the kind of cold that means she doesn't like him. Her eyes gloss over and her face freezes in some sort of unseen determination. It looks like fear in the face of fire.

Whenever they train, Salem flinches each time Bran starts a fire. It never touches her; she's untouchable in fights. He doesn't hold back, either, but he's starting to wonder if he should.

"It would be like taking a hammer to sand," Kabet had told him. Bran knows that he's not going to break Salem. She's been ground into pieces so fine that they won't shatter any further.

But he thinks that it has to hurt, getting hit with a hammer, no matter how sand-like one is.

Either way, he doesn't dare to ask her. He saw how she reacted to Kioh, when she pushed too far. It was the most harrowing expression he's ever seen on a person's face. It was like watching a dead body dance: lifeless and grotesque.

Bran never wonders what happened to Salem; the pieces are easy enough to put together. He just wonders how her eyes can be so cold.

One day, he talks to Kioh about it.

"Do you think Salem hates me?" Bran jokes half-heartedly. The aforementioned mind reader is currently training Jaz in the woods.

"Yeah," Kioh says. "But I wouldn't take it personally." She eats another dried piece of fruit. "She doesn't hate you as a person, she hates what you can do."

"What's that?"

Kioh looks at Bran like he's stupid. "Make her feel powerless. Salem has a carefully crafted kind of control over everything, and you take that away."

"*Salem?*" he asks, incredulous. "*Powerless?*" He nabs a piece of Kioh's fruit. "I don't even think she's fully human."

Kioh whirls on Bran, as fast and as vicious as an enraged viper. She stands up from where she was laying in the temporary shelter. "Don't say that."

"What? Have you seen her? She works like a machine. I don't even think she feels when she murders people. She *barely* makes facial expressions." Bran regrets the words even as they come out of his mouth. "She wants to kill the queen of Shka after *ruining* her, and for what?"

"You think your little colonizer queen doesn't deserve it? Who do you *live* with, Bran? Who is your *sister*? Is Kabet not a friend?" Kioh is spitting fire at him and each word rings true. "Parev committed atrocities in Omari that Salem won't even *talk* about." He can feel Kioh's fury building, and his dying out. "Don't act like you're above her. Just because you're not close to her doesn't mean you get to say those things." Kioh glowers down her nose at Bran as he stares at her.

She sits back down on her bedroll. The eyes she keeps trained on Bran are full of righteous malice.

"How many times has Salem saved you? Or Rioz? Or any of us?" Her mouth curls. "Just because you're worthless to this team doesn't mean everyone else is."

"What did you say to him?" Bran hears Rioz say from behind him.

"You heard me, Rioz. Why don't you ask your brother what he said about Salem?"

Rioz's hand is clenched around the dagger at her neck, but when Kioh says that she falters. Rioz looks down at Bran, her brow furrowed. "What did you say, Bran?"

The petulant rage that surges in him is nothing like Kioh's rightful fury. It is childish and selfish. "The truth," he spits.

Rioz frowns at him. "What did you *say*, Bran?"

"I think Salem waging a campaign of terror against the queen is petty. I think Salem herself is inhuman." These words come spilling out of him, unprovoked, and they've been true for a long time.

Bran hears cold, manic laughter coming from the treeline, and then sees Salem surging towards him from the clearing. Laughing her vacant, angry laughter.

"I never asked for you to be here, you idiotic piece of shit." Her eyes could cut steel. She knocks her foot into his hand resting on the ground, and Bran feels his littlest finger shatter from it. "You can leave, if you think that. You are *welcome* to get up and walk away. No one wants you."

He hears Rioz snarling from behind him, but it seems hesitant and unsure. That cuts deeper than any blade of Salem's could.

"Do you wanna know what Atina Parev did to me? To people like me?" She laughs again. "She killed us like dogs! Every single one of the so-called witches in

Omari were murdered in the streets and in their homes. We were *slaughtered*."

She pulls the sleeve of the shirt she's wearing down at the right shoulder. The skin there is so badly burned it looks like there are chunks missing from her shoulder. "My mother was twenty-eight years old. My father was thirty. My brother was a baby. He was born seven months before the fire. Across the country, thousands of families were destroyed, lives ripped apart. All for the sake of power."

"It was senseless, disgusting violence. All because she could. All because she *knew* there would be no repercussions. My body was destroyed. I cannot see out of my right eye. I cannot feel cold, or touch, or pain on the right side of my body. I inhaled so much smoke that my voice is permanently quiet. I have been disfigured and destroyed by fire, so excuse me if I have been cold towards you." She pauses and looks around at the group Bran has grown so familiar with. "I am seeking to give Atina Parev a taste of her own medicine. The world was not created balanced, it was made balanced by people like me. Atina Parev has unimaginable power, and so do we." Salem pauses. "People must face consequences, and sometimes they are not provided by the law." She looks back at Bran. "Sometimes, Bran, villains must be the heroes."

Salem sighs, and reaches towards Bran to help him up. He grabs her hand. "And I am afraid, my friends," she pulls him to his shaky feet, "that I will be the only hero you get."

Δ

Bran is four years old when his parents leave him in the frigid woods. He is cold, unimaginably cold. He cries and screams with all the might a four year old can muster, wishing nothing more than for someone to save him.

Bran hears voices. He hears someone calling a name. "Mom!" he cries out, knowing that it must be her.

"Rioz, love, is that you?" A figure approaches him. She is not his mother. She is followed by a man who is not his father.

"Oh," the woman says softly when she sees Bran. "What happened to you, my child?"

He likes the way she says that. Like she means it. Like he's hers. "I don't know." And begins wailing all over again.

A small person darts from the night within the trees. He cracks his eyes open wider and realizes a girl his age is kneeling next to him. She plops a sticky piece of candy into his hand, unprompted. Bran hesitantly puts it in his mouth. It's spicy.

"I'm scared," he tells the girl.

"I'll kill it," she says. "Whatever you're scared of."

Δ

Later that night, Salem approaches Bran. He freezes when he sees her. Tensions have been running high the whole day. He and Rioz avoid Kioh and Salem like the plague, while Kioh shoots glares his way and Salem is impassive.

Salem sits next to him as he stares into the fire, and stares at it for a while, too. Finally she says, "Rioz told me that I scare you."

Bran says nothing and Salem clears her throat. "I mean, a bit, yeah," he tells her.

She sighs. "Remember that night when I told Kioh not to accuse me of being afraid?" He nods, not trusting his voice. "Not all fears are created equal."

"What does that mean?"

"It means that my fear, when I have felt it, takes over my mind and destroys any facsimile of control I have. My fear is animalistic. A dog fighting for survival." She pauses. "I have realized that not everyone is built like this. Not everyone has something lurking within their past. Not everyone carries the weight I have.

"Immediately after my family was killed, before I could protect myself, I was constantly looking over my shoulder. I was always on edge, waiting for the other shoe to drop. It was awful, that tension of being afraid of nothing. But I took control of my life and I eradicated that experience."

Salem sighs. "What I am trying to say is, that if I have made you feel like this," she pauses. "I'm sorry."

The wind is knocked out of Bran as he feels a wave of guilt swarm through his veins. He chokes on nothing. Salem continues.

"You do not scare me, Bran. Fire scares me. Fire makes me feel a loss of control. That complete inability to protect myself. Fire makes me fight for my life, because the last time I came in contact with it, I almost lost it." She sighs. "My pain is not an excuse." Her voice becomes tight with anger. "But last I checked, I had not wronged you. So I would suggest having a reason for saying such things, should you want to say them again."

She stands up and walks away before he can apologize. He thinks she knows he's sorry. He thinks that was her forgiving him.

CHAPTER ELEVEN

KIOH

SALEM WHIPS HER ARM towards Kioh with impossible speed. She barely dodges it, and swings the thick branch that substitutes for a weapon towards Salem's leg. Salem is already out of the way. Kioh isn't sure if Salem has ever taken a hit in combat in her life.

Salem cracks her empty fist towards her face, and she flips herself backwards off her feet—a maneuver learned from Rioz—and lands neatly on her knees. Salem crashes a foot towards Kioh before she can even recover her breath. She curls her body and rolls out of the way.

She has kept herself from being bested for this long, but really, it's only a certain amount of time before Salem beats her.

Salem relentlessly attacks Kioh, a new style she has adopted for training all of them. Her pure offensive style forces them to think quickly and react. She has dropped her normally flawless defense in favor of making theirs better.

Salem brings a fist into Kioh's stomach as she stands up. Kioh doesn't think Salem's a great teacher. She doesn't have time to make an offensive move before Salem grapples Kioh to the ground. She ends up crouching above Kioh with the capped dagger to her neck. Salem's blank white eye is trained somewhere to the left of Kioh's head, but her left eye is fixed on her, an invisible smile within its black depths. Kioh takes a moment to scan her eye for a pupil, it's barely visible.

"Your eyes are so dark," she tells her.

She quirks her head in confusion. "I can't tell if that was—"

Kioh cuts her off. "It was." Kioh grins.

Salem offers her hand and hauls Kioh up with her as she stands. "Technically, only one of them is dark."

"Yeah, but that sounds weird. I'll say it if it makes more sense to you, though."

The corner of her lip twitches in a suppressed smile. She shrugs. "Maybe it's dark behind the scar. You could be right."

"As usual."

Salem glowers but it's good-natured. "I was saying that to spare your feelings. That's not how scar tissue works, you know."

Kioh laughs. "I know, but by nature I am incapable of being wrong."

Salem rolls her eyes. "I doubt that," she says, and the two of them walk back towards the camp.

Kioh is sparring with Rioz in the forest. She can normally beat her handily, but she is an expert at acrobatic maneuvers. Rioz flips and dodges and twists in ways that shouldn't be possible. She lands on her feet without fail.

Kioh flicks her makeshift weapon towards her. Rioz falls flat on her back, and springs up moments later with nothing but her legs. Kioh hurls a wave of water towards her. Rioz yells and it explodes into droplets, losing the cohesion Kioh provided. Kioh then takes the opportunity to drive her weapon towards her neck. Rioz blocks the branch, taking the blow's full force into her arm.

It continues like this for what must be hours. They take breaks occasionally to eat, drink and chat. The two of them have finished when the sun starts to dip low in the sky, illuminating the snowy forest in an orange glow.

Rioz takes a long drink from her flask, which she insists contains water. "I hate to give Salem any credit as a mentor, but we might be getting better at this."

"Credit where credit is due, and Salem deserves none of it."

Rioz laughs. "I take it you got your ass tossed around like a sack today as well?"

"Oh, most definitely." Kioh sighs. "Maybe there's a method, but it mostly seems like she's just pummeling us."

Rioz is opening her mouth to speak, when they hear the snap of a twig come from the left of them. Kioh whips her head around and sees Salem.

No, that's not right. It's not Salem. She looks like Salem. She has the same strong brow, wide nose, and round, almost circular, lips. But this woman has no burn scars, and looks at least a decade older.Rioz sees her too, but she fades into the shadows and disappears almost instantly.

"Did you see that?" Kioh asks.

"Yeah." Rioz seems dumbstruck. "Yeah. She looked like—"

"I know."

"Should we tell her?"

Kioh shakes her head. "I don't think so." She pauses. "It was probably nothing." They are near a town after all.

Kioh knows it wasn't nothing, though.

❧

Kioh doesn't notice anything else weird over the following three days of traveling. The woman never reappears, and neither Kioh or Rioz tell Salem about it. They continue their trek through the mountain pass as if nothing happened.

But then something does.

The six of them are eating some fried meat and rice, when Salem goes rigid where she sits.

"Someone's following us," she says, shoveling the remains of her food into her mouth and then grabbing her pack. She hurriedly stuffs whatever she took out for the day into her bag.

"We have to go."

No one questions her. Kioh finishes the bite she was taking and tosses the rest on the fire. Everyone else does the same. They all pack up their belongings and while hurling questions at Salem.

"How did you not notice them?"

"I don't know. They just popped within range, but they'd have to be close in order to trail us. I don't know how..." She trails off.

"How close are they?" Kabet asks.

"Close. They're planning an attack. We need to get out of here."

Bran chews anxiously on his lip. "It's almost night." A pause. "We just set up camp."

Salem shakes her head. "We'll have to walk through it."

The six of them pack up the rest in silence.

❧

Kioh is eleven years old again. Which is strange, she could have sworn she was eighteen. She is holding hands with a girl. She looks over. It's Salem. Her face is smooth, both her eyes are black. She is eleven, before her house was lit aflame.

"What are you doing here?" Kioh asks her, in her child's voice.

"I am your guide." She realizes this isn't Salem. She is a child, though, so she lets Salem lead her along anyway.

"This is your house," she points to her parent's large house. It's gleaming, brick, clay walls shining in the Taahuan sun. She leads Kioh by the hand to a pathway lined with fruit trees and dotted with beautiful flowers. She points to the ground. "This is your garden." She points down the path to two figures with no faces. "These are your parents."

Kioh turns to face her, and her eyes have rotted out of her skull. Kioh screams. This is not Salem, but it hurts her nonetheless. "This is the truth," her voice is distorted and ugly. The world strips away into a blank, endless void of emptiness and loneliness. Kioh screams. Thick, tangible silence comes out of her mouth.

"Kioh," she hears Salem's—the real one—voice speak into this empty chasm. The dark world around Kioh starts to swim with life. The ocean of empty becomes an ocean of creatures. She looks down to see her true form. Kioh is holding hands with Salem. The real Salem, and the real Kioh. Something unknown but not unpleasant builds inside her. She screams again, and this time it makes a noise. A small fish swims into Kioh's open mouth.

The Salem next to Kioh cups her face in her rough hands. "Kioh, please," she says. Kioh doesn't know what *she's asking for. Something hot rises in her chest, choking and burning. She screams again.*

"Kioh!"

Kioh's eyes snap open and she sees Salem crouching above her, shaking her by her shoulders. She gasps for breath, clutching her chest which is tight with fear and heat. Kioh lurches to her feet and stumbles towards the edge of the camp. Salem follows after her. Kioh collapses to her knees and Salem instinctively pulls her hair back as she vomits.

When she is finished she stumbles back towards the camp and collapses halfway there. Kioh feels herself changing, and she wants to scream. She resigns herself to mourn another set of ripped clothes.

Fantastic, she thinks bitterly. Her legs fade into a seamless, red fish tail. Thick scales cover her skin in patches, and her hands shift into gnarled claws and webbed fins. Her hair turns into thick, tight tendrils, much like the dreadlocks she used to wear. She feels her teeth shifting into jagged points, and her nose sinking backwards into her face.

Kioh looks back, still dazed from her dream, and sees Salem stop in her tracks. *Guess she doesn't know all my secrets,* Kioh thinks, remembering how her supposed knowledge of this caused Kioh's fight with Rioz. She almost laughs at how pointless she now realizes that was. She fights off whatever emotions forced her to change against her will.

Kioh takes a few deep breaths, and, eventually, feels herself starting to morph into her human form.

Salem opens her mouth to speak but Kioh cuts her off. "Not a word."

Her lips curl into a small smile. "Okay. But I have a question."

She sighs. "Go for it."

"I thought mermaid tails were supposed to be horizontal?"

"When you've seen a fish with a horizontal tail, let me know."

Salem's eyes glint. "Does that mean you're a fish?"

"Do I *look* like a fish?" Kioh regrets the words immediately.

"I mean—"

She cuts her off with a glare. "Not. A. Word."

Kioh sees her fight to suppress a laugh, and thinks maybe it isn't as bad as she thinks it is.

❦

It begins to get cold at night, as they trek onwards. So cold that each of them has to stay up, taking turns to tend the fire. Even Salem will poke and prod the fire to keep warmth alive. Blizzards kick up at all times of the day, Kioh does her best to part the snow around her friends, but the winds are brutal and fast. Pieces of ice freeze her face and sting them with microscopic cuts.

The trees have stopped providing cover because the trees have stopped growing here almost entirely. There is nowhere to hide besides in the mounds of snow and rock. Salem also told them to tread lightly, to talk softly, because they have entered avalanche territory.

They see no more animals. Winter birds do not sing. Their food supply is disappearing slowly. Kioh hopes it disappears slowly enough to get them to Canak.

Kioh is walking next to Salem when she freezes. Her body goes rigid. "Run," she says; quiet. So quiet Kioh almost doesn't hear her. She kicks into action and starts racing up the steep snow. Everyone takes off after her, and Kioh hears an arrow fly past them. It is close, far too close than anyone should be able to shoot in this wind.

They all keep running.

Kioh's lungs are heaving with effort, and the cold air is penetrating her scarf and seeping into her bones when they finally stop. It is beginning to get dark, darker than normal, so Kioh intuits that it must almost be night.

Salem sighs. "They should be off our tail for now. There's no way that they'd be able to track us in all these storms, and they can't get close enough to follow, so I don't..." She seems nervous.

Kioh takes a biscuit out of her pocket and eats it. Nervous Salem means that they won't set up camp for a while.

Then she hears it. It sounds like an animal growling, faintly. And then there is a crashing noise, like ceramic breaking.

That's when Kioh sees it. A mountain of pure force rushes towards them at a speed previously thought impossible. She desperately tries to remember what Salem said about avalanches.

"RIOZ!" Salem screams, her voice raw and ragged with the effort. Kioh sees panic on Salem's face and she knows that they might die in this encounter.

She then remembers what Salem said about avalanches.

"We will most likely die." She bites off of a piece of dried fruit. "We are all powerful, all deadly," she pauses. "But there is no force more deadly, more powerful, than the unforgiving, apathetic force of nature."

Kioh hears Rioz scream, it is filled with rage and desperation and fear, and it knocks Kioh backwards as she screams at the mountain rushing forwards. Bran channels fire from his hands, in an attempt to melt the wall of snow that is barreling towards the group, but it is in vain.

I should do something, but Kioh is frozen in fear.

Rioz shouts again, and force so tangible Kioh can *see* it charges out of her mouth. The avalanche reaches them, and she shrieks louder. Snow parts around them, over them. Rioz has hollowed out a sphere in the avalanche. Kioh can hear snow rushing over the top of them, but Rioz keeps screaming, her voice growing hoarse as she does so.

Finally the thunderous, crashing noise stops, and the six of them are knee deep in snow, a perfect dome around their heads; made of packed ice and snow. The world around is pitch black, they are buried under several feet of ice. Kioh hopes to every god out there that it doesn't collapse, crushing them all.

Rioz's voice trails off as the darkness begins to choke. As the last note of force comes out of her mouth, she falls quiet and Kioh hears a thud as she hits the ground.

Salem speaks, her voice weary, empty, and *tired.* "They're here. I don't know how, but they're here."

Kioh swears angrily. "Rioz is out cold. I could try to move it but—"

Salem sighs. Kioh can't see anything but she thinks she's holding her head in her hands. "It'd collapse and bury us."

"Where are the people?" Kabet asks.

"Close," Salem says. "Really close." The snow above them is low enough that the makeshift ceiling touches Kioh's hair. There's a long, stretching silence, before she speaks again. "In fact, they're right above our heads."

That is the last thing Kioh hears as the world erupts into a roar of grey.

❧

She snaps back moments later, and she's being choked and strangled by snow, but whoever is chasing them must apparently want them alive. The barest trace of light now leaks into the cave, and Kioh can see her surroundings. As the sky breaks open above them, their pursuers seem to be digging, not breaking. Kioh sees Salem tense beside her, who apparently withstood the massive wave of snow.

"Bran, get Rioz up."

Bran nods and prods at Rioz, while Jaz stands over her protectively, wings spread slightly: prepared for whoever is about to come barreling in.

It happens suddenly. It happens all at once.

Rioz's eyes snap open. She's so furious that potent rage seems to swirl in the air around her. She lets out a howl of anger, and this one is like nothing Kioh has heard from her before. The snow erupts around them, and some kind of force lifts her up, like a piece of driftwood on water. Kioh is tossed to and fro, before finally, she lands. On her knees. Safe.

The people who were above them seem shocked with their sudden eruption. There are ten people in total, five of which have black cowls pulled low over their faces. Rioz flies towards them, dagger in her teeth and arms hanging limp at her sides.

Something terrifying simmers in her eyes. Something far more powerful than anything Kioh has ever seen before has started to stir beneath the surface of her skin. She staggers towards the group of people, now splayed in the snow. She seems unsteady on her feet, almost as though she's still asleep.

With a roar, the knife goes flying out of her mouth and embeds itself with a sick thunk in the forehead of one of the cowled people. She then makes a noise like a wounded animal, and the knife goes flying back into her shaky hand.

Jaz screams from behind Kioh, desperate and horrified. He looks towards her, pleading. "Snap her out of it!" He's clutching his leg, and somewhere in the back of your mind, Kioh wonders if it's broken. "Don't just stand there!" he screams at her. She snaps into action.

Kioh opens her hand, palm splayed towards the sky, and lets power surge within her. A massive, ten foot wide hand of ice and water apparates in front of her. She swipes the hand towards Rioz, who screams at it, to no effect. Kioh makes a fist. Rioz is snared by the watery hand, and Kioh drags her backwards, dropping her next to Jaz.

Rioz snarls at Kioh, and she feels a force hit her arm, almost enough to break it. She ignores the pain and looks fervently around for the rest of their party.

Bran is to the left of Jaz. He stands up and rushes towards Rioz, who is now back on the ground, passed out once again.

Kioh sees Kabet standing up several paces in front of her. Just in front of him she sees Salem laying face down on the ground, clutching her knees and shaking violently.

Whatever fear was within her grinds to abrupt and painful halt, and then doubles. She rushes towards Salem and flips her over. Her eyes are open, and alive. However, they're unfocused, panicked, and horrified.

"Salem." Kioh feels terror rising in her throat. "Get up, Salem. We have to go."

Her eyes snap back to reality and she sits up as Kioh leans back to give her space. "What happened?"

"No idea. Let's get out of here." Salem wobbles to her feet, and then falls. Kioh manages to catch her around her waist. She sighs and picks her up. "Arm around my shoulders." Salem looks at Kioh in horror. "Salem, we have to get *out* of here." She does as Kioh said.

Kioh trusts in the fact that the others are following her, and takes off running. She feels Salem's body shaking with sobs, at one point. Kioh knows better than to point it out.

❦

Salem recovers, eventually. They keep running. Everyone followed Kioh, though, she thinks it was Salem they were following.

❦

The six of them run straight through the night and well into the day. They pause occasionally to sit, eat, and drink. Salem never lets them stop for long. Each time she stands up and starts walking back into the unforgiving winds, everyone follows her.

Eventually they make camp, but only because Salem's too tired to put up a fight.

"Why won't you let us fight them?" Kioh asks Salem. She gazes lifelessly into the fire.

"You're of no value to me if you're dead."

Indignancy flares inside her chest. "We're stronger than you give us credit for." A pause. "We'll be fine, even if there are ten of them."

"You're of no value to me if you're mortally injured, either. It's too close to call—Wait? Ten?"

Kioh opens her mouth to answer when Rioz screams. She should be used to Rioz screaming at this point, but she can tell something is wrong. So can Salem. The two of them surge into action and rush over to where she's standing.

Bran is laying on the ground, where he placed his bedroll, but something is terribly out of order. He's twitching and convulsing, his eyes darting back and forth beneath their lids. Black veins crisscross his forehead and neck, and sweat sheens on his skin even in the frigid cold.

"He is dying," Kabet says, voice tight.

And Kioh knows that his words ring true.

PART THREE: CHASE AND CHAMPION

Chapter Twelve

SALEM

ᚯᚭᚯ

SALEM RUNS TOWARDS HER house. *The sun baked mud cracks beneath her small, nimble feet. Omari is unbearably hot in the summers, with winds from the north blowing frigid cold down in the winters. She leaps from crack to crack, trying not to let her toes slip too far onto the pieces of baked mud.*

"Salem!" her mother calls. Salem grins at her, and she grins back. "It's time for dinner!"

She ceases her game of leaping, and runs full force up to her house. It is close to the city, close enough that at the end of the day she can watch the merchants wheel their wares home. Not close enough to play with the other children, though.

Salem's mother catches her in her strong, lean arms as she jumps towards her. She picks Salem up, spins her, and sets her back down on her feet. Salem has her mother's face. Her face is all sharp angles and oddities. The ridge of Salem's brow is strong, like hers. Salem's lips are round and large, like hers. Her nose flat, wide, and pointed at the corners, like hers.

"You may be your mother's still living reincarnation," Salem's father often says. *"But you get your height from me."*

Salem's mother is a tall woman. She has thick, muscular limbs and a lithe, long body. Her father is built more like her: gangly, slender, and short.

Salem is washing dishes from dinner with her mother when her father approaches her. "Salem," he says. "I have something for you."

"Xian." Her mother seems apprehensive. She is excited at the prospect of getting a gift.

"It is time, Zhengli. I know you agree with me." Then, in a quieter voice, "She has your father's spirit. She must learn to use it." Her mother ponders for a moment, and then nods, picking Salem up and walking her by the hand towards the small room they use for everything. The room is connected to the kitchen. There is no dining room, Salem eats and plays and sleeps in the same room. They all share a bed. However, her father has promised Salem her own room in the new house. She will miss being close to them, but is excited nonetheless.

Salem's mother sits her down on the floor, and her parents take their places in the only two chairs in the room. Salem sits at the table that they eat at, now cleared of food.

Her father leans down to the floor table and lays a long leather belt with pouches out on it. She doesn't recognize it, but it looks similar to the belt he wears now, with his daggers.

"This is my old dagger belt," he says. Salem listens. Her parents are serious, so she will listen. "It is now yours." He reaches his hand out to her mother, and she places one dagger into it. He places it on the table in front of Salem. "This is Rage." She nods. "Rage, like its name, is a deadly dagger. It can kill and corrupt and destroy. But it is also powerful, it can protect you and yours, it can *bring you power in bad situations. It can save you, when used correctly."*

Her father reaches another hand towards her mother. She places another dagger into it. He places it on the table in front of her. "This is Wish," he says. "Wish, like its name, is a hopeful dagger. It will fight for your wants and needs. It will be the embodiment of your greatest desire." He pauses. "But wishes can poison your mind, when you do not wish them well."

Salem's father looks at her, gaze full of love. "Salem, I am giving you these daggers. You must never use them needlessly. You must keep Rage and Wish balanced. You must promise me that you will never allow rage or desire to corrupt you, or your soul and mind will become poisoned. Promise me, Salem, to use these daggers well."

She nods and bows her head in thanks. "I promise."

Her mother gives her a warm smile. "They are yours now. You must keep them with you at all times."

She nods again. She will keep her promise to her parents.

Salem doesn't know what happened during the fight after the avalanche. She remembers Rioz screaming, sending them all flying into the air above. And then it goes black, except for that memory, which she hasn't thought about in *years*.

Everything from that fight has been erased from her mind, it lays at the fraying edges of her sanity. She doesn't dare to go looking for it.

Worse yet, Bran is dying. Salem doesn't know why. The medicine Rioz feeds him does nothing. He exhibits no symptoms of anything. The only symptom is dying.

She's almost positive it's the doing of one of their pursuers. Nothing else makes sense.

Rioz is on edge. She snaps at anyone who gets too close to Bran. Her eyes flit nervously across everything she can see, as though she's going to find answers there.

"Rioz," Salem tells her as the others pack up the camp. "We have to go."

Her lip curls in anger. "Of course you would leave him."

"We're not leaving him." Salem pities her, a bit. "But we have to go."

"He's too sick to transport." Rioz seems desperate; her tone pleading.

"We can leave and wait for him to die," Salem says. "Or we can stay, and there will be no waiting." She hesitates, then says, "It is far more dangerous to both him and the rest of us if we stay. I'm not going to lie and say it'll be a breeze, but it is the only shot we have."

Rioz's face crumbles. Her eyes well with tears that aren't there. Salem knows Rioz. She knows she will not cry. She nods solemnly. "Okay. How are we moving him?"

Salem points to the sled that Kabet carefully made with his abilities. She found a fallen tree, and then watched him change it into a perfectly crafted sled. She's not afraid of anything, but it was a bit terrifying. She grimly wonders what else he can do.

She watches as Rioz and Kabet hoist Bran's limp body from his bedroll to the sled. Rioz packs Bran's belongings into his bag, each movement stilted and sad.

I care if he dies, Salem thinks, with a start. She would care if any of them died. She shakes her head, clearing it of any sentimental thoughts.

Rioz straps herself into the harness of the sled. The harness is also crafted from wood, but it is far sturdier than most leather.

The five of them begin walking. Bran follows behind on his deathbed.

The mountain pass has grown brutal. The winds whip so fiercely that Salem stumbles each time they shift direction. The snow stings her face. She cannot see anything except white and the two silhouettes in front of her. There are no trees, no cover. There is nothing. They have entered a barren, snowy wasteland, as empty as their minds as they trudge along at a creeping pace.

Each breath hurts Salem. Her head is starting to swim.

"Why did you guys strap me in?" Bran's voice says from behind where Salem is pulling him. It's lilted in a joking tone. It takes her a moment to realize why that's strange.

"Bran?" Rioz says, her voice clenched with emotion.

"Surprised to see me alive?" He looks better. The black veins are fading into grey. The slick of sweat on his forehead is gone.

"I guess you could say that, yeah."

Bran closes his eyes. He is no longer as sick as he was, but it is clear that each word is costing effort. "If I die," he says, "make sure they bury me in a suit. If they put me in a dress I'll be so mad." He coughs, body convulsing.

"Who's they?" Rioz is laughing but Salem can tell she's barely keeping it together.

"My adoring fans, obviously."

Bran travels in and out of consciousness. Sometimes, when Salem thinks he's asleep, he'll make quips about something someone said. Other times, he'll be mid conversation, and his voice will just trail off, then stop.

The storm stops. Night falls. They keep walking.

"Please," Kabet says suddenly. "We should stop." His voice is hoarse and he looks sickly.

"You okay?" Kioh asks.

"There is no snow in Sunan," he says. "I have never seen it. Now it is all I see. Quite a transition."

Kioh laughs. "Try being fourteen and from Taahua. It's been four years and I'm not used to it."

"Where you are from?" The five of them have started to slow, looking for a place to stop. "I hear it is a beautiful country."

Kioh nods. She seems forlorn. "It is."

The six of them make camp on the side of a massive snow bank. It provides little shelter from the world around, but it's more than nothing. There are no trees to make a shelter, or to start a fire. Salem takes the massive blanket out of her pack and throws it over their group. It is built to stand stiff and not collapse. They all stay huddled close beneath it. Bran is looking far better, and he and Rioz chat idly as they eat a little of what jerky they have left.

Kioh moves over to Salem so they can talk. It is not much of a feat: there is not that much room under the makeshift shelter.

"Do you think he'll be okay?" She asks. Her voice is almost impossible to hear.

"I don't know."

She sighs. "Do you know what it is?"

"I have a theory."

She nods, then falls silent. "Hey, Salem?"

The tone of her voice almost makes Salem nervous. "What?"

"Did you mean it when you said that you don't intend on getting out of this alive?"

Salem feels a bolt of anger jar her. "I don't say things I don't mean."

Kioh sighs and reaches into her bag, pulling out some jerky. She takes a bite, and is silent for another long stretch of time. "Do you think that's what your parents would want?"

"I think my parents are dead," she snarls.

Kioh's voice is quiet. "I don't think your parents would want you to die too."

Salem's anger simmers like ice within her. "I don't think it matters what my parents would want, because they were *murdered*."

Kioh's voice raises slightly. "And why are you so quick to follow in their footsteps?"

"Because I have nothing *left*!" Her breathing comes out ragged. "There is nothing for me after this. Do you understand that? *Nothing*. There is no family for me to go home to, there is no satisfaction at the end of the road. There is nothing beyond *empty* and *dead*." Salem takes a deep breath, pausing to collect herself. "Kioh, I am not a person anymore. Do you get that? I feel nothing. I want nothing. I enjoy nothing. I *am* nothing. I am not doing this because I want to. I am not doing this because it will bring me peace. I am doing this because it has to be done."

Kioh looks at Salem down her long, straight nose. Anger flares on her proud, regal face. "I don't believe that."

"Well it's a good thing it's not your choice."

"I won't let you die."

Salem laughs. Cold and empty. Her mother once told her that she had a beautiful laugh. It's the ugliest thing she's ever heard, now. "You sure can try."

Salem is woken in the middle of the night by Bran convulsing. His body is twitching and shaking. Rioz is trying to wake him up, to snap him out of it. Her attempts are in vain.

As she comes to, blinking exhaustion out of her eyes, she senses a presence, and then four more. "They're here." She shakes Kioh awake, then Jaz. Kabet was awake when she woke up. "They're here." Salem says.

"*Goddamnit*," Kioh mutters. She stuffs her things into her pack. Everyone else begins to do the same.

"How close?" Jaz asks.

An arrow slices through the dense blanket, leaving a deep gouge on Salem's face. It gets stuck halfway through, she follows its point to where it was aimed.

They were aiming for Rioz, Salem thinks. Jaz seems to know it too. Their adversaries learn from their mistakes.

Blood trickles from Salem's cheekbone into her mouth.

With one fluid motion, Salem stands up and pulls the blanket mostly into her bag. She pulls the bag onto her back. An arrow wizzes towards her. She sidesteps before it even leaves the bow. She then reaches her hand out and catches it.

Someone whistles in appreciation from the dark.

"Someone's got skills!" a low, mocking voice says. Out of the darkness steps a figure. He cups a hand to his lips, and Salem sees a flame appear in the night. He moves his hand to the torch he's holding. That's when she realizes the flame is coming from his hand. Something like anger snarls through her. Something like fear.

The figure is suddenly illuminated, both by the light of the faint moon, and the torch. He has flaming orange hair, dark, malicious eyes, and he's wearing a confident smirk. His face is thin, gaunt, and pointed. A cigarette is perched on his lips. He takes a drag.

"Now, when the queen told me to chase down a group of six rebels. I had my doubts." He breathes in through the cigarette. Then exhales: a cloud of smoke and steam floats into the cold, dark air. "But this is shaping up to be *very* fun indeed."

Four more figures step out from the darkness.

And then five more, behind one of them. They have dark cowls pulled over their faces. They encircle a woman, who is standing on the fray of the torchlight.

A horrible, sick feeling of disgust and fear shocks Salem to her very core. The five figures do not have thoughts.

Her mind races as she tenses for a fight, but going in against someone without thoughts is like going in blind, for her.

"Now," the woman says, "I'm not one to battle without a chat beforehand. I believe introductions are in order." She steps into the firelight. Her entire eyes are a solid, unmoving black. "I am Lydia." Lydia has bone white skin. Salem can see grey veins crisscrossing beneath it. Her hair is straight, black, and parted down the middle. It goes to her shoulders. She has high cheekbones with a slender nose that cuts perfectly down the middle of her pointed face. Her lips are painted a perfect, fresh-blood red. They stretch into a crude approximation of a polite smile. She's holding a scythe.

"This," she points to the young boy smoking a cigarette, "is Tomas." She then points to a girl, about the same age as Salem. The girl is holding a bow, arrow nocked, pointed straight at Rioz. Her eyes do not blink. She does not move a muscle. She has white-blond hair, plaited in two tight braids. Her eyes are piercing; as sharp as daggers. Even in the night they glow acid green.

"That is Mira. Forgive her if she doesn't talk much," Lydia says. Lydia inclines her head to the left, where the remaining two are standing.

"My name's Lark," says the girl. Lark is completely bald, and the most beautiful person Salem has ever seen. She has brown skin that looks like dark rust. Her eyes are large and pointed at each end. Her nose juts far out from her face, and crooks halfway down.

Lark's eyes do not look at Salem, or any of them. The irises are an opaque white, and they are completely unseeing. Still, she twirls the scimitar she's holding like an expert.

A man built like a bear with brown hair and beady blue eyes considers them all with disgust. "Rok."

Salem hears Kioh laugh behind her. Rok shifts his gaze over to her and she sees his nostrils flare. "Sorry," she says, not sorry at all. "It's just that your name is Rok, and well, you're kind of as ugly as one!"

Salem hears him growl, starting to move forward towards Kioh, but Lydia holds up a slender hand. He stops, and Salem sees fear flash across his face.

Lydia gestures to the five hooded-figures behind her. "These are, of course, my servants."

"Well," Lydia says. "That's all of us. Tomas, Rok, and I are our queen's devoted subjects." She looks towards Mira and Lark with distaste. "Those two had to be bought."

Lark spits towards Lydia. "Your queen is a poison upon this earth. A thankless killer." Her words are heavy with an accent Salem can't identify.

"And you're not?"

"I do it for money, not pleasure." Lark turns towards them, almost apologetic. "Business is business."

Tomas snarls at all of them. "Can we just kill them already?"

"Yes," Lydia grins, and it looks hungry. "Let's begin." They all tense for battle but before anyone can move, Jaz steps forward.

"Yeah," he says. "Let's." And then he screams. It is not like how Rioz screams. It carries a melodic note, dipping and humming into an unseen rhythm.

The five opposing Salem drop their weapons, then collapse face forward into the snow.

The others seem to instinctively know what's happening. Kabet straps himself into Bran's sled, scoops up his bag, and starts running. Everyone else follows suit. Jaz slowly backs up, but continues singing. When he drops his voice, they run harder.

"I forced them to fall asleep, he says, looking sickly and fatigued. "It should buy us about an hour or two."

Salem nods as she runs. She knows it will buy them thirty minutes, maybe. The best they can hope for is to make it to Canak within the week, and hopefully not die of exhaustion beforehand.

CHAPTER THIRTEEN

LARK

Φ

"THE QUEEN WILL KILL you," a voice says from the darkness. Lark hears the snap of a rope going taut.

"The queen will kill you," another voice says. "The queen will kill you no matter what."

"You will die a thousand deaths. You will scream a million screams."

"Truth will be your salvation."

The voices compete for a spot in her head. The darkness is endless. The darkness is more than endless. The darkness goes on for miles. Miles do not exist. Nothing exists.

Lark sorts through the clamor for snatches of important phrases.

"The Dominoes. You must protect the Dominoes."

"Trust Mira."

"Fire and fire yields only flame." She hears the crackle of tinder and the roar of an explosion. Heat fans her face.

"You will not save them all."

"Death must be killed."

"Your life lay in the hands of the six."

"I get it!" Lark shouts into her mind. "Anything else?"

Two voices seem to be having a conversation. "Truth will not."

"'It is time to leave, Atina.'"

"Dying words. Words to die for."

Lark tunes the rest out. It is too far ahead to make any sense. Another voice speaks. It hits her with such force that she feels her skin tingle.

"The game is in the catching. The win is in the loss."

The bustle of voices goes quiet. Lark hears nothing more.

She opens her eyes. She doesn't know why. Lark has been blind since she was born, but closing her eyes helps her focus. She uncrosses her legs, unclasps her hands, and lay back.

So, she thinks to herself, *the queen intends to kill me, huh?* She reaches over and grabs a piece of roasted meat right off the spit. She has to feel around for it awkwardly, so grease and fat ends up covering her hand. *Eugh,* Lark thinks.

She will not be killed by the queen. She refuses to be another victim of her idiotic power plays. Lark will not swear loyalty to her, either. She has more dignity than that.

"Who is asleep?" Lark asks.

"Lydia."

"Rok and Tomas."

She smiles to herself. *Excellent.* She could kill them here, but something tells her that's not what needs to happen.

"Mira," she says. "It's time to switch sides." She knows that the others won't hear her. She knows a lot of things.

"The other side isn't helping me."

"The other side isn't killing you, either."

"Your pitiful voices tell you that?"

Lark sighs. "I think that you have no reason to doubt me, since you can also do extraordinary things."

"Little overconfident, are we?"

"*How do I convince her?*" Lark asks.

"*Her mother's name is Sella. Her father's name is Edward.*"

"*She is afraid of leeches.*"

"*Her favorite flower is red in color.*"

She dutifully relays the information to Mira. She doesn't speak for a while.

"Well, shit," Mira says. "What's your plan?"

Lark grins and turns towards her voice. "I'm working on it."

Chapter Fourteen

JAZ

Ø

EVERYTHING IS STARTING TO go sideways. Salem seems exhausted, and, for the first time in the long weeks Jaz has known her, she looks nervous. She looks nervous to the point that it sets everyone on edge.

Bran is dying. Jaz doesn't like thinking about it. He doesn't like thinking about death in general, but Bran is one of the closest approximations to a friend he has. Bran's dying seems to have also killed whatever morale and camaraderie that the six of them had scraped together. It wasn't much, in the first place, but now it's nonexistent.

Rioz and Bran were the two Jaz talked to the most. Now, Bran couldn't string together a sentence if he wanted to, and Rioz has fallen mute with him. He tries to talk to her, tries to cheer her up. She looks at him with warmth in her eyes, but it is the warmth of a dying hearth.

Jaz has a feeling that if Bran dies, Rioz will as well.

Bran is growing gaunt. His cheeks are sunken, his limbs too frail to move. He looks like a breeze could snap him in half, and the winds up here are far stronger than a breeze.

It's strange. When the five of them have been walking for a long period of time, he seems to recover. His body stops convulsing and regains some of his color. It's as though walking heals him.

Rioz comments on it one day. "Why is it that when we walk he gets better?" Her voice is desperate and searching.

"It's not the walking," Salem says with a sigh. "It's the distance."

Rioz's eyes grow hopeful. "From what?"

"That woman." Salem looks around. "Let's make camp here, and allow me to explain."

The six of them stop. There's really nothing to make camp against. The pass has grown frigid and barren. Jaz wonders why Salem didn't put this scheme off until summer.

"Timing's key," she says. He's about to ask what that was in reference to, but then he realizes she was just reading his thoughts. He suppresses a shudder.

Salem takes the large, tent-like blanket out of her bag. They all crawl, undignified, underneath it. "Rioz, I know what's wrong with your brother."

Jaz sees pain, anger, and hope spring to her eyes. "What? What is it? How do we fix it?"

"We can't." Salem pauses. "The ten people that attacked us? Five of them are dead. They don't have thoughts. They have the presence of a rotting log, which is to say, none at all."

He can see the anger taking over in her eyes. "What does this have to do with Bran?" Rioz snarls.

"That woman, Lydia, is a necromancer. I heard tale of her powers when I was in the Queen's army. She can resurrect the dead with just an image. I think she's sapping Bran's life force. The only cure is for her to die, or to get away from her."

Rioz looks at Salem down her thin, jutting nose. "Then we kill her."

Salem looks back at Rioz with just as much animosity. "We have to run."

"My brother's life isn't up for debate, Salem."

"Neither are ours." Salem says. "You would sacrifice everyone for a miniscule shot at saving Bran?"

"A hundred times. A thousand."

Salem doesn't react. Her face doesn't change in any decipherable way. "Alright then. We'll fight, the next time they reach us."

A prickle across Jaz's skin tells him this won't end well.

Ø

"We'll run away," Prolok says. He balances finely on the plank of wood that crosses the stream. They are miles from the orphanage. They are miles away from the things that don't matter.

"And go where, exactly?" Jaz jumps across the creek, wings snapping out to help him balance. The thin plank would surely topple him into the stream.

Prolok does a complete backflip, lands on his hands, and starts walking on them. He's built like a cat, pure sinew and bone. "I don't know." He flips back onto his feet. "Anywhere."

"We'd die out there."

"We're dying here."

Jaz sighs. "Maybe someday."

Prolok touches his fingertips to the fresh scratches running down Jaz's face. Prolok's face is unmarred by Lee's cruelty. Jaz doesn't blame him. He's not an easy target like Jaz is.

"Soon," he says.

"Soon," Jaz agrees.

Ø

"They're here." Salem draws her daggers and stands still. She looks unthreatening, at a glance. But Jaz has trained enough with her to know that Salem is likely the most deadly thing alive.

He's not sure how the rest of them will fare.

Rioz seems to have the same realization, and she looks nervous. Salem's lip curls without taking her eyes off of the wasteland around. "You're the one who wanted to fight, Howl." Salem has taken up calling them by their other names when other people are around. They must be within earshot, then.

Rioz says nothing. She pulls her tiny black dagger from the sheath around her neck. She sticks the hilt in her mouth and scans the area around.

An arrow shoots from the veil of white and lands a hair away from Salem's foot. Jaz thinks about how well the shot was aimed last night.

Did she miss on purpose? he wonders, then pulls his garrote from the pocket on his pack and takes his stance. He hears a wet snapping noise, and flicks his eyes to where it came from. Kioh is standing above a body, bloody cane braced against the ground. She looks worried as she shakes blood splatter from her hand.

The blood looks wrong. It looks old even though it's fresh. The body stands back up, recovering from what seemed to be a killing blow.

Jaz feels a chill dance across his spine. *This won't end well.*

Prolok's dead, blank face stares back at him from across the snow. The side of his head is caved in by Kioh's cane, and Jaz watches as it heals itself, still bleeding old blood. His face is now pristine, perfect, and completely vacant.

Jaz chokes on an aborted sob, and somewhere in the air he hears laughter.

"These are five very *special* puppets," Lydia says, right behind him.

"Jaz!" Rioz screams from around the knife. The force shoves him backwards just as a scythe slices across where he had been standing.

"Well that is *very* annoying," Lydia snaps, charging towards Rioz. Rioz dances out of the way, twisting her body impossibly as the scythe crashes through empty air.

Jaz feels a sudden gust of wind kick up, and snow so thick he can barely see through it starts to swirl through the air.

This won't end well.

He watches from the outskirts of the fight, still sitting where Rioz knocked him back to. He watches as the other pursuers step forwards from the storm. Mira has an arrow nocked. Her green eyes scan for something to shoot, and Jaz realizes that they lack pupils.

He flicks his eyes to where Kioh is standing, still sparring with Prolok. Who, in death, seems to have developed overwhelming strength. Kioh bats his fists away with expert speed, the cane smashing whatever bones it collides with. But Prolok just heals and keeps attacking.

Jaz hears a cackle coming from behind him.

"Those are some *interesting* burn scars you've got, girly. Want to add to the collection?" And Tomas surges forwards, intent on death.

Salem evades him easily. She sidesteps each burst of flame he sends her way. Her face is expressionless, as dead as Prolok's. She may not take hits, but with each wave of heat that reaches her, Jaz sees her flinch.

Kabet is dueling with two hooded figures. He morphs his weapon and blocks every blow, adapting to every situation. One of the figures gets him on his back, his weapon shifts into a whip of steel. He cracks it upwards, and Jaz sees the puppet reel backwards from the strike.

"What *are* you?" Tomas snarls as Salem dodges him easily. He's bleeding from the mouth and Jaz knows he'll go down soon.

He stands up, fanning his wings out. He walks towards where Kioh is starting to lag. Rioz stands protectively over Bran's body. Lydia presses her closer and closer to him.

Jaz knows she'll be fine.

He has to kill Prolok. He's why he's here, afterall.

Prolok is preoccupied with attacking Kioh, so Jaz leaps onto his back and wraps his garrote tight around his throat.

Prolok tries to shake him off to no avail. Jaz pulls the wire tighter. He wonders if he will have to see his old friend's head roll. Jaz looks desperately towards Kioh. She meets his pained gaze, and surges into action.

She cuts Prolok down at the knees with her cane. Jaz hears the wet crunch of bone, and Prolok sinks to the ground, incapacitated.

Kioh cracks him once again, in the ribs this time, and he falls to his hands.

Smashed body on the rocks. Jaz screams. He screams and screams and Prolok does not move. His normally mischievous brown eyes are hollow, blank, and dead. His left arm is twisted in a way that shouldn't be possible. His head is crushed. Blood is surging up through his stomach. Jaz screams. He does not move. He screams. He does not move.

Jaz feels tears spilling from his eyes and he blinks them back, refocusing on the fight. Prolok goes down as he chokes him, as Kioh begins to kill him, smashing his body to bits in the way Jaz did two years ago.

"I'm sorry," Jaz lets out a sob. "I'm so sorry." He pulls the garrote tighter. His neck breaks beneath his hands and Jaz screams in agony. "I'm so sorry."

"Jaz," Kioh says. Her voice is clipped and tight. "He was already dead."

"I killed him," Jaz sobs. "I killed him *twice*."

"Jaz," Kioh says. "We have to keep going."

He nods, numbly, getting to his feet. The two of them have done enough damage to Prolok's body that he's having trouble recovering.

For the moment, it seems like they're winning the fight. Every member of their party seems to be doing fine. Mira launches arrows, but none hit their mark. Salem presses on against the fire. Rioz handily holds off Rok and Lydia as she stands over Bran. Kabet, too, is managing just fine.

And then Lydia laughs. "Alright," she says, pausing her assault against Rioz. "I'm tired of this."

A tiny figure, as small as a child, lunges from the storm and crashes into Salem. With one hand they pull their hood back, and with the other, they choke her, pressing her into the ground. Tomas advances on her hungrily and she chokes out a suppressed scream.

How did she get the drop on Salem? And then Jaz remembers her words: *"The ten people that attacked us? Five of them are dead. They don't have thoughts. They have the presence of a rotting log, which is to say, none at all."*

He hears Kabet let out a wounded yelp as the child pulls her cowl back. She's Sunani, and can't be more than ten. Her eyes have the same blank look Prolok's do.

Jaz looks over to Kabet. The two puppets have also paused in their assault. Mira nocks an arrow and aims it at Rioz.

And then Lark steps out of the storm. He almost forgot about her.

"Yeah," she hums, seeming amused. "Let's get this over with."

Faster than he can blink Mira's arrow fires. He does not have time to warn Rioz.

He doesn't have to.

The arrow embeds itself into the forehead of the girl choking Salem. She flies backwards and goes skidding across the snow.

Mira nocks another arrow before Jaz has time to process what happened. She pulls back, and releases within the span of a breath. It flies straight and true.

It is aimed at Lydia, who, within seconds of the arrow hitting the little girl, seems to process what is going on. She grabs Rioz and pulls her in front of her.

Rioz screams as she does this, the tiny black dagger flies out of her mouth and embeds itself in Rok's throat. His last breath gurgles in his sliced windpipe. It then hurtles clumsily back into her hand.

The arrow hits Rioz in the shoulder.

She crumbles to the ground like a broken boulder. She lets out an earth-shattering roar, and instantly Jaz feels blood drip from his ears. The arrow lodged in her shoulder disintegrates into fine dust, which gets whipped up in the wind.

Lark strides towards Jaz and Kioh. Confident and ramrod straight even in the howling wind.

Jaz tenses for a fight but Kioh places a hand on his shoulder. *Wait*, it says.

"Things are about to go to shit," she says. "Shall we get going?"

Kioh doesn't hesitate. She nods, and says, "Where to?"

"Canak, presumably."

And then things go wrong.

Salem shrieks, ear-splitting and horrified. Jaz whips his head towards the noise. She charges blindly away from the fight she was just in. She runs, terrified, into the storm.

"Salem," Kioh whispers to herself. "Jaz, listen to me. We can't trust them, they can't trust us. Crime is my business, and this is the first rule. *Follow her.*" She points to Lark. Her eyes bore into his, determined and proud. She then turns into the wind, and races off after Salem. Lark looks towards Mira, who nods. Mira then walks after the two.

"Traitors!" Lydia howls. And then she reaches into her bag and grabs what looks like a fistful of bones. She throws them into the air. Then, she too disappears after Salem and Kioh.

Jaz watches, enraptured by his terror, as the bones begin to grow dark, dead flesh midair. Sinew, muscle, tendon and bone materializes from nothing. The effect is immediate and grotesque. By the time the creature falls to the ground, the tip of its short yet gruesome tail has just finished growing.

Standing in front of them is a two-headed, twenty-foot high, black, snarling bear. It paws the ground and lets out a furious scream.

"Rioz!" Jaz shouts over the howl of the wind, which is really getting nasty, now. "We need to get out of here, *now!*" She seems to agree with him. She grabs Bran's sled by the harness, and hauls him forwards. Her hands become bloody from the effort.

Lark turns to Jaz, but her eyes are trained over his shoulder, unseeing. Her face is grim. "There's no chance you can fly with these wings you supposedly have, is there?"

"Sadly, they're for decorative purposes only."

Kabet rushes over to what remains of their party. "The two I was fighting. I think they are—" He is cut off by a massive bear paw swiping towards him.

Rioz shouts. "Stop it!" The paw explodes into bloody chunks. She's breathing hard. "I," The ground, the actual ground beneath the snow, starts to shiver beneath them. "am," Another shudder runs through the earth. "*done!*" The noise echoes through the sky and the ground groans in protest.

"Rioz..." Jaz trails off nervously as the very earth itself starts to split. She whirls on him, her eyes bleeding fury into the atmosphere.

"NO!" She shouts and blood springs from his nose. He sees Lark behind Rioz. *When did she get there?* Jaz wonders.

Lark hits Rioz in the back of the neck with two fingers. When she pulls away, there is a needle protruding from her neck. Rioz collapses to the ground in a heap.

Rage surges within Jaz and his voice begins to build in his unwilling throat. He's about to release it when Lark speaks. "She's fine," she says. "Asleep, but fine." She turns towards where Kabet is standing. "Put her on the sled." He complies. "We're getting out of here."

"What about Lydia?"

She pauses, as though thinking before she answers. "Lydia is pursuing Mira and your other two friends. She will not be an issue for us."

"And the other one?" Kabet asks.

She pauses again, considering. "'Truth did quite a number on him,' they tell me. He will not be able to move for a while. That bear is the only issue."

As soon as it is mentioned, it seems to recover from its removed leg, swiveling towards them. It releases an outraged roar as its foot regenerates to the very last hair.

"We're getting out of here," Lark says again. She clips the harness of the sled on, which now holds both Bran and Rioz, and begins to walk forwards through the storm.

Follow her, Jaz thinks. It sounds like Kioh.

He trudges begrudgingly after. Kabet hesitates, and then follows, as well.

CHAPTER FIFTEEN

RIOZ

RIOZ WAKES UP UNDER a roof for the first time in two weeks. She dimly wonders if the entire thing was a dream. If she is home, if she will wake up to her mother's proud eyes and her father's smiling face. If Bran will look at her, eyes alight, as she tells him about a dream that she could've never thought possible.

She feels a dull throbbing pain in her neck. She reaches up and pulls a thick, sturdy needle from deep within her flesh. She realizes she is stretched out across the floor, on top of her bedroll with Jaz's threadbare blanket stretched over her. She sits stiffly up. *Not a dream, then.*

The sky outside the window above her is dark, but they are so deep in the mountains that that means nothing. Jaz is sleeping in a wooden chair next to her, his wings uncomfortably situated. There's a book open in his lap, god knows where he got it.

Rioz flicks the needle off to the side and stretches her sore muscles.

"Finally awake, huh?" an unfamiliar voice says from behind her and Rioz snaps to her feet, jostling Jaz's chair in the process.

Lark's white eyes stare blankly in her direction. Rioz lunges at her, shoving her against the wall and presses her elbow to her throat. She doesn't even flinch.

"Well now, I'm flattered, but I don't even know what you look like." She laughs at her own joke, and Rioz feels the point of a weapon digging into her stomach. "Now let's back off, shall we? I don't want to have to gut you."

"Rioz," Jaz says from behind her as she feels a growl building in her throat. "She's on our side."

"I don't *care*." She is exhausted. She has been walking for weeks. She has been running while her brother dies beside her. She is tired and fed up and enraged. Rioz wants to *kill* her.

"Rioz, please." She's about to snarl at Jaz when she realizes that's not his voice.

Instantly, Rioz drops her arm and turns around to see Bran standing on shaky legs. He's propped himself up on the table, a lazy and exhausted grin stretched across his pale face. Tears spring to her eyes and she forces them down with a hesitant smile. He's *alive*. She walks over to him and crushes him in a hug which he weakly reciprocates.

"If you ever worry me like that again I'll kill you for real."

Bran laughs and says. "You would never."

Rioz laughs, voice thick and choked. "You're right."

He is right. Bran is her heart. If she lost him she would no longer have one.

Jaz tells her all about what happened after she was rendered unconscious by Lark.

"Bran got better after a while." He pauses. "Lark said that Lydia followed Salem and Kioh, so Bran will be fine now."

Neither of them mention whether or not Salem and Kioh will be fine.

It's the dead of night. Jaz explains how Lark knew this cabin was here.

"Wait, so you can see the future?" Rioz asks, incredulous.

Lark smirks without looking at her. "I can't *see* anything."

Rioz raises an eyebrow, then realizes she can't see and feels ridiculous. "Then how does it work?"

"I ask questions and I am provided with answers."

"From who?"

"Why does it matter? We are here and I am responsible." She throws a piece of dried fruit into her mouth.

Rioz scoffs. "You sound like Salem."

"Is that Truth?"

Rioz nods, then once again realizes Lark can't see her. "Yes."

"I've heard a lot about her."

Rioz laughs. "Such as?"

Lark pauses, as if thinking. When she speaks it's not her voice. "'*Poisoned. Poisoned by anger.*'" She pauses again. "'*Truth is more powerful than you can fathom.*'" The next voice is deeper. "'*She can still be saved.*'" Lark waves her hand dismissively. "Stuff like that."

"That all...seems harsh."

Jaz looks at her, amused. "I mean, it's Salem."

Rioz huffs, annoyed. "Just because she's aloof and terrifying doesn't make her a monster."

Jaz rolls his eyes, but seems in good spirits. "I would know that better than you. I'm just saying Lark's not wrong."

"You mean the voices," Lark corrects. "I haven't even met this Salem person, I have no opinion."

"You are not omniscient?" Rioz realizes Kabet is awake, now. She turns to him, and sees light beginning to stream through the small, snow-filled window. It's faint. it's always faint in this weather, but it is there.

Lark grins like a wolf. "Fancy word."

"For a fancy man," Kabet says. He's gotten better at joking.

Lark's grin stretches wider. "No, I am not omniscient. I only know what is known by others. And they will only tell me a fraction."

"Then how can you s—" Rioz cuts herself off, "...know the future?"

"Fate cares not for time. What will happen, if it can be seen, is known."

Kabet shuffles across the small room towards Bran. He stands over Bran and looks down at him fondly. "I am glad he is better," he says, looking towards Rioz.

"Me too," and he couldn't possibly know how much she means it.

♯

Lark tells them it would be unwise to move. She doesn't know why, though. She tells them that Tomas will be easily overpowered by the five of them, and that they have some time before he even finds them.

Bran grows progressively better. The color floods back to his face and his curls no longer sheen with grease and sweat. He has never been thin, but he looked gaunt on his deathbed.

He no longer looks as though he will die any day.

Lark seamlessly worms her way into their group. Rioz thinks she has an unfair advantage, knowing exactly what she should and shouldn't say.

Though, she thinks, *that rarely stops her.*

Lark is easily the boldest brashest person Rioz has ever met. She is confident to the point of stupidity, and frank to the point of being mean.

Her and Kabet get along famously.

Rioz has realized that Kabet's appearances disguise what is actually underneath. He looks distinguished. He speaks foreign languages like a scholar. He carries himself with humility. Kabet appears, in almost every way, refined.

It was about a week into their journey when everyone started to realize it was quite a different story. Kabet is reckless and impulsive. He does idiotic things because he is overly confident. He laughs in the face of danger and takes delight in rash decisions.

Rioz remembers something Bran told her. While she was still figuring Kabet out, Bran seemed ahead of the curve.

"Kabet is kind. He is smart and good. But he lacks any facsimile of sense," Bran told her, laughing.

"How can he be smart and lack sense?"

"He knows more about any subject than any of us. But, Rioz, let's be honest, he'd drink his death on a taunt."

She laughs. She thinks her brother has it right.

Lark and Kabet fill the cabin with laughter and light. It is nice, to see carelessness when it can be afforded.

As Bran grows healthier he also grows angrier, for a reason that Rioz cannot put her finger on. Bran can be mean, she knows better than anyone.

Their mother once said, very simply, *He is nice, until he isn't.*

Rioz saw his point turned on Salem, but Salem is not the kind of person to have anything pointed at her, so that was over quickly.

However, now he snaps and snarls at Kabet. He makes angry quips and says snarky turns of phrase that just *sound* cruel. Kabet cows like a kicked dog each time.

The cabin is one large room, and there is dense feet of snow outside. No one can go anywhere.

Kabet is scrawling in a journal he must've brought with him. Lark is tossing pieces of jerky at him which he attempts to dodge. Her aim is rather terrible.

"You have not even hit me once!" Kabet laughs.

Lark grins. "I'm blind, you fool."

"You should have hit me at least once."

Bran glowers at them from where the two of them are seated, reading one of the (horrible) books that were left in this cabin.

Suddenly it clicks.

Rioz smacks Bran upside the back of his head. (Lightly, he *did* just recover from dying. But he's being stupid.)

He gasps and moves his hand to his head. "What was *that* for?"

"Stop being foolish."

Bran glares at her. "Finally caught on, huh? Took you long enough."

"If you told me I wouldn't have to catch on." Rioz turns back to her dull book.

Bran hesitates, then sighs. "I didn't think I could."

She resists the urge to hug him. "Not my fault you have terrible selection in men."

"Peter wasn't *that* terrible."

"Peter was *horrible*, are you insane?"

"He was nice!"

Rioz laughs. "He was dumber than a dog, Bran!" She grins. "I'm beginning to think you have a type."

Bran huffs and crosses his arms. "Kabet isn't stupid."

"I know."

"I'm just jealous."

"I know." A pause. "I can still beat him up for you, if you want."

"Refrain, for now." He looks back blankly at his book. "Was Peter really that bad?"

"Worse. I approve wholeheartedly of this one, if it helps," Rioz says, laughing, and claps Bran on the shoulder.

He rolls his eyes. "I don't need your approval."

"No, but Kabet does."

Bran sighs, dejected and deflated. "At least Peter wasn't oblivious."

"At least Kabet isn't Kendren," she counters.

Bran frowns. "I'm Kendren."

"Yes," a pause, "but you're my brother, so I have to like you."

♯

Rioz's heart feels full in this cabin. The situation is horrible, sure, but there is joy in the way her and Bran laugh together and there is comfort in throwing Jaz's blanket over him after he falls asleep while reading.

They fall into a routine for the five days they are there. Rioz wakes up when faint, grey sunlight streaks in through the window, then kicks Jaz lightly until he, too, is awake, and the two of them get up and make breakfast for everyone. There is not much for breakfast, only what is left of their supplies and the supplies that Lark had, but they make do.

Rioz spends mornings teaching Jaz to cook. She spends afternoons reading and chatting idly with Bran as he shoots glares at Kabet and Lark. She laughs when he does this. The evenings are devoted to training, and though not quite as intense as what Salem was doing, she can feel herself getting better, stronger.

Rioz is cooking breakfast with Jaz one day when an idea strikes her.

"I have an idea," she tells him.

He groans and looks up towards the snowy sky, as if pleading with a god. "Oh no."

"My ideas are great," Rioz grumbles, scooping the portions of the meager meal they made into bowls.

"What is it?"

"Let me pierce your ears."

He gawks like a fish for a moment before shrugging in feigned nonchalance. "Yeah, alright."

She grins at him, happier than she has been for a while, and he blinks rapidly, as though he's confused. "I was hoping you would say that." Rioz scoops up some of the bowls from the fire and walks into the cabin, Jaz follows after her with the rest.

After everyone eats, Rioz silently grabs Jaz by the hand and drags him over to where her bag sits beneath the window.

"Wait, right now?" She can hear the panic in his voice.

"Is the mystery boy afraid of needles?" she asks, arching an eyebrow.

"I'm afraid of being stabbed like a reasonable person."

Rioz laughs and digs the kit she uses out of her backpack. Bran drops to his knees beside them and gives Rioz a quizzical look when he sees what she has in her hands.

"Something happen?"

"Nah, I'm doing Jaz's ears." Jaz is looking at Bran blankly and Rioz knows that means he's confused. "Piercings are customary in Talir culture, and we normally only get them after an important life event." Rioz pauses. "Earlobes are normally done after the first birthday, so I guess that means Jaz is turning one."

"Happy first birthday!" Bran drawls sarcastically. Jaz glares at both the siblings.

She begins to prepare the needle as Jaz looks nervously at it. Bran grabs her bag and pulls out the cloth pouch of various earrings and passes it to Jaz.

"Pick a set," Rioz tells him. "Nothing with chains, those will hurt like hell and they're also my favorite." He dumps the earrings out onto her bedroll and looks at them.

He laughs at the disarray of her jewelry. "Very organized, you are."

"Wise thing to say to the girl who's about to stab you with a needle." Jaz visibly pales and Rioz laughs.

Jaz picks up a pair of large green studs, with a black ring around the edge. Rioz outstretches her hand and he drops them into it, looking nervous.

"Why doesn't Bran have any piercings?"

Bran laughs. "Do I look Talirian?"

"Do I?"

"No, but you look willing," Rioz tells him, and then, without warning, she grabs his ear. "This might hurt."

"Wait, no—" he's cut off by the needle going through his ear, and he makes a choked noise of pain and surprise.

Rioz quickly places the earring through the hole, and then gestures him to turn his head so she can do the other one.

"That wasn't so bad," he says, once they're done, admiring his new earrings in the sole mirror in the cabin.

Rioz tugs the one that loops through the middle of her nose. "This one hurt so bad." She considers for a moment and then taps the one between her eyes. "This was worse, though."

Jaz winces in sympathy. "I'll bet." He pauses. "I think I'll just stick with earrings."

She laughs and claps him on the shoulder. "That's probably a good idea."

Chapter Sixteen

BRAN

△

BRAN KNOWS IT'S WRONG: he knows his misdirected rage at Kabet and Lark could easily be fixed with some introspection, but he doesn't care. He is filled with such visceral anger at the sight of the two of them flirting that he forgets that being mean is, generally, not the solution.

Bran refuses to be alone with them. He spends most of his recovery with Rioz. The two of them read dry, dull books and Bran forgets all about his pathetic infatuation with the boy across the room from him. Ignoring Kabet has proven to work the best in taking his mind off things, but occasionally Bran snaps when Kabet attempts to drag him into a conversation.

His face falls each time Bran does so, and he instantly regrets it. Without fail. Every time.

And, still...

Rioz laughs at him, which is to be expected from her. She tends to think issues like this are trivial.

"If you're keen on him," she tells Bran after he complains about her nonchalance, "then that is your problem. It's up to you to decide what to do with that."

He groans. "That's exactly the problem."

"I haven't made my point yet," she glares at him. "Once you decide what to do with your feelings, it's no longer your problem."

"That doesn't sound right." Bran frowns.

"Let's say hypothetically, you tell him." Bran shrivels further into his blanket at those words. Rioz is undeterred. "You've done all you can, and all you should. After that, it's over."

"It's not that *simple*," he complains.

"Yes, it is."

"It's not that simple for me!"

"That's your issue, then." She smacks him lightly on the arm. "So stop taking it out on Kabet."

Δ

"Bran, would you like to play card games?" Kabet asks Bran timidly after the dishes from dinner have been cleared.

"No," he says, glancing at Lark, who is standing behind his shoulder.

"Are you posit—"

"Yes," Bran's voice is clipped and tight. He does not look at Kabet.

Suddenly his book that he was not reading is knocked from his hands and onto the floor with a thud. Lark is standing over Bran, now, her face curled into fury.

"Alright that's it," she snarls. "Kabet has done nothing to you, so stop acting like a child and at *least* be courteous. It's the minimum you can do, considering you can barely do *anything*."

Bran's arms erupt into flame. His vision narrows with rage. "Who are *you* to say that to *me*?" Lark looks afraid, oddly. His eyes feel strangely hot and his face burns with anger. "You tried to kill us for *weeks*. You tried to kill me. You tried to kill my *sister*!" Lark backs steadily away from Bran and he feels fire licking at his scalp.

"Bran," Rioz says, looking nervous. He pays her no heed.

"Yes, Lark, if I do remember correctly all of us almost *died* because of you." Bran steps closer to her, crowding her with fire. His back prickles with heat. "So *excuse me* if I'm a little touchy Kabet seems to like *you*, of all the goddamn people, more than us."

"Bran look in the mirror," Jaz warns carefully.

Bran whirls on him. He feels a scream building in his throat. He releases a pained noise and hot breath is expelled from his lungs with a huff.

Rioz says, cautiously: "Look in the mirror."Bran turns towards her, where she has placed herself next to the mirror. And he sees himself.

His eye sockets have been filled with bright green fire. He doesn't understand how his eyes haven't burned out of his skull. Skeletal wings of the same burning green stretch from his back. What look like stag antlers protrude from his skull in the same, molten green.

His entire body is coated with green fire. He starts to notice the heat rolling off him in waves, realizing how intolerable it must be for everyone else. When he breathes, fire comes out of his parted lips.

"Bran," Rioz says. "Please calm down."

Bran then notices that the cabin around is slicked with fire in the places he has stepped. It doesn't spread but it burns, throwing off heat of deadly temperatures.

He takes a deep breath. The air around is hot and he can see the others struggling but he drinks in the heat. Bran takes another inhale; drawing heat into him with each ragged breath. The fire begins to die down, until the room is dark again, and the last flicker of flame seeps through his skin into his insides.

Bran takes a look at the fearful faces around him.

Then, he blacks out.

Δ

"—was terrifying."

"I know. I've never seen him like that."

"It was my fault?"

"In a sense, yes. But, no. It wasn't your fault."

"That does not make sense."

"They told me to 'be very afraid' right before it started."

"Of what? Bran? He wouldn't hurt you. He wouldn't hurt *anyone*."

"A lot of stuff is about to happen, I think." A pause. "I wish I knew what."

"Rioz...Why is Bran upset with me?"

"I can't tell you that, but it's not really anything you did."

Kabet sighs. Jaz speaks. "You two are capable of ridiculous things."

"And you're not? You have wings, you know." Rioz's voice lilts. He tries to tug together threads of consciousness.

Jaz doesn't pick up on her joking manner. "Not like that." Another pause. "Not yet."

He is pulling together his comprehension when an unseen force rips it from his unsteady hands, and he falls back into a black, dreamless sleep.

Δ

Bran wakes up in the middle of the night. Everyone around him is asleep. His mouth feels like it's been stuffed with hot coals, and his stomach protests angrily.

Bran sighs and rolls over, determined to go back to sleep.

His determination lasts all of four minutes. He clicks his tongue and drags his pack towards his bedroll, clawing around inside of it for food.

It is devoid of any sustenance. Rioz must've raided it again. Bran drags himself to his unsteady feet, wobbling carefully towards where she lay, asleep. Her bedroll is normally right next to his, but she must've moved it to talk to Jaz while he was unconscious.

Her arm is thrown haphazardly over his chest. Jaz looks relaxed.

Salem and Jaz are very similar, Bran thinks. *Except Jaz is scared, and not angry. And Jaz finds reprieve when he sleeps.*

Bran thinks, deep down somewhere, Salem might be scared too. She might be more scared than all of them.

He can't be sure.

He finds Rioz's bag in the dark and manages to grab some food, when the door behind him clicks open.

Bran feels fire roiling beneath his skin as he whirls around, heart racing.

Kabet is standing there, looking like a terrified wild animal.

"Oh," he says. "You are awake."

"And so are you...what were you even doing outside?"

"Oh. I was. Um."

"It's okay, you can say you were pissing."

Kabet laughs and Bran feels lighter for the first time in days. "No, actually. I was praying." He sighs. "I couldn't sleep. I pray when I cannot sleep."

"Recently, you must be praying a lot, then." Kabet laughs again. A smile dances warily across his lips. "You could've done that inside, though."

"Ah. No. The cold makes me uncomfortable."

"All the more reason to stay inside?" Bran arches an eyebrow.

"Praying for me is a very formal affair." Bran only smiles in dumbfounded confusion and Kabet rattles on. "In Sunan, we have...I think you call them churches? anyway, we attend churches daily, for one hour, in our finest clothing." Kabet laughs, almost fondly, at what he's going to say next. "You must be quiet, pious, and careful with everything.

"I am not a very careful person, so doing so feels... stiff. Praying with my...family, has always been cautious and reserved. The clothes make me feel, well, not at home. The quiet makes me scared." He pauses. "Do not get me wrong, I love my gods with every ounce of myself, but praying to them while in a warm lodge, surrounded by people who I care for in a way I never cared for my family, and *comfortable*. Well. It does not feel right." He sighs. "You feel too much like home."

Bran's heart quickens at his words but he reminds himself that he means all of them. "Shouldn't you want to feel at home, though? I'm not religious but Rioz says her gods always feel like peace."

Kabet smiles and shakes his head. "I love my gods, but they are like parents. Respected. Overwhelming. Discomforting." He shrugs. "I believe that there are many kinds of love. Love for my gods needs to be distanced. Reserved, like churches. I am not like them, afterall."

"Some would disagree," Bran points out.

Kabet smiles at Bran fondly. "When it comes to certain things, only select opinions matter. It is what I believe." He pauses. "Do you think I am a god?" he jokes.

"No," Bran laughs quietly. "I think you're just a boy." The atmosphere shifts. "A stupid, sad, lonely boy." Bran isn't sure which of them he's talking about.

"Correct on all counts," he laughs but it seems sad. He opens his mouth, then closes it. Kabet seems to be struggling with himself to say something. "I was not afraid."

"Not afraid of what?"

"Of you. Tonight."

"Shouldn't you have been?"

"Some would disagree," he echoes Bran's words from earlier. "I suppose that I was afraid. But not of you."

"Are you saying that wasn't me?" Bran tries not to let hurt seep into his tone.

Kabet frowns. "No, not at all." A pause. "I am saying that I was not afraid *of* you. I was afraid for you. I was worried."

Bran doesn't quite know what to say to that. "I think Rioz said I wouldn't hurt anyone, while I was asleep." He lets the silence stretch, hoping not to fill it. "I don't know if that's true."

"It is not true for anyone, Bran."

"What do you mean?"

"Everyone hurts people." Kabet pauses. "It is not if we hurt people. If is irrelevant, when is absolute. Neither matter. Why matters. Who matters. What you do after is what matters. If you only hurt people who deserve it, you are not bad."

"I hurt you," Bran whispers.

"Yes, but you have your reasons, I am sure."

He chokes back tears. "They aren't good ones."

Kabet shrugs, but he seems upset. "Then you must fix it."

"What do I do to fix it?"

Kabet smiles fondly at him and Bran's heart swells. "Apologize."

"I'm sorry. I really am."

"I forgive you. And you owe me a favor."

"What's the favor?"

Kabet smiles at Bran, seeming careless again for the first time in a while. "I do not know yet. Ask again later."

"That can't be good."

Kabet laughs and then turns to Bran, looking at him so intently his skin crawls. "You said I liked Lark more than you earlier."

"I—I did say that, yes."

"I do not."

"It's alright if—"

"I do not."

"Even if you did it's not my business."

"Bran," Kabet is laughing now, trying and failing to be quiet so the others don't wake up. "I do not."

Δ

Kabet is sitting next to Bran, writing, when he tells him.

"I have no family," he says plainly.

He's been doing this a lot, recently. Telling Bran snatches of his past and his emotions. It does nothing to help Bran's situation. "What happened?"

"They do not claim me." He pauses. "I was too wild. Too reckless. I put my family into too much danger, being a rebel. I was thoughtless. It did not help that I was created and not conceived."

This gives Bran pause. "Wh—what?"

"Ah. My mother told me that a witch placed me inside her. I have no reason to doubt her, either." Kabet frowns, but it seems commonplace. It is far too natural on his face for what he is saying. He shrugs. "Rema was not unkind to me," he says simply. "She was merely fearful."

"That still seems mean," Bran remarks.

Kabet looks at Bran like he knows something he doesn't. "I do not think Rema was bad. I do not think people who lash out are bad. I think they are only afraid."

"That's not an excuse."

"We are all afraid. Compassion does not mean forgiveness. You can care about someone's struggle, realize the humanity in it, and not like them all the same."

Bran doesn't speak for a while, pondering what to say to that when Kabet speaks up again. "I shall say it this way. I feel no pain for dying scoundrels, but I recognize that death affects us all."

He nods quietly. Then decides to be brash. He leans over towards what Kabet is writing and attempts to read it.

Kabet closes the journal quietly, and grins at Bran. His face is bright. "It must be a secret for a while longer."

Bran rolls his eyes and slouches against the wall in defeat. Kabet turns towards him and stares at him for a moment, before sighing and reopening his journal.

"Later, yes?" Kabet says carefully, kicking Bran's foot.

Bran kicks him back, harder. "Yeah," he grins at him, and he doesn't look up from his journal, but Bran sees a smile tugging at his lips. "Later."

Δ

Later that same day, Lark sits bolt upright and rushes to her bag, beginning to stuff things into it. "We have to go!" Everyone stares at her, dumbfounded. "*Now!*"

Bran snaps to attention and begins to pack when the wall behind him explodes inwards in a wall of blood red fire.

There's a terrible laugh that fills the room as a figure steps in. He knows, intrinsically, this is Tomas. "I'm looking for a Monroe Fehner?" A chill runs down Bran's spine as he turns around. Cold sweat springs to his forehead. He hasn't heard that name in years. "The rest of you can die, though." Tomas laughs maniacally, and unnatural red flame erupts in his hair, coating his head and feathered wings made from fire arch out from his back. Tomas glances around the room, a sick grin on his face.

Rioz steps in front of Bran, tensing for a fight she knows she cannot possibly win. "What do you want with him?"

"Him? Oh this is *very* interesting." He bats Rioz aside with a fist coated in flame. She screams in pain. The windows on the cabin erupt into minute shards.

"Hello, dear sister." Tomas looks at Bran like he's evaluating how much he could sell him for.

Bran puts his confusion aside and leans into anger. "I'm not a girl," he snarls, rage chokes at the back of his throat.

Tomas waves a dismissive hand. "I am Tomas Fehner. We'll be going now." He grins. "I'll kill your friends on the way out." He grabs Bran, and it *burns*. He's never felt *burned* like this before.

Bran gives into the heat that roils beneath his skin, in his gut, about his mind. He erupts into a column of green and grabs Tomas back, channeling the fire into his skin. For a moment, Tomas looks surprised, and then afraid.

He roars in rage and pain, and Bran hears Rioz scream his name. He hears everyone else in the background, too.

The world erupts into red and green fire. Heat crackles in Bran's ears and singes his hair. He watches as, in slow motion, the cabin is leveled to the ground. He sees fire barrelling towards his friends, his *family*. Bran screams, and the fire reverses in its tracks, and crashes into his body. His insides feel hot: his brain feels like embers rattling inside his skull.

The worst thing Bran sees is three hooded figures stepping onto the ruins of the cabin. Kabet is collapsed face down on the floor. Rioz is helping Jaz to his unsteady feet. Lark is standing tense, her face grim.

Their skin is red from the heat. Bran feels guilty, somewhere in his failing mind.

Someone picks him up. He sees Rioz scream, but doesn't hear it. She lunges for him, screaming what looks like his name. But a figure catches her by the hood and drags her back.

Red fire erupts around him again.

The last thing Bran sees before he blacks out is Kabet pulling himself to his shaky knees, looking around.

Chapter

Seventeen

KABET

KABET STANDS UP WHEN he hears Rioz screaming Bran's name.

Tomas laughs, but he seems winded now. "You're not getting her back, sorry." One of the hooded figures they sparred with earlier grapples Rioz to the floor. Tomas strolls lazily out into snow outside.

That's when Kabet notices Bran draped over Tomas's shoulders, unconscious.

That's also when he notices the small, slight figure standing in front of him.

The figure tugs their hood back, and the breath inside his lungs is stolen; his world knocked sideways.

Adena.

Kabet is ten years old. He is far too young to know anything about witches and family and loss. He is far too young to know about almost everything.

Adena delights in Kabet's powers, and that is all he cares about. He shifts random silks into lovely clothing for her. He causes her turtle figurine, bought from a foreign merchant, to swim haphazardly in the sand you sit in.

He would do it all for her. He would do it all for her and more. She is his family. His only family.

"We're getting out of here, one day, Kabet." He loves how she says his name.

"Of course we are," Kabet says, because it's true. He glances around the street market and gives her a nod. The two of them grab some imported fruits from a merchant and bolt in opposite directions.

"You little bastards!" Kabet cackles the whole way back to their spot, knowing Adena will be waiting there for him. She's always been a better runner.

She is there when he gets back, of course. They swap fruits and spit seeds and laugh until their lungs feel tight.

Their "spot" is really just a treehouse the two of them made in Adena's backyard. The tree is a one of a prickly desert, but it holds them all the same. Her parents are traveling merchants, never home, and she said they wouldn't mind when they were home, anyway.

"You are my family, Kabet."

"And you mine," he tells her.

"Don't you ever leave me."

Kabet smiles at her. "Of course not."

Looking back on it, he wishes he had asked her the same.

Kabet and Adena had met when they were six years old. It took four years to get to this point.

It took three days for her to die.

They were playing their stealing game when Adena got lost. She wandered into the wrong part of the city. The sick part of the city.

She caught the plague. She died. And a part of Kabet's heart died with her.

He always blamed himself.

Adena stands dead in front of him. Her lively brown eyes are dead. Her brown skin is pallid and unhealthy. Her black hair is ratty and coarse.

And yet, she is standing in front of Kabet. Ten years old. Dead.

He saw her during the last fight, but dismissed it as hallucination.

"Adena," Kabet whispers. She lunges towards him with inhuman speed, swinging her tiny fist towards him, *fast*. He takes the hit, and feels pain surge through him as he is thrown across the burned, destroyed room.

"*Don't forget about me*," this thing that is decidedly not Adena hisses her last words. Her last words as Kabet clutched her dying body, praying that tomorrow he would catch the plague and die with her.

His prayers were not fulfilled.

Kabet feels the tears crawling down his face before he understands that he is crying. "I never did. I never will."

"*Don't forget about me*," she says again. She then delivers a kick to Kabet's ribs, and he feels bones break.

"I never will," he sobs. The face of his past continues to beat him until he is bloody.

Suddenly, Kabet feels her hand around his throat. He feels the air stolen from his lungs as he heaves what will likely be his last sob.

"Please, Adena," Kabet mouths, unable to speak for many reasons. "Come back to me." His vision starts to narrow. "You left that day, while we were stealing. You never came back." His silent words fall on deaf ears. "Please, Adena." Kabet says, anyway. He does not attempt to fight back. He would never fight Adena.

Through his dying vision he sees someone rushing towards her. *Don't*, he thinks. *Don't hurt her.*

Adena goes flying off of Kabet and air rushes into his lungs. It is robbed, moments later, when he rolls to his knees and vomits onto the ground. Jaz grabs him under the armpits and hauls him to his feet. One of his eyes is black and swollen shut. His other eye is empty. His wings look ruffled, somewhat like an angry bird.

Jaz sighs. "We have to go."

"Adena," Kabet whispers, then his empty stomach heaves again.

"It's not her, Kabet."

For a moment, the four of them regain their balance in the fight. Lark knocks one of the figures down. Rioz saws through another's windpipe with her tiny dagger, looking increasingly angry.

And then Kabet realizes Bran is missing.

He's gone. He's nowhere in sight. He's gone.

Rioz seems to recognize this as soon as he does, and he sees her die. She dies, in every way but one.

"Stop," she says. Her voice is cold and empty. This is not the Rioz Kabet has seen before: an enraged force to be reckoned with.

This Rioz reminds him of Salem.

"I said stop, now," she says, calmly. And suddenly the room is filled with gore. The figures... disintegrate. A spray of dark blood explodes from the three places where they were standing, then falls to the ground in a mist. There is nothing left but blood on the scorched floor of the burning cabin.

It's over.

It's over and Bran is gone.

Rioz collapses to her knees, her eyes are alive again but filled with immeasurable pain. She screams. She screams again, and again, and again. The house is leveled, the world flattened in every direction, force kicks up like a hurricane and rips everything to shreds. Rioz keeps screaming.

Kabet, Jaz, and Lark are somehow untouched by this devastation. As the very earth beneath Kabet's feet cracks open, falls away, disintegrates, the three of them feel none of the pain.

The earth opens, creating a cliff where there was none. Jaz grabs Rioz, pulling her away from the earthquake she caused. She turns her face into his chest and sobs.

He starts walking. Starts walking to where they know they have to go. Rioz is cradled in his arms, sobbing and screaming. Kabet follows after him, and after a moment, so does Lark.

They start walking towards the heart of Duskra. Kabet sends a silent prayer, hoping Bran can find them there.

Kabet knows he probably won't. He knows he will likely be another tally on the long list of people who have left him, of people he has left.

But still, he hopes.

CHAPTER EIGHTEEN

RIOZ

HE'S GONE. HE'S GONE. He's gone. He's gone.

Not dead. He can't be dead. *He can't be dead.*

Her heart has been ripped from her still living chest, but still, she knows it beats. She knows. She knows. He *has* to be alive.

She *will* get him back.

And she will rip apart everything that stands in her way.

CHAPTER NINETEEN

SALEM

∆|∆

WHEN SALEM COMES BACK to herself, she is running. She doesn't know why she's running, but continues regardless.

Her mind is an empty ocean. She knows that if prodded, even slightly, she will lose herself. Something is haunting her and it swims just beneath the surface tension of her mind. Salem doesn't dare peer at it.

Salem trudges through the snow as quickly as possible. Her breath heaves ragged and cold in her chest, and the water in her mind swells to bursting.

"Salem!" She hears Kioh's voice. Why does she hear Kioh's voice? "Salem!" She hears again.

Suddenly, Kioh pulls even with Salem. When did she get there? Her mind itches. "Salem, what's wrong?"

Salem opens her mouth to reply, halting in the snow. She turns towards Kioh. Her mind itches, feels foggy. Kioh's eyes widen but she can't react before a cold arm is wrapped around her throat.

Reality comes crashing in all at once and Salem fights her assailant off. Drawing her daggers, she flips them to the correct position in her hands, then levels them at her opponent.

Then the world burns.

Salem sees flames licking up the sides of her face, sees them crawling up her arms and legs. She cannot feel the fire, but it is all around.

And standing in front of her is the perfect face of her mother.

Salem cannot scream. She cannot stop screaming. The fire has robbed her breath and she's dying. She's so afraid and she's *dying*.

Salem can't hear Kioh scream her name. She can't see Kioh get thrown violently away from her.

All she can feel is the fire. All she can see is her parents' charred faces. All she can hear is her house crackling like impossibly loud tinder.

All Salem can feel is the burn, the ache, the fear, and the end. It's ending. She knows it's ending, because it's ended before.

Salem is brought crashing back to reality when she feels her ribs shatter. She feels at least three of them snap inside her body as her father, *her father*, brings his boot smashing into her chest. Salem gasps a ragged breath, one that is robbed when her mother grabs her by the throat and lifts her into the air.

She weakly brings her hands up to fight. Then drops them almost immediately. She deserves this. *She deserves this.*

Salem let her parents die because of her. She let their bodies burn and then let herself survive. They are dead because of her. They burned because of her.

She doesn't struggle. She lets her arms hang limply by her side. She bows her head to her mother. She accepts what has been coming to her for a long time.

Distantly, Salem hears Kioh screaming her name. Through the flashes of the past that swarm her head, Salem hears her fighting.

She writes out a letter in her mind. She whispers the last words that she cannot say: they cool the world around her and warm the frigid within.

To my parents: I am sorry. There is nothing I can say that hasn't been said already.

To Kioh Taa: I am sorry. I think you were my friend. I am not sure if friends exist for people like me.

To the rest of my team: I am sorry. I was never your leader. I was just a girl. I think you were my friends, too.

To Atina Parev: I am sorry I could not kill you, but it is better this way.

To my brother: I am sorry.

To the world: I am sorry. Death will be my forgiveness.

Salem is choking. Her vision is blackening as she prays to every god that Atina Parev dies like a dog. But really, it is better this way. Her mother tightens her grip and Salem's consciousness begins to fade.

"They're not your parents, Salem! Salem!" She knows this: her parents would never hurt her. She doesn't care. It's better this way.

Death will be my forgiveness. Death will be my forgiveness. Death will be my forgiveness.

Salem loses her grip. She enters a dreamless sleep.

♨

Salem's back hits the ground and she hears a furious scream. Water washes over her, but leaves her completely untouched. Her head feels clear for the first time in a long time, and the melancholy feeling that swims in her mind makes her want to bash her skull in. She curls into a ball and begins to sob. Her parents are dead. Her parents are dead and it is her fault. She has nothing left and it kills her. It *kills* her.

Kioh screams again, and Salem sees her standing over her. It's a terrifying sight, but it is one that comforts her, oddly.

Kioh's teeth gnash as fangs in her mouth. Her hands have turned to claws. Her eyes are black with red slits. She lets out an enraged roar and what seems like all the water in the world builds at her command.

Kioh thrusts her hand forward and Salem watches as it encloses her parents and freezes. Salem screams. She drags herself over to Kioh's leg and claws at her to stop. She closes her gnarled hand and Salem watches her dead parents shatter. They split into bloody, frozen chunks and fall limply to the ground. She realizes that they have met their end in both fire and ice.

Salem chokes out a sob which quickly turns into a retch. She vomits onto the ground, bared of snow because of Kioh.

She feels Kioh pick her up and start walking. She remembers this happened after the first time she saw her mother, the time she forgot about. Kioh carries her and she sobs into her neck. And then Salem realizes she's speaking.

"Salem? Can you hear me?"

Salem doesn't know how to respond. She doesn't know if she can. She nods into Kioh's neck, almost against her will.

"After all of this is over, after Atina is dead and I've made sure you're alive, we're going to go fishing."

"Fishing?" Salem's quiet voice cracks.

Kioh speaks, and her voice sounds soft but it's wet with sadness. "I grew up in a coastal city. Fishing was how we city made our money. My mother owned a boat with a crew. I went with her when I was old enough."

Salem doesn't know how to speak, everything she says feels wrong. "You must be really good at it."

"I haven't been in five years, I'm not so sure, anymore."

"But you want to go?" She pauses. "With me?" She doesn't know why she said that.

"Yeah," Kioh says, and then she laughs. Her laugh is sad and painful to listen to. "With you."

♯

Kioh carries Salem until she collapses. Salem doesn't know how she knows what direction to go, but the snow has started to thin, the air grown breathable. She can see a treeline in the distance. They're getting close. She's getting close and she doesn't have it in her to care.

The sky has darkened when Kioh sets Salem down. It's actually dark, not the grey of the winter mountains they have grown used to. Kioh rolls over onto her back, and stares at the sky. Salem's tears have long since stopped, but there's a horrible gnawing sadness that digs at her guts. She lays, cheek pressed into the deep snow, and waits for the emptiness to come back. Salem's eyes are tilted towards the ground: she does not look at the stars.

"Salem," Kioh rasps. Her voice is hoarse and ragged. She's exhausted. Too exhausted to pretend she's not.

"What?" Salem feels Kioh's hand clawing at hers in the dark night. She grabs it through her gloves, holding it like something precious.

"I told you I wouldn't let you die." Kioh says it like a promise. She grips Salem's hand tighter.

Salem laughs, and for some reason, it doesn't taste bitter. "You've still got a lot of work ahead of you."

Salem hears a smile in Kioh's voice. "I've put too much effort in now. Too much effort to waste." She pauses, silent for a long while. "What's it like? Reading minds?" she asks suddenly.

She doesn't know how to answer. How does she tell someone that something feels horrible, exhilarating, unnatural, and routine all at once? Jen once asked her if she would choose mindreading. If out of anything, Salem would pick it knowing what it was. What it felt like.

Salem wanted to say no. She wanted to not want. But she said yes. Jen asked why.

"Why? Didn't you say it felt like someone else's blood dribbling from your ears?"

Salem shrugs. "It does. It feels awful. It feels like trying to drink a waterfall. It's the worst thing to have in your head. Everyone else's thoughts."

"Then why choose it?"

She pauses. Then sighs. "Jen, you're a very powerful person." Jen preens a bit at this. "You've kicked my ass many times, though I don't think you could beat me anymore." Jen glares at her. Salem barrells on. "What I'm saying, is that you are powerful, in your own right. But nothing, and I mean nothing, compares to knowing someone, intrinsically, without even trying."

Jen scoffs and takes a sip of her ale. "You have the advantage without even trying. Don't think it makes you special."

"It doesn't make me special." Salem smiles angrily at her. "But it makes me unstoppable."

"We'll see, kid. We'll see."

"It feels like having the advantage," Salem tells Kioh. "It feels like winning."

Kioh scoffs, and she is reminded of Jen, once again. "You'd know a lot about that."

"I'd know a lot about loss, too."

"Everyone knows about loss."

Salem thinks of Atina. "Not everyone." She pauses. "Everyone loses things, but not everyone mourns them." She thinks of herself.

"I think sometimes," Kioh says, "that you lose so much; that you lose everything. And after all that loss, you forget how to mourn. Forget what you lost in the first place."

Salem curls her face further into the snow. "I don't think I forgot how to mourn." She heaves the beginning of a sob into her lungs, but cuts it short. "I think I forgot how to stop."

Kioh squeezes Salem's hand again. "Do you have anything left to lose?"

I think I'm starting to. "No."

"Then you win," Kioh says, shoving Salem's bedroll towards her.

She drifts off to sleep somewhere between breaths. Before her consciousness fails for the second time that day, however, a thought intrudes into Salem's head. It's not her own, she knows.

The most cunning thief in Rowak turned soft for a sob story. How pathetic am I?

Salem decides to forget she heard that, and falls into a fitful sleep.

♛

"You should wake her."

Salem hears a sigh. "She needs the sleep," Kioh says.

Her eyes flick open and a knife is in her hand instantly. She jolts to her feet and gets into a defensive position. One of them is *here*.

Kioh is sitting on her bedroll behind Salem. To the side of her stands Mira. Salem considers attacking, but Kioh seems relaxed albeit uncomfortable.

She doesn't drop her knife, but she lets the poised tension slip out of her shoulders a bit. "Why's she here?"

Kioh opens her mouth to speak but Mira cuts her off. "I've changed tactics." Salem notes the use of the word tactics. Not sides; tactics.

"Money, I'm assuming?" Mira's eyes flash angrily as she says this.

"Money is not what I seek."

Salem decides to push. "Atina was paying you, was she not?"

"The queen was paying me in protection. I have discovered she is not one to keep her word, and I have thus altered my approach."

Who is this girl? Salem wonders. Talking like a playwright?

"What do you want from us?"

Mira smirks, lips pulled back in something that resembles a snarl. Salem can see wolf sharp canines within her mouth. "I do not require your assistance." She turns towards Kioh. "I need her."

Kioh starts a little at that, so Salem figures they haven't been talking much. "I'm not in the business of giving out my help for free," she says, each word measured and cautious.

Right about then is when she notices Mira's eyes. They're acid green, with nothing in them. No pupil, no coloration except the flat, glassy green.

Mira does snarl this time, turning her ferocity on Kioh. Something angry stirs inside Salem. "You wouldn't be helping me for free. I do not ask for hand-outs." There's an edge to her voice that gnaws at her.

Salem scoffs. "You really think you can threaten us? Threaten me? I could kill you before you could draw that bow of yours. I could kill you before you even had time to think. *Why* should we help you? Why should Kioh?"

"I have not threatened you, though I have doubt in your violent promises." She pauses. "Kioh is the leader of a rather notorious group of thieves, are you not?"

Kioh straightens. "When I was sixteen, I inherited a gang, The Jacks. It initially belonged to a man named Dalton. He died and left his money to his family, who had no idea where it actually came from. But he left everything important to *me*. I revamped the gang to be more suited to my tastes: new members, new rules. Less blood. So, short answer, yes, I run a gang of thieves." She pauses. She seems sad. Salem wonders if Kioh likes her life.

"I do what I need to do to survive. I try my best to give back to the world in the same way I take." Kioh sighs. "So," she says, "yes, Mira. I am. But I find no pleasure in it."

Mira shrugs, Salem feels like growling. "I care not for semantics. I need protection."

"From what?"

"My parents found trouble with a landlord. He owned the property we were staying on, at the time. We couldn't afford it. I'm sure you know the rest. He also happens to be a higher ranking member of a gang. A less...tasteful gang. To abbreviate, my parents and myself need protection." She pauses. "If I join The Jacks, will you provide it?"

"The Jacks provide extensive protection to all its members." Kioh's gaze turns harsh and sharp. "But what can you provide for me?"

Faster than Salem can blink, Mira draws her bow and knocks an arrow, she lunges for Mira, but the arrow fires helplessly into the snow before she reaches her. Mira dances out of the way, and Salem allows her to pass by her. She wants to see where this goes.

She grabs the shaft of the arrow and yanks it from the snow. Impaled on the head of the arrow, is a fat, bloody vole. The arrow goes right through its skull.

"I was blessed with senses that go far beyond that of a human," she slides the vole off the arrow and tosses it to Kioh, who snatches it out of the air seamlessly. "I can hear your heartbeats, from where I'm standing. I can pick out human whispers from blocks away. I can read chicken scratch at a distance that one wouldn't be able to make out a pencil. I can do all of this and more. I have not the skills of a spy, but I have the makings to be a great one."

Kioh nods. She seems devoid of her usual cheeriness. She seems like a businessman. She looks gravely at Mira and says, "You will be my eyes and ears. You will tell me anything and everything. You will act as an extension of myself, of The Jacks. The Jacks are one organism, and you will *never* betray your body, your comrades in crime. If you do, my protection is null and void."

Mira looks far too calm for the threat she has just been posed. "I shall serve you faithfully, so long as you do the same."

Kioh kneels and roots around in her pack. She pulls out a loop stacked with rings. The rings are simple black bands, identical to the band that Kioh wears on her right middle finger. She glances at Mira's hands, evaluating, then sorts through the rings until she finds one she's satisfied with it. She flings it at Mira, who catches it effortlessly.

"Read the inside," Kioh says.

Mira squints at it. "Mirrors have your eyes. Fear them. They have your teeth, too."

"It's a good one. You can make your own, when we get back to Rowak."

"What's it mean?" Salem asks.

Kioh looks sad. "Hell if I know. It was an old member's. He died on a job. We all called him Bull. His real name is one he said never mattered."

Salem gestures to the loop of rings. "Are those all old members'?"

Kioh looks amused and affronted simultaneously. "How bad of a boss do you think I am? Mostly just extra, not all of them have words." She glances towards Mira. "You can change it later, if you like. Put it on your fourth left finger, you're a new member. It'll change if you get promoted."

Mira does so obediently. Salem glances at Kioh. "What's yours say?" she asks.

She smiles sadly. "A lady must have some secrets, you know."

Funny, Salem thinks, *it seems like you have them all.*

⚕

"Do you know what the most valuable currency is, kid?" Jen asks Salem. She is still covered in bandages and salve for her burns. Breathing still hurts.

"The Sunani haic?" She has no idea, really.

"The haic is worthless in the face of what I'm talking about." Jen pauses. "The most valuable currency, the most priceless prize, is meaning."

"Meaning?"

"Yes, meaning. Meaning, well, it means things. People will fight their entire life searching for it, abandon all the world's gold for it. People will do anything for meaning, and do anything to protect it. Secrets are a part of meaning. A man's secrets generally equate some form of meaning: something they would do anything to protect."

"My family," Salem starts crying. Pain erupts as tears flood her ruined face.

"Your family meant something to you, yes? The most valuable thing to you has been stolen. Your meaning has been taken and used to buy something. It's degrading. It's horrible. That is the true cost of meaning. It can be used to buy anything, to obtain anything, to leverage whatever you want. But you will hurt people in the process."

"What should I do?" She sobs, her lungs ache from it. "To get it back?"

"You can't get it back. You have to rebuild it. You have to make it." Jen pauses, considering. "Do you want to know who did this to you? To your family?"

Salem is eleven. She doesn't know what weight those words bear, yet. "Yes," she sobs.

"A woman named Atina Parev has killed your family, stolen your meaning for power. I can teach you to take hers right back." Another pause. "Atina Parev is the queen of Shka. She has more power than you can fathom. Do you have anything that can level the field?"

Salem is eleven. She doesn't understand what Jen is asking her. She can barely grasp this concept of power. Of using it to hurt people. But then something occurs to her. Something her father once said. He said she had a powerful gift.

"A powerful gift," she echoes.

Jen seems surprised. "And what is it?"

"I know your thoughts. I know what you're thinking. I know what everyone's thinking."

Jen blinks, her eyes widened to that of saucers. Regardless, she says, calmly: "What number am I thinking?"

"Two hundred and fifty-six. What?"

Jen blinks. "Generally, people like proof, when presented with the impossible." She sighs. "And proof you have just provided."

Jen heals Salem. Treats her. Trains her. Jen teaches Salem everything she comes to know.

Salem learns that she has the direct key into the most protected thing under the sun: meaning. Secrets. Information. Whatever name it is called by, she can know it. One day, when she is thirteen, Jen sits her down.

"You will grow close to people."

"No. I won't."

"You will. And when you do, these people will try to keep things from you. Even if they know they can't, they will try to keep things from you. They will guard their secrets, their meaning, with everything they have."

"They can't. I won't let them," her body screams defiance. Salem will never allow anyone to keep anything from her. She has to know what's coming.

"But you should. Salem, you have to learn to turn it off. Because people will try to keep things from you, and as misguided as their reasoning may be, you must let them keep their secrets."

"Why?"

"Your family meant something to you, correct?"

"Of course."

"Secrets mean something to people." She pauses. "It would be like if someone reached into your head, and took everything that you don't want to talk about, and brought it into the light. It would be like someone taking your meaning. Granted, on a much smaller scale, but it would happen constantly, and without repent," her voice is grave.

"I wouldn't like that," Salem admits.

"No one would. So if you ever come to care about someone, Salem, please, please, let them keep their secrets."

She nods. She keeps her promise to Jen. She never goes rooting around in people's heads without a reason.

Jen teaches Salem every fighting style she knows. She trains her on how to survive in the most desolate places. She mentors Salem, raises her. And throughout it all, she tells Salem to rebuild meaning.

Salem doesn't. She never gets the hang of finding something that means as much to her as her family. Even Jen, who she considers to be close to her, will never fill that void. There's a horrible pain inside Salem's chest. She can't replace it with another feeling. So she replaces it with nothing.

After a while, Salem becomes bitter. She stops searching, stops trying. She becomes a tool to execute her family's revenge. Nothing more. She tells Jen this, one day. Jen says nothing, but Salem sees tears shining in her eyes. She feels nothing.

Jen teaches her so many things. So many things that save her life.

But Salem's frigid anger? That's something that only she knows.

♟

They are walking towards Canak when Kioh asks Salem.

"Do you know everything I'm thinking?"

"No," she answers without hesitation. And it's true.

She hums thoughtfully. "Why not?"

Salem shrugs. "I don't read someone's thoughts without purpose. I'm very good at filtering out what I need. It's a conscious effort to grant people some privacy, I suppose."

"You turn it off?"

"Not really. It's more like I have a filtration system. Sometimes important things get through. Sometimes drivel. It's very unreliable, but it generally prevents me from knowing things I don't need to know."

"Why? If I had what you had, I'd be doing it constantly."

"Because I wouldn't like it if someone had my secrets. I wouldn't like it if someone took something dear to me, without asking. Without me knowing."

Kioh laughs. "You're a very moral person, for a thief and a murderer."

"I think those two things prevent me from being moral." Salem feels a quirk at her lips.

"Obviously. But you've got to be the most moral criminal I've met."

She smiles, glad her scarf conceals it.

"Who taught you to fight?" Kioh asks suddenly.

"Jen Van Otto, my mentor. She raised me from when I was eleven to the time I was fourteen." Salem doesn't want to say more. Kioh has other ideas.

"What happened to her?"

Something pricks at her throat: ugly and emotional. "She was a deserter. She had me turn her in." She chokes silently, then regains composure. "She had me turn her in so I could be granted a place in the queen's army at a young age. She said she'd escape. I'm not sure if she did or not."

Kioh is staring at Salem in horror. "Did you want to do it?"

"I didn't want to, no. I needed to. And I trusted her enough to get out, at the time. The older I grow, the more I realize she was far from infallible." She hesitates, then adds, softly, "I hope she got out."

Kioh pauses for a moment. "Me too." She barely gets the words out before adding, panicked, "Did you hear that?"

And then Salem does hear it: laughter. And then something knocks her to her knees. She feels teeth tearing into the back of her neck. The laughter grows closer, and Lydia appears in front of them. The wolf (she thinks that's what it is) is knocked from Salem's back with the whiz of an arrow. Salem collapses into the snow, and rolls over onto her back. She's bleeding profusely from her neck, and her vision is growing fuzzy.

"You know, for all the talk, I really expected that would be harder."

Salem growls and pulls herself to her feet, haltingly. Next to Lydia is a pack of five wolves. They have no fur or eyes or skin. Only bone and sinew and bits of muscle. All of the flesh is dark and degraded. It's a horrifying sight.

"I'll kill you," Salem snarls. Blood dribbles down her face and into her mouth, down her chest.

Lydia laughs again. "You're not in any shape to do so."

Salem feels anger clouding her senses, and she rushes Lydia. Wolves charge at her. Three are knocked flying with arrows before they reach her. One is batted away with a wave of water. Salem smashes the final one's skull with nothing but her fist, and sends it skidding through the snow.

She reaches Lydia, and she draws her scythe. Their scuffle lasts about thirty seconds before Salem has her knife pressed to Lydia's throat.

"You're *nothing* without your puppets."

Lydia laughs. "You have to admit, it was genius: using the dead faces of your pasts." It *was*, Salem thinks.

She spits in Lydia's face before saying. "You desecrated the sanctity of death." She feels a wolf rip into her right calf. She kicks it away, feeling nothing.

Lydia laughs again. "There is no sanctity in anything. It's best you learn that now." The wolf reappears at the arm clutching Lydia. Salem doesn't let go. She lets the beast hang from her forearm and clutch onto her with everything she has. She feels her muscle ripping. She doesn't care.

Lydia seems panicked now. "Are you even *human?*"

"Clearly *not*," Salem snarls. *Why haven't I killed her yet?* She starts to crash the knife towards the woman.

"WAIT!" Lydia pleads. Salem feels another wolf tear open her left thigh. She lets it hang. She will not be cowed by filthy half-animals. "I can bring them back! I can bring your parents back!" *Oh, that's why.* Salem's grip almost slackens. Almost.

She feels Lydia attempt to tear away from her. It was a trick. She can't bring them back. Salem tries to not let that eat at her.

In a final, desperate move, Lydia fights with all her strength. She bats Rage out of Salem's hand. She can't grab Wish without letting go. Salem feels a surge of hate. Of such powerful ire it blinds her.

"Die like a dog, then," Salem hisses.

And then Salem tears Lydia's throat open with her teeth. She sees her die in an instant. She goes limp in her grasp. Salem spits the blood out of her mouth, and drops her unceremoniously to the ground. The wolves go slack on her, and fall to the ground as heaps of random bones.

And then she passes out.

The last thing she hears is someone screaming her name.

Salem can't help but imagine how her parents will welcome her home.

⚓

She dreams of fire. She dreams of ice. Familiar faces swarm her, wreathed in flames that boil her skin. She dreams of pain and death and loss. She mourns her family, but most of all, she mourns herself. She mourns the girl she used to be. The girl who was made of summer and warmth without fear and without rage. Salem cries for the girl who she killed. She could have saved her, maybe. But it was so hard to look her in the eyes; how could she possibly save her?

Salem weeps for a future that was torn from her. She sobs for a life that was stolen.

Kioh invades her dreams, too. Kioh and her secrets. Her and her charm that hides something Salem doesn't dare to pick at. She thinks she might want to know Kioh. Salem thinks she might want Kioh to know her.

But no one would want to know her. She is filled with destructive rage and fueled by blinding fear. She is a bomb waiting to go off. Anyone who wants to know her is only a fool with a death wish.

Salem dreams of all of this. She wonders, dimly, if she will ever feel loved again. If she will ever love, again. She sees a wish in her mind's eye, bright as a newly born star.

It dies, exploding, birthing a universe into itself. She is blinded by its death.

"Is she going to be okay?" A nervous voice.

A sigh. "I couldn't tell you, Kioh."

Kioh, the name sharpens Salem's blurry consciousness.

As she becomes aware, she also becomes dizzy. Her mind buzzes with agony. There's so much pain.

Everywhere she can fathom *hurts*. Her body feels like it's burning, from the inside, this time.

Salem feels a cold rag wipe at her face, and the perpetrator seems to realize she's awake. "Oh, Salem," that's Kioh, she thinks. "Go back to sleep."

Salem focuses on the cool sensation of the rag, instead of the horrible sting that overwhelms her senses. Her mind comes back in bits and pieces, and with each thread of coherency, her body only hurts more. "No," her voice is choked.

"Salem," Kioh says, forcefully this time, "sleep."

"No."

"Why not?"

She swallows back an agonized scream. "Because if I sleep, it will burn." Why did she say that?

Kioh wipes the rag along her face again. "You sleep all the time."

"That's different," Salem sobs, pain ripping through her body. "I have control, then"

"Trust me enough to give me the reins for a while, please."

"No," Salem hisses. She feels Kioh flinch ever so slightly.

"Please, Salem."

"No!" Salem shouts and immediately regrets it. "I can't trust you. I can't trust anyone. The world will burn." And then, because she's feeling cruel, "You mean nothing to me!" She feels tears running down her hot face. "The world will burn. I can't!"

"Please. Just sleep." Is she crying? She sounds like she's crying.

"No," Salem hisses. But her body betrays her. The pain is overwhelming. She passes out.

♔

Salem wakes up again an indiscernible amount of time later. Kioh is dozing in the chair (chair?) next to her bed (bed?). The pain overwhelms her immediately, and she lets out a tortured scream. Kioh jolts awake and Salem screams again. It's so much and it feels like how it did when she was eleven and it's *so much*. Dimly, Salem feels Kioh stroking her hair and shushing her and telling her to sleep. She listens to Kioh whisper and hum. She fights back another scream. Salem wants to be able to hear Kioh. She turns her face into Kioh's arms and sobs. *It's so much.*

"Hey shhh. It's alright Salem. It's all temporary." *Temporary.* Salem likes the sound of that. She feels like forever, and always, and never have been wearing on her nerves. She finds some peace in *temporary.*

"Shhhh," Kioh tilts Salem back into her bed, and Salem mourns the loss of her touch. How long has it been since she's been touched? Kioh's touch reappears, clutching her arm, and Salem feels a small prick, a needle. "Go to sleep, Salem," she whispers.

"Okay," she says. The pain has faded, a bit. She sleeps.

CHAPTER TWENTY

BRAN

△

BRAN WAKES UP IN a metal chair. He is lashed to it with several chains in places all over his body.

Rioz, Bran thinks, desperately. *Kabet. Jaz. Lark. I have to help them.* He jolts uselessly against the chains. There's a cold and frightening laugh from behind him. He inhales shakily and tries not to scream.

"Don't let me stop you," Tomas says. "By all means, escape and show us how *strong* you are." A pause. "At least then you'd be worth something." He stalks from his position behind Bran and places himself in front of him. Bran fights down terror.

Tomas sighs. "But really, I think we can be mutually beneficial to each other." He crouches in front of Bran and Bran feels a visceral rage. This man could have killed his *sister.* He spits in Tomas's face without even thinking.

He regrets it instantly. Tomas roars in anger and stands up, wiping his face clean and reaching for Bran, who thrashes desperately against the chains. Tomas grabs Bran's right middle finger and it snaps, painfully. Bran screams and fights. He wants out. He wants *out.* Tomas laughs and brings his face level with Bran's.

"That'll teach you to-" He is cut off by Bran smashing his head into Tomas's with as much force as he can muster.

Bran decides in that moment he will not be cowed. He will not be disheartened by some power-hungry, soulless monster. There's something defiant stirring inside of him, and he gives into it. Bran will prove everyone wrong. He will not break. He will not snap.

He may not be strong, but he will not be feeble.

Bran will stand straight, even as he is dying.

Tomas rears back in pain, clutching his head.

"Fucking idiot," Bran snarls at him.

Recovering, Tomas reaches forward and snaps Bran's other middle finger. Even as he screams, his eyes bleed defiance.

Tomas walks back behind him, placing his hands on the chair Bran is sitting in. Dimly, through pain, Bran realizes that the chair isn't bolted to the floor.

"Put it in the worst cell we have." Tomas pats Bran's face condescendingly. Bran's feet don't reach the ground, but he rears all his weight forward and then throws it backwards again. The chair topples onto Tomas, crushing him beneath its weight.

Just as Tomas is pinned beneath him, two guards rush over and drag him off of Tomas, chair and all. Tomas is practically sputtering with rage when he stands up.

"You little whore," he snarls. And Bran laughs. He laughs and can't stop laughing. Something like fear passes over Tomas's face, replaced quickly with rage. "I'll kill you! I'll kill you, you get that?"

Bran laughs as the guards get him out of the chair and to his feet, arms pinned behind him, hands bound tightly. Bran keeps laughing. "Tomas," he lets a sick sort of joy seep into his voice, "I'd love to see you try." The guards turn Bran towards the exit and he laughs, calling over his shoulder, "Maybe get a little practice? Hm? Try killing yourself, first. Should be easy enough."

Tomas screams obscenities after him, and all he can do is laugh.

After walking for a while, the guards throw Bran in a cell. It is filthy and cold. His hands are still bound.

He waits, kneeling for a while in the cell, until he hears the door slam behind him, and footsteps pattering away.

And then he cries.

Δ

"I'll kill it," she says, "whatever you're scared of."

This only causes Bran to cry harder. He doesn't want anything to die, scary or not. He dislikes destruction. As a child, he would take out his buckets of lavish toy figurines and estates, and set them up in a perfect arrangement. He cried whenever his parents made him put it away.

His parents. He wonders where they are now. Bran cries some more.

The girl just takes his hand. She grips it tight and fierce. Like something precious and worth protecting. He hesitates in his sobs.

"You will be okay," the girl says defiantly.

"Do you promise?" At four years old, a promise means everything.

"Always," says the girl, with all the gumption a four year old can muster.

Bran lets a tentative smile slip onto his face. He squeezes her hand back.

Δ

I will be okay. I will be okay. Iwillbeokay. The words he tells himself all run into one sentence. One incoherent loop.

Three of his fingers are broken. He forgot about the third, temporarily. The one Salem crushed. He wonders if it will ever heal right. If any of them will. *It could be worse*, is what he tries to tell himself. He's not sure it could, though.

It has been an unknown amount of time since the guards threw him in this cell. He stopped crying a bit ago. Instead, he just screams. He screams with all his righteous fury and blinding fear. His hands are still bound behind his back: tight. He fell on his face a while ago, and has been writhing around in the dirt since. He screams. He does not stop screaming.

Δ

The days begin to bleed together. Bran doesn't eat at all. He is not given the chance. He is also not given the chance to sleep, when he tries. When he tries, the guards come in and beat him bloody. No doubt at the order of Tomas. They pour water down Bran's throat, occasionally. He stops caring. The days bleed together. He's not sure how long it has been.

Bran's hands have been bound behind his back the entire time. His muscles have begun to atrophy, growing so painful and unbearable that sometimes he just passes out. Then the guards come in, and beat him bloody.

It is halfway to starvation when a loaf of stale bread is thrown into his cell. He can tell it's stale by the hard thunk it makes against the grimey, blood covered floor. Bran doesn't care that it's stale. Bran looks to the guard in the doorway, expecting him to unbind his hands. He simply laughs, and slams the door. Bran worms his way over to the bread and starts eating it off the ground, without his hands.

He realizes, in a deep pit in his mind, that this is degrading. He can't find it in him to care.

Δ

They unbind Bran's hands, at some point. He can't move his arms for a day afterwards.

Δ

They begin to feed him more. He knows this is leading up to something. Something he doesn't want to confront.

Δ

Tomas comes into Bran's cell personally. He grabs Bran by the hair and drags him limply out of the cell. He stumbles along as best as his ruined body can handle.

They reach a room, the same room he was in before. Bran doesn't keep track of directions. He has accepted that he is going to die here. Bran notices that the chair is now bolted to the floor, with metal cuffs in places, instead of chains. He starts laughing hysterically. It hurts.

Tomas strikes Bran across the face, then shoves him towards the chair. He stands the best he can.

"Am I supposed to sit in this?" Bran laughs as he says this, amusing himself at his own joke.

Tomas strikes him again, harder. He collapses onto the floor next to the chair.

Bran laughs harder. "Now, that's hardly a way to treat a guest!"

Tomas reaches for a gun that Bran now notices is strapped to his waist. He hesitates. Then stops completely.

"Get in the chair, Monroe."

The name doesn't even register with him. Bran does as he says. Tomas bolts him in. Then pulls up a cushioned chair and sits across from him.

"Are you ready to cooperate?"

Bran ignores his question. "That a gun?" He nods towards the gun. "You should give it to me."

"And why should I do that? So you can shoot me?"

"No," Bran laughs, "so I can shove it up your ass."

Tomas's face morphs into one of hatred so quickly that Bran can't help but feel pride. Tomas grabs his collar and gets in his face. Instantly, Bran slams his head into his with every ounce of force that exists within his body.

Tomas stumbles backwards and falls. Bran laughs. "You really ought to strap my head down, too, you know."

"You *whore*," he snarls. Tomas draws his gun and shoots Bran in the foot faster than he can think. Bran screams. He then nods towards someone outside Bran's line of sight. "Yank one of her top molars out." He pauses. "Sorry, *its*." He seems amused at his little joke, implying that he's a thing. A monster. Bran will show him how much of a monster he can be.

Two people come over and hold his mouth open, a third reaches in with a pair of pliers.

Bran doesn't know what's about to happen next. He just lets it happen.

It all erupts at once.

The pliers melt in his mouth. The person holding them pulls their hands backwards, but the other two don't get the memo quick enough. Bran clamps down, molten metal between his jaws. One of them yanks their hands out, fast as a viper. The other is not so lucky. Bran bites down, the person, a man, he realizes, begins to scream. He bites down harder and tastes blood mixing with the burning steel. He bites down until he feels his teeth snap through tendon. The man screams, removing his hand, now devoid of two fingers. Bran spits them onto the ground.

Tomas is looking at Bran in terror. He opens his mouth. Bran spits a column of fire and liquefied steel right into his face. The fire is green.

He watches with glee and horror as the steel begins to seep into his face. As his flesh begins to sizzle and pop and mold with the melted metal.

Tomas screams in pain, but draws his gun and pins it to Bran's forehead. The smell of his burnt flesh chokes Bran's senses.

"Any last words?" He hisses.

Bran laughs. He glares upwards at Tomas, letting his triumph ring throughout his eyes. "I cannot *wait* for Rioz to kill you."

The world goes black.

Δ

Bran wakes up in a chair, again. It is the same chair. He really thought he died. He feels a bit disappointed at the fact that he didn't. Better sooner than later.

Tomas is out of the room. Bran attempts to crane his neck, but his head has now been fixed to the chair as well. He smiles inwardly.

The door swings open, and a beautiful woman walks in. She has auburn red hair and freckles smattered across her cheeks. Her face is cut into sharp angles: all elegance and poise.

Bran recognizes her instantly.

It's his mother.

"Monroe," her voice is sweet and thick, like honey.

"Mom," he chokes.

"I'm going to offer you a choice," as soon as she says those words, Bran knows that she is not his mother.

Not really. His mother is back in a cabin in the woods, fretting over a letter he left. It's both disappointing and freeing.

"What is it?" Bran asks anyway. He is so tired.

"You can join me and your father. You can join us, and you can be happy. And you can be *strong*," her voice is so sweet. It's sweet enough to be rotten. "You would be working under the queen herself. You would have so much power. I know that you are the weak link. I know that you don't know how to use this incredible power you've been given, but, Monroe, you could be *unstoppable*." She pauses. "I would normally give you more time to make this decision, but we must act soon."

She sighs and continues. "The queen needs us. She needs *you*. I am so sorry we have put you through all of this, but you must realize that you have been working against us. We must take the utmost precautions." She hesitates. "I never wanted to leave you. But the queen wanted you to die. I had no other choice. Tomas had already been taken from me by the queen, I wouldn't let her take you as well." She smiles fondly at Bran. "But now, the queen has seen the light. And we can be together again, all of us. As a family. I missed you, Monroe. What do you say?"

Bran considers it. He does. He could get out of that cell. He could eat. He could sleep. He could *heal*. And this is his *mother*. She is offering him *everything*, and she seems nice. She rescued him from Tomas, even if they are working together. And, maybe, with time, they would come to accept him. Maybe they *could* be a family.

A voice that sounds like Rioz's tells him not to be selfish. Even if they accepted him: the atrocities against the people of Omari would never be erased.

But Bran gave up hope of anyone finding him days ago. This seems like the best offer he's going to get, in this lifetime.

He's so afraid. He is so *tired* of being afraid. He wants to be able to never feel this way again.

And then he remembers something.

"*You feel too much like home.*"

"Mom?" Bran asks, timid.

"Yes, Monroe?"

"You wanna know something?" She nods. Bran takes a deep inhale. "You are so much *uglier* than I remember." Her face morphs. "Go fuck yourself."

Faster than he can blink she has a sharp, slender knife drawn. She slashes it across his left eye in a vicious X, and tears his eye from its socket. He doesn't even scream.

"*You feel too much like home.*"

This is not his home, and he would rather die than live in a false one.

He needs to get back to them.

Bran feels the metal wrapped around him begin to melt. He rips his arms up through their constraints, slicing through steel like butter. His feet begin to melt through the floor.

As this happens, his mother, no, Alice Fehner, steps back in horror. He's sure he must be a terrifying sight. He's sure he must look beautiful.

Bran kills her. He kills everyone he comes across. The floor melts in his heat, the stone castle walls liquefy when he touches them. Bran kills them all. Burning and melting and branding everything he comes across. At some point, he kills his father. He begs for Bran to spare him. He has Bran's eyes. He barely notices.

By the time Bran finds Tomas, he feels...calm.

His face is destroyed, with bits of metal still embedded into it. He's fleeing the estate, as is everyone. Bran's destruction does not go unnoticed. Tomas is running; running away from *him*. That brings a horrible thrill.

As Bran reaches for him, he shouts. "I can tell you things! I can help you! Don't you want to know why you're like this?"

He stops. "Tell me."

"It has to do with the energy around birth circumstances. Our parents, they were able to replicate this energy, and they were able to *create* us."

"How?"

"It's all in this book," he scrambles around and holds out a leatherbound journal. "I can, help, Monroe—"

Bran snatches the red leather journal out of his hands. "Thanks. It's Bran, also." And he kills him.

By the time he has destroyed everything, it is starting to wear on him. By the time he starts walking towards Canak, (It's so *close*. He is *so* close.) he has vomited three times and not stopped crying.

Bran killed people. A lot of people. It makes him want to throw up, again. He does. There's nothing in his stomach, at this point. He's just heaving up acid. He keeps going.

At some point in time, he bandages his missing eye. He wraps his ruined shirtsleeve around his head, hoping his coat is enough to keep him warm.

Bran tries not to ponder it too much. He finds the river that flows through Canak and drops the sickle Salem gave him into it. He's weapon enough, himself.

PART FOUR: DOMINOES AND DELUSIONS

Chapter Twenty-One

KIOH

BY THE TIME THEY are just outside of Canak, Kioh can barely walk. She drags her bad leg behind her, leaning her weight on *Kahiji*. The mountain finally caught up with her limp. She doesn't care, she will cross it. Conquer it. She will face this challenge as she has every other: without a choice.Because, really, there is no choice. She does or she dies. She does or someone else dies. She succeeds or she fails.

Failing, in her line of work, is generally not an option.

It took years for her to get into this mindset. It took ages for her to kill whatever reservations lived inside of her. Because, no matter what, no matter how much pain she's in, or how much she detests it, she has to survive.

Kioh used to be nice. She used to be 'the brightest sun in the sky', as her mother used to say. She was warm. She shed light and heat like rain.

There's a desperate part of her that clings to that girl. That holds tight to her shining smile and cheery demeanor. That won't let go of the desire to help people.

There's a more desperate part of her that has its hands dirty. That has taken everything it wants. That steals from others for the sake of itself.

Kioh trudges her way down the last slope towards Canak. Salem and Mira are ahead of her, and she knows she's slowing them down. A part of her feels bad. Most of her doesn't care.

Salem officially woke up yesterday. She had bouts of consciousness between getting herself ripped to shreds and now, but Kioh tries not to think about them.

"You mean nothing to me!" she said. *"The world will burn. I can't!"* she said. Kioh knows that neither are true. She knows Salem believes both to be.

Kioh's not sure which *she* believes at this point.

Some of Salem's already short hair has been ripped out, leaving scabs behind. Her wounds are barely healed, flesh still gaping and healing beneath bandages. Kioh's shocked that she's not dead: the infection was severe, and they didn't find anyone even resembling a doctor until two days ago. Her fever broke less than a day ago. The doctor's apprentice said that she would probably lose some function in the affected areas.

Kioh's not even sure how Salem is standing.

She knows Salem's been through worse. The burns scars are the screaming evidence for the physical pain she's been through.

The times she woke up after the fight with Lydia are a testament to something else entirely.

The one that sticks out to Kioh the most is one that she knows Salem doesn't remember: if she did she would be unable to look Kioh in the eye.

Kioh is reading in a chair beside the bed that Salem is laying in. Salem woke up a few hours ago, screaming. She thankfully fell back asleep.

Kioh's not even aware that she woke up again when she says: "Are you my friend?"

Kioh starts and turns to look at her. Her voice is clear and empty of pain: but her seeing eye is delirious and foggy. "Why do you ask?" Kioh says, because she is incapable of making anything easy.

"Because I don't have any friends," she says, quite frankly.

Kioh sighs. Everything Salem does and says during these episodes makes her feel melancholy.

"I'm your friend if you want me to be your friend, Salem."

She frowns. "I don't think that's how it works."

"You don't have any friends, how would you know?" The snarky, playful words slip out of Kioh's mouth before she can stop them.

Kioh's about to panic when Salem bursts into full blown giggles. Her face splits open in something Kioh has never seen on her. Something gorgeous.

"You're funny, Kioh. I like you when you're funny," she says. Her eyes start to clear. "Why does everything hurt?" She asks, now meek. Kioh sighs and reaches into the bag for the painkiller the doctor's apprentice gave them. She knows it's not long until she's screaming in pain.

Salem sits up suddenly and glances around desperately. "Where is my family?" She asks suddenly, panicked and horrified. "Where are they, Kioh? Where are my parents? They should be here."

Kioh doesn't say anything. She simply waits until the pain overwhelms her. It doesn't, though.

"They're dead aren't they? They're dead and I didn't even get to say goodbye."

Kioh's heart hurts. "Yes, Salem. I'm sorry."

Salem frowns. "I think my family died a long time ago. My meaning was stolen." She looks at Kioh. "They were worth more than you. But you're worth more than everything right now." Her words are a riddle Kioh can't possibly hope to solve. *"Will you help me rebuild meaning? Jen always told me that's what I needed to do. I think I need help, though."* She's rambling and Kioh sees tears streaking down her scarred face.

Salem sighs and lays back in the bed. "I miss Jen. I miss my family. I want you." Kioh doesn't know what to say to that. She doesn't know what to think, even. Salem turns to her and looks Kioh dead in the eyes. Her good eye is now clear, and swimming with all sorts of pain. *"You can give me the shot, now."*

So Kioh does.

❦

They reach Canak just as dusk is falling. Salem's strides have grown more sure, more confident. Kioh can tell she's itching to get started. She knows how badly Salem craves revenge.

At the edge of the city, Kioh collapses. Her leg gives way to pain, and she falls, kneeling, clutching her cane. She begins to pull herself up. Mira eyes Kioh warily. She probably thinks she's going to ruin the plan. She won't. She never does.

Kioh stands, jerking her leg forwards as she limps towards Canak. The even ground is bliss to her leg. She walks hastily, as if trying to prove something.

Kioh has gone aways when Salem pulls even with her. "Arm around my shoulders," she says, her voice plain.

"I don't need your help."

Salem looks at her. "You do. Consider it payback."

"Technically, you'd have to carry me twice," Kioh says, relenting and wrapping her arm around Salem's shoulder as they make their way down the street.

Mira follows them. The three of them stride into the city as darkness begins to descend, wrapping them like an icy blanket.

❧

Kioh doesn't know when pickpocketing became a routine for her. All she knows is that it eases the itch at her mind. It kills the boredom that follows her everywhere. The thrill she gets from stealing is native to her energy. She needs somewhere to put it: she needs to find something to do.

So she starts stealing. No one in Port City expects theft to come crawling out of a child. It's not that kind of place. Port City is a place of prosperity and peace. Like most of Taahua, it is utopia for its citizens.

But she needs. She wants. She itches.

Kioh begins to observe how people behave, while her mother is off on fishing trips that are too dangerous for her to go on as well. She is old enough to leave the house alone, and at the time she thinks she is old enough to do anything. Twelve years is quite a bit, after all.

So she watches. She watches how people bustle about the streets, focusing on the person next to them, the task in front of them. She watches how they can walk right through a throng of people, never taking note of the things around them.

And she notices. She notices how things small enough to fall between the cracks of people's consciousness are ignored completely. It's strange, how the brain only notes what it deems important. She once watches a woman run towards a man, right past a street performer juggling knives, right through danger, never noticing. Kioh figures she must not have seen the man in a while.

But it's thrilling. It is exciting to see everything that people missed. To simply know that she knows more. To take in the finer details, connect them into ideas, and bring those forth into a truth. It sharpens the dullness that surrounds her mind. It allows her to focus on something other than nothing.

Soon, it's not enough. She starts itching again. She wants to use what she sees. She wants to put it into practice.

If Kioh could just confirm that she was right. If she could just use the knowledge she could obtain within a glance.

She tries several things at first. Talking to strangers on the street is not welcomed. Neither is anything else that forces them to take note of her. She needs something where they wouldn't see her. Where she can interact with them without them ever knowing.

It starts innocently enough. A woman pushes a wooden cart down the street; selling candies and fruit. Kioh strides right past her, walking confidently, ignoring her in the way she ignores anyone who isn't a customer.

Kioh drops her left hand right as she pulls level with the cart. She uses her quick fingers, the ones obtained from tying fishing knots, to snatch a morsel of fruit off the cart, right as the woman exchanges a bag of candies for money.

Kioh waits for her to notice, waits for her to yell at her the way other children are yelled at when they steal things off carts. It never happens. She is never caught.

Kioh is shocked. Stunned at the fact that she slipped between the gaps in the woman's mind. The excitement from being successful makes her forget all about the restlessness that lay within her. She sits on a bench and eats the fruit, swinging her legs.

She starts doing it more and more. She nabs things off carts, and stands. Soon, she graduates to taking things out of satchels and coats. And then she starts taking things right off people's bodies.

Kioh accumulates a collection of watches, wallets, jewelry, and other valuables. She does this for almost two years. She has a fortune in stolen goods sitting in a threadbare bag in her room.

And she's never caught.

And then, one day, she is.

It's Kioh's mother who catches her. She finds hordes of stolen items in Kioh's room while cleaning one day. She normally never lets it get that messy, because of this. She grew careless.

Kioh comes home, one day. She greets her mother and father cheerily, as she always does. She loves them more than anything in the world. They do not respond.

Kioh peaks her head into the living area and sees stolen items laid out across the table. Tears spring instantly to her eyes.

Her parents stare gravely at her. She can feel the weight of her crimes bearing down on her. Kioh can feel the guilt and shame that she does not want to face; will not face.

"Why would you do this, my child?" Kioh's mother asks. "We have provided everything you ever needed? What can you possibly gain?"

"I...I don't know," Kioh sobs, taking a seat at the cushion across from her. "It made me feel better."

"You've hurt people for your own gain," her father says morosely. "You have failed to hold empathy for those around you."

"You have disappointed us," her mother says. "You've done something very, very wrong. Aren't you old enough to know better?"

The weight of their expectations, the weight of Kioh's failure, the weight of the fact that she has hurt the people closest to her; it bears down on her like an elephant. It crushes her. It makes her shrink. Kioh cannot bear it.

Kioh's mother stands. She walks towards Kioh and kneels in front of her. Kioh waits for her to touch her: she doesn't. "You have never done something like this. I thought you were the perfect child, Kioh. I see now that I was wrong."

And she is broken. Something in her chest twangs with the sound of a failing musical instrument. She does not scream. She won't hurt her parents any longer. Instead, she runs.

A bag of stolen goods is propped by the steps down into the living room. Kioh grabs it, swinging it over her back wildly.

"Kioh!" Her mother calls, just as the door slams behind her. Kioh hears her father starting to follow after her, but she knows these streets far better than he does, and she slips between the cracks. She fades into the darkness.

Kioh makes her way towards the ports. People are moving about, even at this late of an hour.

"Where is this ship going?" she asks the first person she sees, pointing towards the first ship in the dock.

"Fishing trip. We don't need more workers, sorry."

She keeps walking. "Where is this ship going?" she repeats to another. She receives the same answer.

"Where is this ship going?" Kioh asks, a sixth time.

"Shka, why?"

"Just wondering," she keeps walking, she slips into shadows, away from the light.

Kioh waits until everyone has boarded. She waits until the night around begins to grow deeper.

She makes her way onto the ship, silently. She finds a spot behind a few crates of what seem to be Taahuan cloths, and curls up to sleep.

Kioh manages to stow away for a few days. She is sleeping when the crew finds her.

She jolts awake as one of the crates is pulled aside. The man looks down at her and laughs. He is Kendren. His face is foreign and his words are strange. He's shouting at her, but she cannot gather anything else.

And then he's reaching for something at his waist. A gun, Kioh realizes. She grabs wildly for something to protect her. She finds a broken plank of wood, and brandishes it in front of her. He laughs, and cocks the gun.

Kioh swings the plank at his hand as he shoots. The bullet hits her in the leg, pain courses through her: more pain than she has ever known. He yells and cocks the gun again.

She braces herself for death. Kioh apologizes to her mother and father one last time in her head. She says her goodbyes to the world she loved and lost. She has lost so much.

Her savior comes in a shape she would not have expected.

Three people round the corner. They take a look at the situation and smack the gun out of the first man's hand and begin shouting at him. Kioh catches none of it. She presses her hands to her eyes. The weight of leaving her family has finally sunk in. She misses them desperately. She cannot go back.

Someone speaks in her mother tongue. It is horrible and stilted but she understands it.

"Who are you?" he asks. His voice is grave, but not unkind.

"No one."

"'No one,' is stowed away on my ship. Who are you?"

"A thief," Kioh supplies. She will not give her name. A name means something.

However, the man brightens at this. "What kind of thief?" Kioh grabs the pack of stolen goods and throws it at his feet.

Gold, money, jewels, and other valuables spill from its opening.

The man laughs. "You have come to the right place," he tells her. "We are all thieves here." He turns and says something to the rest of the crew.

"What did you tell them?" Kioh asks. She is not sure if she wants to know what the future holds, but asks anyway.

"I told them to get in touch with Dalton," the man laughs again. "You'll fit right in with him, kid."

It takes three more weeks to arrive at the ports of Shka.

During the three weeks, the sailors teach Kioh as much of the language as they can. They're not horrible to be around, actually. They are by no means kind or good, but they are not evil.

They quickly pick up on the fact that she knows her way around a ship. She tells the only man who speaks Taaish her background in fishing. He puts her to work.

She becomes a member of the crew. She is paid, as is the rest of the crew. It feels strange to become acquainted with them. They are thieves. They are both like her and unlike her.

She likes to think she has more morality than them, but she is not sure how long that idea will last.

Kioh appreciates the stolen money she is paid with, at least.

They remove the bullet in Kioh's leg. It's a bloody, painful affair. The captain tells her that it hit bone. He advises her to rest, knowing full well she can't. She cannot sit still. She cannot be idle. It has always been impossible for her.

Kioh limps about the ship for the three weeks, propping herself on the plank that she found that day. She knows her leg will never heal right. She doesn't care, she will never be caught sitting still again. She drags it about with her, never slowing down.

One of the kinder crew members asks Kioh about her parents, one day. She chokes back tears as she tells him how dearly she loved them. How devastatingly she lost them.

The only other woman on the crew is the one who explains Kioh's fate to her. The captain translates her words to Kioh.

"I'm friends with Dalton," she tells Kioh. "We go way back." She asks the captain, Arnel, what that means, he explains. This is how most of her conversations with the other crew goes. The woman, Frenya, continues. "He's getting old, though. So he's looking for a prodigy to take over his gang." Kioh doesn't know what a gang is, she'll ask later. "Tons of people volunteered. But they're all too old, apparently. Dalton says he took over the business when he was sixteen, and he wants someone around that age. And those who are that young, aren't 'right' I guess. Dalton's always been picky. Anyway, he's searching for someone to take over the business."

She sighs. "It's not a bad fate. Probably not one someone might choose, but Dalton is a good boss, and an even better thief. He's nice. You're free to leave whenever, too. Hell, you don't even have to do it. He'll care for you while you work for him, but he won't make you do anything you don't wanna do. Not something you see often in that business." Frenya pauses. "He'll explain the rest to you when you get there."

Dalton is waiting for them when they arrive at one of Shka's ports. She picks him out of the crowd immediately. He has a shock of white hair with a pale cutting face and a sharp gaze. His posture is ramrod straight, and his gait is confident, but not overly so. He has a brown tweed suit on, with a golden tie pin in the shape of a jester's hat. He's wearing a gold watch with a black face. He screams luxury, but no one else seems to notice him.

He catches Kioh staring at him, and he smiles. It's not menacing or cold. It's just a smile. She feels oddly comforted.

The crew begins unloading the ship while Arnel and Frenya walk Kioh over to him, with her bag of valuables clutched in her hands.

Dalton turns towards Arnel. "You could have contacted me once you were ashore. I do not enjoy having pigeons show up in my home. I also do not enjoy mail."

The words register as Kendrak to Kioh, but she doesn't understand most of them.

"Didn't want to make you wait," Arnel shrugs. Dalton ignores him and shifts his gaze to Frenya.

"Good to see you, old friend. Though, I never thought I'd see you in this sort of position."

"It's temporary," Frenya snaps. "Do you want to meet the kid or not?" Dalton smiles at her.

"Let me speak with her," Dalton turns to Kioh. She is almost tall enough to look him in the eye. He then addresses her in Taaish. It's bad, but not as bad as Arnel's. "What do you have in the bag?"

Kioh shrugs. "Anything."

"May I see?" She hands him the bag. He looks into it, then looks back at her. "Did you steal all of this?"

She thinks of how few of her crimes that bag now holds. "And then some."

Dalton's eyes sharpen and for the first time Kioh feels afraid of him.

He turns back towards her. "Who taught you to steal?"

"I did."

"How?"

"I watched people. I realize they notice less than they think."

"Why do you steal?" he asks, suddenly.

A jolt of sadness shoots through Kioh. She squashes the morality that lives inside her. She will not be cruel. She vows to never be cruel. But she will survive at all costs.

Kioh looks him in the eye as she answers his question. "At first I stole because it was something to do. Now I do it to get back to where I belong." She doesn't elaborate. She doesn't want to speak about Taahua and how dearly she misses it.

He nods. "Do you think you'll ever stop?"

Kioh smiles, somewhat sad and somewhat mischievous. She hands him Arnel's wallet. "Probably not."

Dalton's face splits open into a warm grin. "Arnel, Frenya, Kioh," he says in Kendrak, as Arnel flounders and snatches his wallet back, "you have just made me very happy indeed."

❦

Night cloaks the three of them as they meander about the slow streets of Canak. Salem seems to be looking for something. Kioh's not sure what.

Canak is a dull town: Duskrans tend to be dull people. They have bland food and a disregard for anything fun. They also dislike technology, she notices. Walking around Canak feels like walking around in Rowak four years ago. Everything is old and obsolete.

Salem suddenly takes a sharp left, veering towards one of the few stores that seems to be open. Kioh notices even some of the bars are closed.

Ridiculous, she thinks. *If they were normal people, this would be the time to make money.* Kioh then realizes that Rowak is hardly normal, and neither is the way she makes money.

They follow Salem into what looks like an artisan's shop. Salem approaches the man who is reorganizing items on the shelves.

"Do you have board games here?" Salem asks.

Board games? Why would she need board games? Kioh wonders. Despite her knowing better, she wonders about Salem a lot.

The man looks at her in confusion, and then says something in Duskran.

Salem sighs. They're in the heart of Duskra now. Kendrak will not be spoken easily, and though the words are similar, they are not the same.

Salem tries some fragmented Duskran, but she falters on board games. That's not a very common word, and Kioh knows that she doesn't know it; none of them do.

Suddenly, yet another language pierces their ears. It's words are sharp and pointed, all harsh angles and no rounded edges. Kioh cannot identify it for the life of her.

Salem, however, whirls towards the noise, and replies in the same tongue.

Kioh turns to where Salem's gaze has landed, and sees a young Zhidish girl. She's tall, much taller than Salem, and her face is so mirthful it almost seems cruel. She has long straight hair that falls to her waist. Her skin is much darker than Salem's.

Salem and her speak rapid fire Zhidish. The girl laughs and says something, at which Salem pales.

"What'd she say?" Kioh asks in Kendrak. The girl turns towards the shopkeeper and says something in Duskran. He bustles off, probably to go grab something.

"She said I speak Zhidish like a criminal."

"I mean. You are."

Salem turns towards her, her expression grim. "You're forgetting that I learned Zhidish from my parents."

"Well, what did your parents do?"

"That's the thing," Salem sighs. "I don't know."

The shopkeeper returns with a box. He hands it to Salem and waits patiently.

That's when all of them seem to realize they don't have any money.

The Zhidish girl brushes past Kioh, who hesitates for a split second before nabbing her wallet. *Maybe I can make it up to her later*, Kioh thinks, discreetly passing the wallet to Salem, who draws a few bills out of it and hands them to the man.

He nods thankfully and them all depart the building. Kioh glances around for the girl but she's nowhere in sight. She feels a minute twang of guilt.

Salem glances around the empty street before kneeling down on the cobblestones and prying a stone loose with her nails. She opens the wooden box and pulls out a domino. She then jams it into the crack with the loose cobblestone and stands up.

"The others will be here," she says. There's not an iota of doubt in her voice but Kioh is still not sure if she believes the words she's speaking.

"Where are we staying?" Kioh realizes suddenly they have no money and, based on Salem's vague words, they will likely be staying in Canak for a while.

Salem turns to her. "That's up to you, I suppose."

Kioh opens her mouth to infer further, but then catches Salem's meaning. "You want me to steal an apartment?"

"Or a house. Whichever's easier."

Kioh rolls her eyes and Salem begins to walk. They make their way through the streets of Canak, Salem stopping every so often to wedge a domino somewhere. The three of them have been walking for an hour, remaining largely silent when Kioh sees it.

A massive building wrought from shiny red brick and black iron stands proud among the otherwise humble streets of Canak. The double doors have polished handles and a doorman dressed in finery standing next to them. A glance further up the street shows similar buildings. Even Canak has a rich district, she supposes.

Kioh walks up to the doorman with a confidence only a professional criminal can have.

"Excuse me, sir, I seem to have forgotten my identification. If you'll allow me into the building, I have a key to prove ownership."

"Who the hell are you?" the man asks, warily.

"I haven't been here in about seven months," she's taking a gamble but intuition tells her it's a correct one, "I'm not sure how long you've worked here. I'm a tenant of this building, you see. I've been on vacation to see my family in Taahua."

"You're speaking Kendrak," the man points out, eyes narrowing.

"I'm not familiar with Duskran. I'm a merchant trader. Primarily based in Taahua. We don't do a lot of trading with Duskra. Hardly any, in fact. However, I do live here. How long have you worked here?" She tilts her head in a friendly way.

"Almost three months." He seems to be softening. Kioh decides to push her point home.

"I just love Duskra, so I decided to settle in this wonderful city. I'm hoping to stay for a tad longer this time; maybe we can get to know each other?" Kioh hears Salem cover a laugh with a cough. The man leers at her. *Pervert*, she thinks, and then prattles on. "Unfortunately I seem to have forgotten my identification. I do have a key to prove residency, to..." she roots around in her pockets and pulls out the key to her apartment in Rowak. Kioh hands the key to him and prays to the earth itself that she's lucky enough to pull this off. "Apartment two thirty-eight!" She recites the number on the fake key. "I always forget, my apologies. anyway, I assume you don't want to wake your supervisors for such a paltry issue? As long as two thirty-eight is still vacant, I'll be able to move in promptly, no?" Kioh bats her eyelashes at him and grins like she doesn't know how to do anything else.

He hands the key back to Kioh. "That apartment is still vacant, however I'm not supposed to let anyone in without identification..." He glances at her, clearly expecting something.

"Please?" She asks, giving him exactly what he wants. "You'd be my hero. I've been traveling all day, I just want to get home with my compatriots here." Kioh gestures to Salem and Mira. Salem glares at her, clearly not playing along. Mira, however, smiles dumbly and flirtily. A *natural*, Kioh thinks.

The man huffs, clearly faking annoyance. "I suppose." He opens the door behind him, the three of them make their way in. Kioh nods her thanks and begins to walk towards the stairs.

"I'll see you around, yeah?" he calls after them.

Kioh smiles coyly and nods, then begins to head up the stairs. *In your dreams, idiot.*

Kioh leans over and whispers to Salem. "Remind me to fake some paperwork to give to them. And to get him fired."

"You dug your grave."

Kioh ignores her. "I need to come up with a name. I'm thinking Huapal Aori."

Salem ignores her in turn. "You're probably going to have to go on a date with him."

"If I have to go on a date with him, I'm killing you, personally."

"Can you kill someone impersonally?" She jokes, then pauses. "Nevermind, don't answer that question."

Kioh laughs. There's a beat of silence before she says: "Huapal Aori was my eighty year old neighbor, in case you were wondering."

"I wasn't, thanks."

Kioh picks the lock into the apartment. It's completely unfurnished, and clearly hasn't been cleaned in months. She scrapes her finger across the floor. A thick layer of dust is picked up.

"I'll clean," she volunteers. Kioh refuses to sleep here until it's been cleaned. She starts rifling through her pack to find something to use for said task.

"Can you conjure some furniture while you're at it?" Mira remarks dully, clearly not impressed by the state of the place.

"I'll get you furniture."

Mira arches an eyebrow. "How?"

Kioh rolls her eyes. "I do this for a living. I think I know how to con a moving crew into giving me a couch." A pause. "I'll get it done by tomorrow."

"We're going to need a lot of stuff," Salem looks at her, almost apologetic.

"Write me a list. I can probably get it within the week. Small stuff within the day."

Salem nods tightly and starts to unpack. Kioh finds a shredded shirt in her belongings and runs it under some warm water with soap from her pack.

Kioh starts to erase the grime from the place wiping down the walls, the countertops. *I'll give it a proper cleaning, later*, she thinks to herself; remembering how her mother used to clean for days.

Piece by piece, she starts to scour the apartment. Piece by piece she starts to click together the puzzle that Salem has been building around them.

When she's done she throws the makeshift rag in a corner with the others. Mira is asleep. Salem is sitting on her bedroll, twirling *Mao* absentmindedly, staring off into the distance.

"Salem," Kioh's voice is hoarse. She doesn't want to think about why. "Why are we doing this?"

Salem looks at her, confused, for a moment. Her face clears and returns to its natural grim expression. "Because wrongs must be made right." She sighs. "Because the world deserves justice."

Something painful inside Kioh thumps against her ribcage. "You're not the only one who lost parents, Salem," she says. "Not all of us have some sort of hero complex. Some of us are just trying to live our lives. I don't need your goddamn *justice*." The words hiss out of her. She doesn't know why she's so angry. She doesn't know why she feels so horrible. "If you're going on some twisted, self-serving revenge quest; at least admit that you're doing it for selfish reasons."

Something about Salem freezes. Kioh's seen her like this before. She's seen Salem shut down and ice the world around her. She's about to apologize but Salem turns her empty gaze towards Kioh and the words are knocked out of her.

"You can leave, you know." Her voice is so *cold*. "I don't need you. I don't need any of you, in fact. I would like help. I would like to execute my 'self-serving revenge quest' in the most brutally efficient way possible, and for that I need other people. But you need to understand, Kioh, is that even if I have to take innocent lives and do horrible things, even if I am cut and bloody and *broken*, even if I am sent to hell for my crimes...Even in the face of the worst thing you can possibly imagine: I *will* do this."

She takes a sharp breath in. "I would kill *anyone* if it meant Parev would die. I would do anything."

"Why would you say that?" Kioh gasps out. She doesn't know when she started crying.

"You know why, Kioh." And she laughs. She laughs that horrible dead laugh. "You've spent weeks with me.

Surely you've riddled it out by now? Surely you understand?" She laughs again. "In every way but literal: I am dead. Everything important, everything worth living for, everything that made me who I am? It was all stolen, Kioh. I was killed when I was eleven years old.

"You know what I am, you know what I feel. You know that I am merely a weapon to deliver justice." She laughs and Kioh feels like screaming. "Look in my fucking eyes, Kioh!" She laughs and laughs and laughs. "There's nobody home!"

Salem turns away from her and lays down to sleep. Kioh is sent back to the moments when she was sick. When Salem cried and she held her. Kioh thinks about her leg. She thinks about hauling it over an insurmountable mountain.

Two million is a lot of money, she thinks.

Two million is a lot of money, she thinks, again. *Enough to let me leave Rowak.*

Two million isn't enough money for this. Kioh doesn't get up to leave. *Why am I doing this?* She wonders.

Kioh thinks about Salem's smirk. About her silent way of taking in the world. She thinks about the rare moments when she's seen Salem happy. She thinks about the fact that Salem twitches slightly when she approaches her from her blind side. That she's unbeatable in a fight. Kioh thinks about her expression when she's nice to her. About her not having any friends.

Why am I doing this? Kioh wonders, again.

She thinks she knows why.

Chapter Twenty-Two

MIFENG

THOSE LITTLE PISSANTS STOLE her wallet.

Chapter Twenty-Three

KABET

ARRIVING IN CANAK FEELS hollow. They have crossed a nearly insurmountable mountain in the winter. They have dodged death and defied...well, they've pretty much defied everything.

And Kabet has always loved rebellion. But arriving in Canak still feels hollow. It feels sickly sweet, like fruit gone rotten. Like winning everything he wanted but losing the only thing that matters.

Kabet knows it's because Bran isn't there. He knows that his absence gnaws at all of their minds. Rioz has been inconsolable since they left the ruined cabin.

He has never quite understood how someone could grow to be like Salem. He thought Salem may be an odd case.

Kabet sees now that is not the case.

Rioz transforms into a different person. Her face grows empty and devoid of emotion. She snaps and snarls at anyone who tries to approach her. She rips into anyone who mentions Bran. When she's not screaming trees into splinters, she's just cold.

Kabet never quite understood how someone could be so completely destroyed by loss. He lost Adena, but he was young. He was young and knew nothing of the emotions swirling inside of him. It hurt Kabet, it cut him so deeply he can still feel the scars today, but it did not control him.

Kabet knows that had he been older, had he been more afraid of the world, grown more wary of strangers and more trusting of friends, he would be exactly like Salem.

He knows Salem was only eleven when her family was ripped from her. He also knows Salem's pain didn't end with their deaths.

He figures being burned alive would put a different sort of spin on things.

Kabet watches Rioz transform. She goes from bright and burning— common sense but hot-headed nonetheless— to dim and dull.

The moment they lost Bran, they lost Rioz, too.

So, yes. Their arrival in Canak feels hollow.

Kabet walks nervously up to the edge of the town. He unconsciously rubs at the bruises that lace his neck, and chokes back tears at the thought of Adena. She was alive again. Hurting him, killing him, but alive.

He knows she wasn't actually alive. But it feels horrible knowing how close she was to it.

Kabet tugs his collar up and tries to assess how suspicious they look. He wonders if news of a foreign renegade would have reached a place like Canak. He decides not to take any chances.

Bran's absence chews at him, in the back of his mind. Kabet tries not to think about it.

"So?" Lark asks, dejected. "What now?"

"This is fucking ridiculous," Rioz snaps. "We don't even know if they're here. We don't even know if they're coming. We're lost in Duskra with no money, no plan, and a target on our backs. I want to go home and grieve my brother." She snarls the words and looks murderously at all of them.

Kabet sighs. "I would think they would be here, now." He looks nervously around their group. "We can look for them, if they are here."

Jaz nods. He turns to Rioz, expression soft. "Rioz, we need to recuperate, anyway. And if Bran comes anywhere, he'll come here. We can stay for a while, look for them, and hopefully come up with a plan, if they aren't here."

Rioz glares at him. He holds her gaze. She turns her eyes downwards and nods, softly. Jaz is the only one who can even come close to having a rational conversation with her.

Rioz stalks up ahead of the group, likely going to scour the city for Bran. Kabet turns towards Jaz. "Do you really think he will come back?"

Jaz shrugs. "I have no idea. I'm not all-knowing. I can't tell you one way or another." He sighs. "Do you think it hurts to hope, though?"

Anger snarls through Kabet. He just wants him *back*. "Yes," Kabet snaps. "It always hurts to hope."

They follow Rioz down the busy street. Her eyes dart around the crowd, desperately searching for something Kabet thinks she won't find.

He ducks his head and pulls his scarf up, resigned to keep hoping.

♂

They have been in Canak for two hours when Kabet trips for what is probably the tenth time. The city is antiquated. The streets are outdated and rough. He falls into a kneeling position. As Kabet goes to pull himself up, his hand snags something. He glances at the ground, and sees something odd.

"Look at this," Kabet says, pulling the domino out of its slot in the ground and presenting it to his compatriots.

Rioz barely glances at it. "It's a coincidence. We're outside an artisan toy shop."

"No," he says, defiantly. "Look at the back."

Rioz snags it out of Kabet's hand and flips it over.

"What's it say?" Jaz asks. Before, he would have crowded over her shoulder to peek at it. That was before, though.

"'*Watch your step*,'" she smiles, faintly. "Typical."

"Salem, I'm assuming?" Lark asks.

"Yes," Kabet says. "She probably put some under every loose cobblestone, knowing we would trip over one, eventually."

Lark gapes for a second. "That's...I don't know? Terrifying?"

Rioz snorts, amused for the first time in ages. "That's Salem." She seems energized. "Let's look for them."

Kabet nods, whirling around to look for more clues, and smashes right into someone.

It feels sickeningly familiar. It feels right and horrible and perfect all at once.

Kabet glances down at the person who he just so rudely crashed into, and his heart snags in his chest. His breath catches in his throat. The world halts in its tracks and Kabet is thrown wildly off the train.

"Bran?" he asks softly. Softer than he has any right to be.

Bran glances up at him, seeming startled. His face instantly tenses, then relaxes, then tenses again. He looks...well, he looks horrible.

Before Kabet can say anything, Bran wraps his arms around his torso and sobs into his chest.

"What happened?" Kabet is frantic. "Are you okay? What happened to you? Where were you?" He's about to continue his onslaught of questions when Bran raises a battered hand to his mouth and clamps it over his lips.

"For once in your life, Kabet," he laughs, it's sad and relieved and soft; it makes Kabet ache, "just shut the hell up."

Kabet gets to hug him back for a fraction of a second when he hears Rioz sobbing. Bran wipes his eyes, releases him, and walks over to where she's kneeling on the road.

"I'm back," he says, lightly. "Hope you didn't miss me too much while I was off on vacation."

Rioz's sobs transform into hysterical laughter for a few seconds before she composes herself. "I didn't miss you at all, don't flatter yourself." She looks at him with so much love in her eyes that Kabet wonders if he's even capable of loving someone like that. She reaches up and cups his face. Her expression shifts to concern.

Bran shrugs. "You should see the other guy," he jokes. His tone is airy and dismissive but he winces at the words.

"Is your eye okay?" Jaz asks.

Bran snorts. "What eye?"

Rioz doesn't seem to hear him. She's gripping him tightly, both of them kneeling on the cobblestones. She's back to hysterically sobbing. He sighs and pulls her to her feet.

Jaz, however, understands. His expression flashes with sympathy and something like fear. "You can't be serious?"

Bran shrugs again. He tips his head towards Rioz, who seems to be recovering. "Tell you later."

Then he looks at Kabet, and for a moment his neutral expression grows frantic and sad. Kabet opens his mouth to ask Bran...anything, he supposes. But by the time Kabet is about to get the words out, Bran has recovered from whatever it was.

Rioz separates herself from Bran. Lark claps him on the shoulder. "Good to hear you, Bran."

Bran smirks. Something about him is different. "Funny," he says. "I was under the impression we hated each other."

Lark laughs. "You just got kidnapped. I decided to cut you some slack for today."

Bran shrugs, again. "Sorry, can't return the favor."

Lark grins at him and then turns to the rest of them. "So, are we finding the others or what?"

♂

They find twelve more dominoes before they arrive at a red brick apartment building. It looks ridiculously lavish.

"This can't be the place," Jaz says, but he seems unsure.

"How would they even get in?" Rioz wonders.

Bran, however, scans the area for clues. Kabet glances around as well, and then he sees it.

"Look," he points to the writing on the flag that hangs out one of the second story windows.

"What's it say?" Lark asks.

"*Everything that can happen, is possible because of a choice you made when you were four years of age. Everything takes care of everything.*" Kabet tries not to let delight seep into his voice.

"What does that even *mean*?" Bran asks.

"It is a line from a philosophy book written by Duphi Owreshi. She is a renown Sunani scholar, one of my favorites. She is known for her work on the subject of choice and free will, mostly the existence and the definition." A pause. "The line references the idea that there is no free will. Everything is connected in such complex ways that we cannot possibly begin to understand our own fates, let alone influence them. Everything takes care of everything merely means that every single breath you take has an outcome. Every event in the world is responsible for everything else."

Bran looks at him, owlishly. Jaz and Rioz mostly seem confused. Lark isn't paying attention. "Isn't that sad, though?" Bran asks.

"In the next chapter, Owreshi insists that we must know that we have no control, and we must continue to make choices despite that. And that is the true definition of free will: being aware of your insignificance, but making things important despite it." Kabet smiles at Bran. "It is not sad. Enlightening, but not sad. Because making meaning in the face of obscurity is what makes us human."

Bran looks up at him with an unreadable look in his eye. He wavers there for a second, and then turns away. "You know all of this but you can't sharpen a knife." He grins up at Kabet, walking towards the building. "Some revolution leader you are."

Kabet laughs. "I am an intellectual leader. I educate people, I do not force them to arms."

"Oh, so you write pamphlets?" Bran mocks Kabet, who laughs again. "You write pamphlets for a living?"

"I own an artisan leather-working shop. That is my main source of income."

Bran rolls his eyes. "Of course you do."

They're growing closer to the building, when Kabet halts in his tracks, realizing something.

"How are we going to get in?"

Everyone falters. "We give them their names?" Lark suggests.

Rioz shakes her head. "They would have used aliases, which we have no way of guessing."

The four of them stand there thinking for a while when Jaz suddenly jolts.

"Oh," he says, laughing. "I'm not very bright."

"What do you—" Rioz starts to say, then stops. "Oh."

Jaz tugs his cloak tighter over his wings and walks up the remaining distance to the doorman. He then lets out a jaunty tune. The rest of them quickly follow behind. The doorman opens the door.

"What apartment are they in?" Bran asks once they step inside. Kabet attempts to recreate the floorplan in his head, when Lark speaks up.

"Two thirty-eight. Also, Salem and Kioh are not getting along, currently."

"Your little gift couldn't have helped out earlier?" Rioz jokes.

Lark shrugs. "Not really up to me, after all."

The four of them make their way up to the room. Kabet hesitates when he reaches it. "Should we knock?"

Rioz shrugs. Bran stares at the door blankly. Kabet decides to just knock.

As soon as he raps on the door, it flies open. Kioh is standing on the other side, looking much better than all of them.

"Decided to finally show up?" She arches an eyebrow at them and opens the door wider. "You guys are just in time. I was about to throttle both of them."

Salem steps into view. "You couldn't throttle me if you tried," she says playfully, smiling at Kioh.

Rioz elbows Lark. Lark shrugs.

Salem turns to all of them. "So," she says, smirking, "are we ready to get started?"

♂

Salem explains their immediate future to them. She remains vague about the rest of the plan. However, when pressed on it by Kioh she sighs and begins to tell them the plan.

"So we're not stealing the money?" Rioz asks, seeming affronted.

"No," Salem says. "We're pretending like we're stealing the money."

"But don't you want to rob her?"

"Of course," Salem nods. "And you're still getting your money, more of it, in fact."

"What are we stealing, then?" Bran asks. Kioh opens her mouth, likely to fill in, when there's a rap at the door.

Salem stands and strides over to the door. She seems to have been expecting it.

The door swings open and on the other side stands a tall, dark Zhidish girl, she can't be older than the rest of them.

Salem starts upon seeing her. So does Kioh.

"You're Mifeng?" Salem asks, backing away from the door slightly.

Mifeng squints at her. "You're the crazy sons of bitches who are going to steal the crown jewels? I want my wallet back, by the way. Pissants," Mifeng says in harsh and jagged Kendrak, her words stilted and uncomfortable in her mouth. She glances around the room. "Shit! Is that The Hare King?"

"That would be me, yes." Kabet shifts uncomfortably, having no idea what's going on.

She ignores him and turns towards Kioh. "My wallet. I want it back."

"I tossed it."

"Who tosses a wallet? Are you kidding me?"

Kioh glares at her, just barely. "I mean, I kept the money. And spent it."

Mifeng bristles. "I don't care about the money. I have money stacked to my chin. I want my wallet. It was a nice wallet."

"Buy a new one," Kioh suggests.

"*You* buy me a new one."

They're about to continue bickering when Rioz interrupts. "Did she say we're stealing the crown jewels? Did anyone hear that?"

"What are the crown jewels?" Kabet asks.

Mifeng whirls on him. "How do you not know what the crown jewels are?"

"I do not really care."

Salem steps in before Mifeng can pick another fight. "The crown jewels are a selection of forty different stones. Twenty are sapphires. Ten are emeralds, and ten are colored diamonds. Each of them have perfect clarity, stunning color, and each of them are all larger than your thumbnail.

"Combined, they are estimated at some price over thirty-six million *metlins*. In the jewelry they are currently set in, that price is elevated to over fifty million *metlins*. The diamonds and ten of the sapphires are set into the crown she had made for her coronation, which is, technically, a wolf mask. The other ten sapphires are set in a solid gold bracelet cuff. The emeralds are set in a similar piece."

Salem glances at all of them. "With a little extra outside help, we're going to steal them and frame Parev."

Mifeng nods. "But to fence jewels, you need a jeweler. And that's what I am."

Salem nods. "A very crooked jeweler." A pause. "And she has connections to people we need to get in touch with. Speaking of which—"

"She's on her way," Mifeng cuts her off.

"Not to be particular," Lark says, "but, how, exactly, are you supposed to pull this off?"

Salem sighs. "I've had most of this plan in motion since I was fourteen, just trust me on this?"

Kabet knows any sane person wouldn't trust Salem, but none of them are quite sane, so he nods.

Suddenly, there's yet another knock at the door. Mifeng brightens, and goes to open the door.

A girl who looks like a younger version of Lark steps through the door. They have the same skin tone and the same long, hooked nose. The obvious similarities end there, but they look quite similar.

This girl has hair, however. It's cropped at her chin.

Lark startles about five seconds after she walks in and says something in a language Kabet has never heard towards the girl. Her eyes stare fixed at the now closed door, not seeing anything but maybe hoping to.

The words she says are deep, spoken from the chest. The syllables are long and rounded, but they jab pointedly.

Kabet has familiarized himself with almost every dialect in Sunan. He taught himself Zhidish, Duskran, and Kendrak. He knows enough of Talirian to get by. Taaish escapes his grasp, but he knows what it should sound like, and it's not this.

The girl looks blankly at Lark. "My parents moved here before I was born. I don't know a lick of Evallian."

Lark's face falls. Kabet decides not to inquire about it.

Mifeng clears her throat and speaks. "Now that my associate is here, I think formal introductions are in order," she says. "I'm Mifeng Guang. This is my friend Moe. She doesn't have a last name."

"Salem Aotuo." Kabet has noticed she's stopped saying Oto.

Kioh nods at the two of them. "Kioh Taa."

"Rioz Tamen."

"Bran Fehner. I'm her brother," he points at Rioz.

"Jaz Westfen." Jaz gestures vaguely to himself. He's clearly exhausted.

"Kabet Oreh."

"Lark," Lark says. She also doesn't give a last name.

"Mira Elak." Kabet starts at Mira's voice. He barely even knew she was there. She fades seamlessly into the background. Stealthy in a way that he's really only seen from Kioh.

Salem hops off the small table she was sitting on. "Now that that pointless affair is over: shall we get started? We have quite a bit of work to do."

Everyone squares their shoulders and straightens. Something about Salem commands attention. Salem is not what Kabet would call a leader: she is not charismatic, well-spoken or inspiring. But there's something about the way she holds herself. The way she speaks.

He thinks it's because pain demands to be seen, in one way or another.

They all get to work.

⚥

It is late at night by the time Salem has laid out every detail she considers essential knowledge. It wasn't a lot: it's Salem. However all of them hounded her with questions and particulars, most of which she ignored.

The sun has vanished from the sky. The moon is a sliver in the night sky, backlit by countless stars.

Rioz and Jaz are passed out in the living room. Everyone else seems to be making use of themselves doing various things about the apartment. Kabet notices Bran is missing from the group, and a bolt of terror goes through him as he frantically scans the room for him.

The balcony door is open. Kabet didn't even know they had a balcony, despite seeing the flag that signified Salem's location hanging from it earlier. He sees Bran leaning on the railing, his short stature forcing him to stand on his toes to peer fully over the edge.

Kabet slips out the door and closes it behind him. He expects Bran to start at the noise, as he's always done. But he merely keeps his eyes trained on the ground below.

"What has happened to you?" Kabet asks, suddenly. The words slip from him as most things do: desperate, reckless, without permission.

Bran shrugs. Then sighs. "I guess I can tell you."

"Of course you can."

"I can't tell my own sister. But you're not my sister." Something in his expression seems amused. Kabet smiles at him. Bran shrugs, unprompted, then sighs again. "How long did it take you to get from the cabin to Canak?"

"Almost two weeks. Why?"

He laughs, but it's wrong. It's not humorous, but frigid and miserable. "Two weeks, huh? Bet they'd be surprised I lasted that long."

His face is pained and broken. "Who, Bran? Who?"

He shrugs. Kabet is tired of seeing him shrug. He doesn't want Bran to be unsure, any longer. "Everyone, I guess." He pauses. "You really want to know what happened to me, Kabet?"

His voice isn't accusatory. It's merely frank. Bran is giving Kabet a choice. He's offering him a way out.

Kabet doesn't want it. "I really do."

Bran nods and reaches behind his head. He unties the bandage, which Kabet now recognizes as part of his shirt. As it slips off Bran's face and into his hands, Kabet sees his ruined eye-socket. Two vicious slashes criss-cross his left eye. There is barely dried blood and still raw flesh. He winces, he can't help it. Bran doesn't seem to hold it against him.

"I got out today. The castle is a day's walk from Canak, luckily. Otherwise you probably would have left me for dead." Kabet doesn't correct him, Bran's not wrong. He's not right, either, though. "I'm not a doctor but I think seven of my ribs are broken. I can feel them."

"Bran—" Kabet starts, Bran cuts him off.

"Don't interrupt. You wanted to know." A pause. "I don't think I've eaten in three days. Before that they only fed me four times, most of it squished towards the end."

"Who—"

"I said don't interrupt!" he snaps. Then sighs and continues. "They gave me water seven times, I think. I haven't slept for days, at all. I haven't slept properly in... well, two weeks." He gnaws at a scab on his knuckle absentmindedly.

"He broke two of my fingers. Bad. I know it's bad because Salem broke my pinky and it didn't hurt that much. There's a hole in my foot. I'm not sure if the bullet's still in there. I should probably get that looked at." Kabet wants to say something, but he won't interrupt.

"Most of my skin is bruised. Somehow my gorgeous face escaped the beatings. But then my eye got cut out, so you know. Win some, lose some." Bran's starting to grow frantic and angry, but Kabet thinks he needs to be frantic and angry. "I was called a girl or a thing consistently for two weeks. That does things to my psyche, you know? Speaking of which, I've been hearing things. I didn't notice them until I got out but I keep hearing things. I keep seeing stuff, too. Like that fucking chair." Bran laughs and it shatters Kabet. Tears start to spill from his eyes. Bran continues on.

"But enough about what happened to me. What about the things I did? I killed fifty-five people. I melted my brother's face off. I bit someone's fingers off. I saw my parents. Then I killed my parents. I got a book! And then found out my birth was a science experiment ordered by the very person we're about to murder. I threw away my sickle because I'm pretty sure I'm dangerous enough without it. I'm afraid of myself now! What if I kill Rioz? Or you?" Bran is crying now. Kabet glances to the apartment beyond the balcony doors, but no one seems to be paying attention.

"So yeah, Kabet. That's what happened to me. Oh, and I think I have a concussion, but that's really more my fault." He sinks to the ground in a dejected, exhausted manner. He sits on the cold balcony and holds his head in his hands, tears streaking silently down his face. "The worst part is that I can't...I can't get out of there. I mean, I'm out, obviously. But I just keep waiting for the other shoe to drop. For me to wake up to someone kicking the shit out of me and figure out it was all a dream." He heaves a muffled sob.

"And I can't feel anything else. I can't feel relief or joy at escaping. I can't feel anger or amusement or sadness." Bran's lungs shake and he chokes back a scream in his throat. "All I am is fear, Kabet."

Kabet sits down across from Bran and takes his hands. Bran's eyes clear somewhat, and he turns his gaze to Kabet's.

"Bran, I say this in the kindest way possible, you are too impatient." He laughs and it seems wrecked, but fond. "You need medical attention, food, and sleep, in that order." Kabet grips his hands tightly. "There will be a time to process this. It will be hard and arduous. It will not be easy, and it will not be pleasant. But now is not that time."

Bran holds Kabet's gaze for a while, and then asks, meekly. "Does it get better?"

Kabet is unsure of how to respond. He thinks for a moment, and then says: "I lost my only family when I was ten years old. My life would be irrevocably different had she not died, and most of the time, I believe it would be better."

He tilts his head towards the sky, not letting go of Bran's hands. "You will grieve. You will mourn the future that you have lost. You will lose the person you once were." Kabet drops his gaze back to Bran. "You will suffer like you have never suffered before. But you must believe me when I tell you it will be worth it."

"How?"

Kabet smiles warmly at him. "We have no control over our lives, remember? While fate is not up to us, *we* are up to us. Meaning and exhilaration and love... these things are not inherent. They are not found. They are built. Life gives you the cards, but it is up to us what we do with them."

Bran smiles at Kabet, but there's still that haunted look in his eye. Kabet thinks it will be there for a while. "What if I have a really shit hand?"

He releases Bran's hands and stands up, offering to help Bran to his feet. Bran grabs Kabet's hand and Kabet pulls him until he stands.

"If the hand is not good...Cheat. Change the game. Build a house of cards." Kabet opens the door back into the apartment. "They are *your* cards, afterall." He pauses. "I was serious about getting you medical attention, you know," he says, gesturing into the apartment. Bran nods and walks in. Kabet isn't even sure how he's standing.

He thinks pain has likely become an afterthought in Bran's mind. He shudders to imagine what's at the forefront.

The door shuts behind them and Kabet notes that more people have fallen asleep on the bedrolls on the floor.

"Kabet?" Bran whispers.

"Yes?"

"Thank you. For everything."

"I would do it one thousand times, for you," Kabet says, cursing his reckless tongue. "I will do it as many times as you ask."

Bran stares at Kabet for a moment, then turns his head and nods tightly. "I may have to ask you a lot," he says, after a moment.

"That is perfectly alright with me."

CHAPTER TWENTY-FOUR

BRAN

△

BRAN HAS HAD THE journal for three days now, and still its presence grates on him. He reads it cover to cover twice. He's still not ready to share it with everyone else.

Bran's not even quite sure if he understands what he's read.

He picks it up off the floor where it sat while he stared at it. He then flips through it and reads some of the portions he underlined.

ENTRY NO. 1

Atina believes there to be a link between birth circumstances and abilities. Alice and I have been ordered to investigate if such a link exists. This journal will serve as documentation for our progress and research.

ENTRY NO. 4

I have done some more research and found several links between natural disasters and the frequency of children with these inexplicable abilities. More specifically: children born in the years of natural disasters have a higher rate of abilities.

I have included some newspaper clippings, and bits of Atina's research in Omari. Of course, the gifted in Omari are in the process of being terminated, which Atina says could take as long as ten years. Hopefully she takes power soon to decrease that time. She wants me to do further research.

The link between birth circumstances and abilities is currently tentative, at best. However, if there does prove to be a correlation, it will be a groundbreaking and useful discovery. Atina could breed armies of people with these abilities. Shka would be unstoppable. Shka could control the world if we could figure out how to harness this possible correlation.

I am eager to do further research. My wife is currently pregnant. The queen told me if we can make any discoveries before she gives birth, my child could be the first to bear witness to it.

There are pages upon pages of scientific jargon that Bran can't wrap his brain around between that entry and the next important one. He underlined the portions that made more sense to him: those that mentioned the birth circumstances and the powers born of them. He nearly vomits at the thought of the countless children that gave precedence to this information. Choking back disgust, he flips to the next entry he has marked.

ENTRY NO. 19

Alice gave birth to our child. A baby boy. We named him Tomas, after myself. We did our best to imbue him with powers. It was a hard decision to decide on what. We decided the ability to control and produce fire would be best. We induced labor while staying at an inn near the royal palace during the Kendren Festival of Fire. The energy in the air, we hope, is enough to imbue him with abilities, but we will see.

We're going to try to have another baby this same time next year. The festival is supposed to be especially heightened next year, if all goes according to Atina's plan. She's going to murder the royal family and take power alongside Viktor. Viktor is somewhat naive to certain aspects about Atina. I doubt that will be the case for long.

Also, Atina has halted the extermination of those blessed with abilities in Omari until she takes power. She says it is too long of a process to be carried out silently while she remains where she is at. She would much rather have a force of soldiers to carry out the genocide than the people she has now.

Bran shudders in disgust. Throughout the journal his father discusses the slaughter of children easily and without remorse. Bran does not feel bad for killing his parents. They were evil, without a doubt.

He still recoils at the thought, though. He doesn't want to acquire a taste for murder. Not like his parents. Never like his parents.

ENTRY NO. 30

Atina has taken Tomas, to the distress of Alice. However, I believe he is in good hands and have unwavering faith in my new queen, though she has been flighty since Viktor was killed as well. I pity her. Being at fault for his death cannot be easy.

Alice is pregnant again, also. All is on track for the new baby to be born during the festival, which is also near Atina's coronation. Tomas has shown an affinity for fire, proving our theory correct. Atina took him for further research, and I do not blame her. He is an exceptional child.

As for research, there is not much to report. Abilities have a direct correlation with birth circumstance, as Tomas has proven. Atina believes it has to deal with the mass energy of the people and world around. She says that celebration, natural disaster, and other events that collect a large group conscious to rally around an idea gives a child born in or around that idea power over what that idea holds. She also says it can happen on a much smaller scale, but that is more rare and depends more heavily on the individual. It all seems like speculation to me, frankly. Believable, but speculation nonetheless.

ENTRY NO. 34

Alice gave birth to our second child today. We are overjoyed. Everything went according to plan, and, hopefully, this child will show an affinity for fire just like Tomas.

She had a baby girl. We decided to name her Monroe.

Atina has been crowned, also. My last entry was the day before the coronation, but she is now queen of Shka.

The future holds much. This will be my last entry for a while. I will report back on the child's status regarding abilities later.

ENTRY NO. 35

Monroe shows an exceptional talent for fire summoning, control, and tolerance. We placed her in the fireplace while she was only nine months. Not a mark on her. Prior to that, she was summoning small flames before she could even walk. She is quite talented indeed.

This will be my last entry. I need to focus on aiding my queen and sharing my research with her.

The next entry is the actual last one. It's just as faded by time, but Bran knows for a fact that it was written four years after the previous one. There is not an entry number on it.

The queen has stated that she's resuming extermination efforts in Omari. She also wants any known blessed children wiped out. This includes Monroe. Atina has stated it will take roughly five years for the project to be complete, with the new soldiers stationed in Omari.

As the queen has aged, I have watched her descend into paranoia. She is now seeking to kill any gifted within her own country, not just Omari, which presents a threat of rebellion due to their ruined economy and our leech-like presence on them. I do not feel guilty: we will do what we must. But to kill your own citizens seems insane to me.

Atina is twenty-one, now. I was that age six years ago, right before all of this began. I am unquestioningly loyal, however I do worry if her sanity may be fraying. It cannot be easy. I worry about her.

She has made Tomas one of her future personal guards. I am very proud of him. He is currently undergoing rigorous training, though even I know he has not the natural affinity Monroe does. She is exceptional. Hence, the queen has ordered us to kill her.

We're leaving her in the forest tonight. Hopefully she dies, it would be impossible for her to live too long, especially in the cold. I don't want to bear witness to her death, but Atina has said she must die.

The next part is spaced out from the rest, clearly written after they abandoned Bran.

I want out of this whole abilities mess, frankly. I have lost two children to it now. I want to live the rest of my life in peace and power: serving my queen faithfully with my wife on our large estate.

I will serve my queen well, but I am done with this whole affair.

Bran thumbs through the book again. Then he shuts it, and lays it on the ground next to him.

Alice and Tomas Fehner tried to murder him. The people responsible for his existence wanted him to die on the whim of someone responsible for the deaths of thousands. Alice and Tomas Fehner were complicit in the deaths of thousands. Alice and Tomas Fehner were his parents.

Bran killed them. Reading the journal makes him feel better about that, at least. It makes him feel worse about a plethora of other things, however.

He was a science experiment designed to help hurt people. He was "bred" for the purpose of a scheme that would advance a genocide. That would bury the world and have Shka on top of the bodies left.

He feels guilt and shame at these facts. He feels reprehensible for the crimes of his parents.

Bran swallows those emotions. If he has learned one thing over the past couple of days, it is that emotions get him nowhere. He cried for days in that cell. His tears were not the thing to get him out.

Action must be taken if he wants to accomplish anything. If he wants to atone for the sins of his family, he will have to work at undoing the effects.

Bran scoops the book up, careful so none of the separate papers that were mashed into its pages fall out. Standing shakily from his bedroll, he straightens and walks over to where Salem is rooting about in the kitchen.

She turns when he approaches. Before she can say anything, Bran cuts her off.

"We're friends, Salem." She opens her mouth but he prattles on. "Hostile friends, yes. Friends that barely get along, but we're friends. We all are. And as friends I'm going to tell you some things. A lot of things."

Bran takes a deep breath in. "Kioh and you need to get your shit together. I don't know what that whole mess is, and frankly, I don't care. All I know is that Kioh is the nicest, warmest, most caring person here. She struggles to show it, but she cares more than any of us. She feels the deepest and hurts the most. She doesn't deserve you being cold to her. Not when she's only ever been warm."

Salem is gaping at him. He continues. "My sister thinks you're impressive. Hell, I think you're impressive. You're the most powerful fighter I've ever met. You can read minds! That's insane. Every single person you've hired thinks you've hung the moon whether that be a good or bad thing. Stop acting like we don't care about you. Stop acting like you don't care about us.

"I was tortured for two weeks and during those two weeks it gave me some time to think. Before, Salem, I thought you were insane and violent. But I've realized something." A pause. "When human beings are pushed to their limits, we don't break. I *wish* we broke, but we bend, instead. And, because of this, it is *impossible* to ever get back to how we once were. I will never be the same person. I will never be the same as I was before. I am twisted so out of shape, I would be unrecognizable to the person I was before. I understand, now, that you were never broken. You are only mourning. I'm telling you this as a friend, Salem: you will never be the same as you were before. You need to stop trying. You need to stop mourning and start living life as your new and unrecognizable self."

She tries to interrupt him, but Bran doesn't allow her to. "People care about you. About us. This strange little team you've assembled for this insane revenge plot? We work. I don't know how and I don't know why, but we work. I know your parents are dead, Salem. And that fact won't ever get any easier. Stop expecting it to."

He hesitates. "I know your family was murdered. I know that must hurt. I cannot fathom how much that must hurt. But you would never put your parents in pain, right? You would never hurt your family." Bran takes a deep inhale. "Your parents and brother are dead. You can't hurt them. I know this. You can still hurt us. We're your family, too. You have to know that."

Her eyes seem sad. For once, she doesn't seem angry. Just resigned. She's waiting for Bran to say more, he does. "Kabet is scholarly and impulsive. He's reckless and dangerous and bright. He's read more than all of us put together, and, for someone who thinks so much, he always acts first.

"Rioz is my sister. I love her more than life itself. She's all common sense. She takes the most direct and practical solution. She loves to laugh and have fun but she knows when to stop. She's everything she needs to be, exactly when it counts. She's not perfect, though. Far from it. She's hotheaded and overprotective and, when she lets her emotions rule her, they *rule* her." He pauses. "She will never yield to anything. Anything that gets in Rioz's way gets shouted out of existence." Salem laughs at this.

Bran smiles. She seems...different, now. Maybe it's him who's different. "Jaz is...Well. Jaz is Jaz. He's aloof at best and awkward at worst. He feels bad about something, what I don't know. But he's haunted by himself. He's funny and snide and grim. He's also lonely. He misses something he never really had. He acts like he's dark and brooding, but he's just scared. Scared of a lot of things. Of everything."

Salem smiles knowingly. "You don't seem to like him too much."

"I like him fine. He's just a little too fascinated with my sister, if you know what I mean." Salem laughs. Bran smiles. He really doesn't mind Jaz. "Kioh is a famous thief. She's *the* famous thief. But for all of that, she's probably the most morally upstanding one out of us. She's kind and warm. She cares immensely about all of us. About *you*. She's energetic to the point of being insane. She's curious about anything and everything. Kioh is also sad. She doesn't like it here. She doesn't like her life. She's very prideful but she finds it hard to take pride in herself. In who she is today."

Salem nods. Her eyes seem far off and forlorn. "And you, Salem." She looks at Bran again. "You're more than you think. For one, you're funny. You don't realize it but you have a way of viewing and interacting with the world that is amusing to an outside view. And you're smart. Well, witty. I don't think you know how to do math, but you're cunning." She laughs. Bran's voice drops as he speaks the next part. "And you're very angry. And you're very sad. But you're also so many other things. Other things that matter more than your anger, and your sadness."

Salem seems to think about that for a while. After a beat, she nods. She's then silent for a long moment before speaking. "Hey, Bran?"

"Yeah?"

"You're not flirting with me are you?"

He lets out a startled laugh. "No! No. I like men."

"Good," she tells him. "Because I don't." She pauses. "You're very good at reading people, you know?"

"I just think I have too much time on my hands." Bran hesitates. "I have something I think you should see," he says, remembering the journal in his sweaty hands. He hands it to her.

"What is this?"

"A journal that belonged to my parents."

Confusion flashes across her face. "Your parents? But —"

"You were informed that I was kidnapped, right?"

"Yeah, what does that have to do with..." She trails off and her eyes widen in surprise.

"A revelation, yes. What's in the journal is even more shocking." Bran shrugs. "Some of it made no sense, but I know one thing. It belongs to you."

"Why?"

"Because your tragedy is the one outlined within the pages." He shrugs, again. "And because I don't really want it."

She nods at that. Bran is glad she understands. "I should probably go read this," she says.

"Most definitely."

She turns to leave, but hesitates. "Earlier, when you were listing everyone's flaws and such?" Her voice is questioning.

"Yeah?"

"What about you?"

I want to be known. I want to be loved. He said that, once. He's not so sure now. Before, Bran would have jumped at the opportunity to share something close to him. Now he feels as though he must guard it with everything he has. Bran doesn't want to be known. He doesn't want to be loved. He wants to be left the hell alone.

Bran is starting to understand where Salem is coming from.

He shrugs, again. "What about me? There's not much to tell."

She frowns, but nods and walks away.

Bran let go of who he was before. He only hopes Salem can do the same.

Δ

Bran's fingers are breaking, again. Tomas is snarling down at him. He can't make out the words, he's delirious with fear. They're reaching into his mouth with pliers, again. The smell of burning, sizzling flesh reaches his nose and he retches. Did he do that? He can't remember.

Bran still can't make out any words. It sounds familiar, he recognizes what they're saying, but can't put them together into thoughts. His mental stability is degrading with each second. Tomas is snarling down at him. He's not a girl. He knows this. He's a boy. Why is this important, again? His fingers are breaking and everything hurts.

Suddenly, words pierce his ears. They are as unwelcome as not being able to make out anything at all.

"You're going to be just like your big brother, dear Bran." Bran realizes he's having a nightmare. Tomas never called Bran by his real name. "Just like me." He doesn't like the sound of that, even if it is a nightmare. Bran screams. He cannot stop screaming. He keeps screaming.

Bran wakes up when his hand collides with something firm.

There's a vague noise of pain, and then Kabet is looming over him. Bran feels tears streaking down his face, and quickly blinks them back. Kabet looks down at him worriedly.

"Are you alright?" he asks.

"Yeah," Bran lies. "Sorry for punching you."

"It was more of a slap." He grins.

He laughs. It feels awful. It feels worse than screaming.

"Did I wake anyone else up?" Bran asks. Kabet shakes his head. "Go back to sleep, Kabet."

"Do you really want me to?"

He doesn't respond. Kabet doesn't go back to his bedroll. Bran sits up and rubs his eyes, curling into himself. He doesn't want to do this, right now.

Kabet sighs. He looks sad and weary. It's foreign on his mischievous face. "It is not bad to need people."

Bran feels rage and sadness contort his face. "I didn't need people while I was being *tortured* and I don't need people now. No one was there for me, then, Kabet. I don't *want* anyone here for me now."

Kabet looks at Bran, his face morose and melancholy. "You assume I want to help only for your own sake. I care, but I am selfish too, you know?"

Bran ignores him. He tries desperately to fight down whatever emotions that are trying to surface right now. There's something burning in his throat, and he will only let it out in the form of fire.

"Bran," Kabet says, "please just—"

Bran doesn't let him finish. "Listen, Kabet," he snarls. "I'm not asking for your help, so please do not try to provide it. I can handle this on my own."

Kabet's nostrils flare indignantly. "I will not let you." Bran is about to snap at him again but he cuts him off. "You are not as good at hiding your pain as you seem to think. You must think me cruel, Bran, if you think I will bear witness to your suffering and do nothing. I will not do that to you. I will not do that to myself. I am not as callous as you seem to believe." His face has grown taut with anger and it's the first time Bran has seen anything like it on him.

"My best friend, my family, my Adena: she died when I was ten years old. I clutched her diseased body in my arms while she wasted away. I felt her last breath stutter out of her ruined lungs. I watched her go from bright and stunning, to a frail and fragile slip, to dead." Kabet's lips are pulled in grimace. Bran can tell he hates talking about this. "I should have died, too. The plague was highly contagious and almost always fatal."

Kabet frowns. "But here I am," he says, bitterly. "I am here, and I will not allow myself to lose another friend. Not to something like this."

"I'm not asking for your help," Bran hisses, more pain than anger.

"So ask!" he snaps. "I told you you could ask. You said you would. So *ask*."

"No."

He throws his hands up. "Why not?"

Panic clutches Bran. Terror seeps through his veins. "Because it's dangerous to be weak," he chokes.

Kabet's face softens. "You cannot live your life in fear. Not of the ones who care about you." He sighs. "I will not pretend that I understand everything that is going on in your head. I will not pretend to even understand a fraction of it. But one thing I know with certainty is that if you push away every person who cares, is that, soon, there will be no one left." He pauses. "I am not sure if asking for help is weak. It may be. But if you face everything alone, then one day, there will be something that has friends."

Bran turns away from him, but he still can feel Kabet's eyes on him. "So, Bran, ask for help. Humans are stronger together." He hesitates, then adds, voice lilting, "Even Salem asked for help."

The tension in the room dissipates. Kabet has the miraculous quality of making everything feel lighter. Bran laughs. He turns back towards Kabet. "Okay. You win this round." He's suddenly exhausted. "Can we go back to sleep now?"

Kabet laughs. "I was very much hoping you would say that."

The two of them lay back down. Kabet scoots his bedroll closer to Bran's.

"Can't believe you compared me to Salem."

"You deserved it."

Bran shuts his eyes and dreams of nothing in particular.

Chapter Twenty-Five

KIOH

CANAK IS A BIG city, nearly the size of Rowak, but it still surprises Kioh to find out they have a beauty district. She passes through it while pick-pocketing rich people who pass her by on the streets of the well-off district. Her interest is piqued, to say the least. She spends the rest of her day out searching the district for a Taahuan hair-braider. To Kioh's shock, she actually finds one.

The braider is part of a larger establishment, and has a little shop tucked away between the two larger establishments of the same salon. They also boast traditional beauty techniques unique to cultures that are decidedly not Duskran.

There's a small sign signifying that she's open and listing the services she provides. Kioh opens the creaky door with the large window and steps carefully inside.

There's a woman writing on a notepad behind the counter. She has dyed green hair which is pulled into several tight *Tulaa* knots. Kioh's heart aches at the sight of it. The woman's eyes are dark brown, darker than Kioh's, as is her skin. Plus, Kioh's face is sharper but still, her heart hurts at the familiarity of it all.

The woman seems almost surprised to see Kioh. "Hello! It is not often I see new faces in here." She's speaking in Taaish and the authenticity of her words almost makes Kioh weep. There's a broad grin on her face, and her words are innocent enough but Kioh catches her meaning and laughs.

"It can't be fun living in Canak," she responds in Taaish. The words greet her like old and charming friends. "I live in Rowak, so I'm not one to talk much. But at least the stores there stay open later than dusk."

The woman laughs, warm and fond. Kioh understands how she feels. It's alienating and impossibly lonely to be in a country full of people who are nothing like her. It's a welcome relief to see a face similar to hers. "Are you from the coast?" she asks. Kioh nods, grinning at the fact she recognizes her dialect. "Where at?"

"Port City," Kioh responds. "My mother owns a boat and runs her own crew." She's not sure if that's true anymore, but her mother lives preserved in her heart. She can't be sure of anything except of how she used to know her.

"An ambitious woman!" she exclaims. Kioh has forgotten how expressive her culture is. How expressive she used to be before it was squashed out of her. "Would you like an appointment?" the woman asks.

Kioh beams. "Does tomorrow work?"

"I have one other appointment, a regular, but I can likely do two at once," she grins. "I *am* that good. You may have to wait a bit, though. What are you hoping to have done?"

Kioh remembers the thick, tight braids her mother used to wear her hair in on fishing trips. How she would take a day to go get them done before she left, to protect her hair from the elements. Kioh doesn't know the actual name of them, everyone in Port City just called them port braids. Sometimes people would braid yarn into them.

Her mother had laughed when she suggested it. *"They are to protect my hair from the seawater. If the yarn gets soaked, that defeats the entire purpose!"* Kioh blushed and told her mother she just thought they looked pretty. She agreed with her.

"I only know them as port braids, I'm sorry," Kioh tells her.

"No worries, I've heard the phrase, however there are several kinds." She pulls a thick book down from the shelf near her head and flips to a beginning portion. She beckons Kioh over.

The book is filled with different sketches of different kinds of braids. Kioh realizes that the whole book is braids. She glances up. Sure enough, there's other books for different types of hairstyles.

She remembers her mother taking her to hair stylists when she was young.

"There are thousands of ways to wear hair. There are thousands of kinds of hair," she tells Kioh one day, on the way to her new regular hair stylist. *"It can be arduous to acknowledge all the different styles, the best hair stylists put in the effort. The best will have thousands of questions."* A funny look crosses her face. *"Never get your hair done by someone who is not Taahuan."* She laughs. *"I made that mistake once, in my youth."*

Kioh nods towards the pages. "May I?"

She beams at her. "So polite! Of course you can."

She begins to flick through the pages, looking for something that catches her eye. It's overwhelming, frankly. Her natural upkeep, though extensive, is minimal, compared to this. Kioh cringes thinking about how her hair must look, right now. Their month long mountain journey can't have been kind to it.

Kioh sighs and turns towards the woman.

"What's your name?" she asks, feeling rude for not asking earlier.

"Juqula, you may call me Juqu. And yours?"

She hesitates, unsure whether she should give her real name. "Kioh," she says, ultimately.

"Am I to keep that to myself?" she asks, perception uncanny. Kioh smiles, then nods. "I am excellent at keeping secrets. Thank you for sharing yours. Now, did you decide on a style?"

"I need something strong," Kioh says. "Something that won't get in my way too much, and something durable. Not a lot of upkeep. I can come in for the foreseeable future to get them redone, but I am not sure when I will be leaving, so nothing that is too terrible if I'm late on care." A pause. "Maybe something with yarn?"

Juqula nods at Kioh, jotting something down on her notepad. "How many braids? How thick? What kind of maintenance?"

Kioh dutifully replies to all her questions, only for Juqula to rattle off more. Kioh remembers what her mother told her, and there's little doubt in her mind that this woman is one of the best.

Once finished, the woman tucks the sheet of paper she'd been writing on away. "I'll see you tomorrow. Bring friends!" she says.

Kioh smiles. "I don't have any Taahuan friends."

"Bring them anyway, they'll find something on this street they like."

Kioh nods and exits the shop. For the first time in a while, she feels at peace with the world and herself.

❦

Kioh manages to convince everyone to go to the beauty district with her for her appointment. Rioz, Kabet, and Lark are the only two who actually seem excited at the prospect. She thinks Mifeng would like the idea, but she has a life in Canak, unlike the rest of them. Everyone else decides to tag along anyway. It's not like there's much else going on.

Salem stands awkwardly next to Kioh while Kioh tries to make her hair as presentable and undamaged as possible. Salem keeps opening her mouth and closing it, trying to say something but clearly struggling.

"I'm not a very nice person," Salem says, finally. "I'm not a very nice person and I'm not very easy to be around." She hesitates. "What I'm trying to say is—" She cuts herself off. "I guess I'm—" She stops again. She opens and closes her mouth a few times like a fish, again. Kioh tries not to laugh. She fails.

As Kioh bursts out into giggles, Salem sighs. "Salem," Kioh says, out of breath. "You don't have to apologize."

Salem glares at her momentarily before dropping her gaze. "I feel like I should," she says softly. Then, softer, "I made you cry."

"I didn't take it personally." A pause. "That's a lie, I took it very personally, but I know you didn't mean it."

Salem frowns. "I still shouldn't have said it."

"That's true. But the very next morning you let me teach you how to cook, no matter how bad you were at it. So I know you didn't mean it."

Salem shrugs, falling back to her normal cold self. "Still," she says, "I'm sorry."

Kioh grins at her. "Yeah, I know." She quirks an eyebrow at Salem. "Now, are you going to come get your hair done with me, like a real criminal, or are you going to apologize all day?" She breezes out of the bathroom's open door and tugs her shoes on.

"I don't even *have* hair," Salem protests.

Kioh can't help but grin. "That's cowards talk."

❦

It takes hours for her hair to get finished. It basically takes all day. She doesn't mind it, though. It's familiar and commmfortable and she chats in Taaish with Juqula and the other client, who's name she learns is Zaliha.

Kioh's friends muck around the rest of the district while her hair is braided. They come back a few hours later, like she told them to, just as she finishes up paying Juqula.

Juqula gives her a mirror to examine her new hair with. Her hair has been braided into six thick braids, a severe part down the middle of her head. Two large braids rest on either side, with two smaller braids underneath each. Dark red yarn has been braided seamlessly into the ends. They fall just past Kioh's shoulders.

Kioh grins widely at Juqula. "They look wonderful, thank you so very much." She pauses, and then says, in very bad Duskran, "These are my friends." She sweeps an arm towards the large group of people who have amassed in the small waiting area.

Juqula hums thoughtfully. "They seem very strange," she finally says, in Taaish.

Kioh laughs. "You can't even imagine," she tells her. Juqula laughs with her, and her heart feels full.

They all leave the salon with different destinations in mind. Lark and Mira split off to go look at a large jewelry store, Rioz drags Jaz and Bran towards another jewelry store, one that sells predominantly Talirian products. Kabet shrugs apologetically and follows Bran.

Kioh and Salem stand there for a while. Both silent.

"There's nothing you want to do?" Kioh asks.

"Not really."

Kioh ponders for a moment. "This one has some Zhidish beauty," she says, pointing to the larger store next to Juqula's shop.

Salem considers this for a moment. "Yeah, alright."

The two of them head into the store with little fanfare. Salem seems to be quieter than normal. Kioh talks a lot about Juqula and, eventually, Taahua itself.

"It's a very nice country. It's warm and bright and there's so much good food. Not that you would understand the value of that." Salem scowls at her when she says this. Kioh prattles on. "I mean, I'm probably just nostalgic. But it's my *home*. I want to go back."

"I understand. I want to visit Zhidi, even though I've never been. It feels close to my heart, somehow."

Kioh nods, feeling somber about Taahua and the home she abandoned. Then she realizes Salem referenced the future, which she almost never does. She decides not to point it out.

The two of them wander for a while. They're approaching the end of the store when Salem stops in her tracks.

"Oh," she says, voice soft and hesitant.

Kioh turns her gaze to where Salem's looking, and sees some pieces of small metal, arranged in different sets and sizes. The sign for them is in Zhidish, and Salem is staring at them transfixed.

"What are they?"

Salem blinks. "My mother used to wear them. You put them over your nails."

An elderly Zhidish woman seems to apparate out of thin air and begins speaking with Salem. She smiles at the woman and says something back. The woman beams and replies cheerily, but Salem frowns.

"What'd she say?"

"The nails are for great female fighters. They've been somewhat commodified, though. They're a very old tradition that female warriors employed a long time ago. She asked if my mother was a warrior. I said yes. She asked me if I wanted any."

"Do you?"

She frowns, again. "I don't know." She then speaks to the woman in Zhidish again. They have a long conversation and Kioh takes the time to sort through the nails.

She finds a set with rounded but still lethal points. They're a shiny black, but they don't look painted. Kioh thinks they're made out of iron.

Kioh nudges Salem when she stops speaking and her face softens, nearly imperceptibly.

"Those look exactly like the ones my mom wore."

"What can I say? I'm gifted." Salem takes one of them from her and hands it to the woman, who nods courteously and bustles off.

There's a beat of comfortable silence before Salem breaks it. "It looks nice," she says.

"What does?"

"Your hair."

Kioh is silent for a long moment; contemplating. "I think that's the first time you've ever complimented me." Her voice is cheery and playful. She then spots the woman coming back with the nails.

Salem scoffs. "It is not." She pauses for a moment, then pales. "It can't be."

"I think one time you told me I had a nice fighting style while you were kicking my ass."

She elbows Kioh, but there's no anger behind it. The Zhidish woman hands Salem a small cloth bag, which jingles gently when she takes it. She then explains something, and hands Salem a paper handwritten in Zhidish. She points to various parts of the paper as she talks.

Salem nods, hesitates, and then bows stiffly. The woman smiles and bows back. Salem hands her a fistful of *drunes*, then turns to Kioh. "I haven't done that since I was eleven," she says, seeming awed.

"What does it mean?"

"You're supposed to bow whenever favors are exchanged." She pauses. "There's different rules of courtesy for different situations, but that's the most important one. Whenever an equal exchange is made, you bow. That's pretty much the only one I remember." Her voice is sad.

They walk out of the store together. "Well," Kioh says, "you could always learn them again."

"I suppose that's true," she concedes. Kioh counts it as a win.

They meet back up with the other six heathens Kioh calls her friends, and the eight of them wander around the city for a bit. At some point, everyone realizes they're in dire need of new clothing. They find the largest apparel store, and spend the rest of their trip cleaning it out.

All of them head back to the apartment under the cover of evening, bags laden with various finds. Kioh's nervous hands snatch a few wallets and watches on the way back. Rioz notices her doing so and gives her a curious look.

"Nervous habit," she says, just as she nabs another wallet out of a nice woolen coat.

"That's an awfully nasty nervous habit," she prods. There's no judgment behind it, though. They're all crooks.

Kioh slips the money out of the leather wallet and drops it discreetly to the ground. She pockets the money. "I guess so."

"Why do it?"

Rioz stares at her intently. Kioh's not sure if she has an answer for that question, anymore. "Because I'm good at it," she says. "And, sometimes, when you're good at something, it's hard to be good at anything else."

❧

As night falls and drags into the wee hours, Kioh learns more about her fellow criminals. That's been happening a lot, lately. She learns about their cultures and family and the lives they left behind. She also learns inane things, like the long lists of what foods Rioz won't eat and what books Kabet doesn't like.

Rioz is laughing at something Jaz said when she turns to all of them and asks a question that Kioh never really thought she'd hear asked.

"So we've all killed someone, right?"

Everyone nods. Kioh assumed as much. "Actually," she says, "I've never killed anyone."

Everyone except Salem gapes at her. She knows all their secrets and assumes nothing. "Really?" Bran wonders. "But you run a gang!"

"Of thieves."

Kabet stares at her. "You said you were a criminal, no?"

Kioh laughs. "Last I checked stealing was a crime."

"What have you stolen?"

"Anything and everything, Kabet. I have a business to run, after all."

Salem finally chimes in. "If you can name a crime, Kioh's committed it. The only exception to that rule is murder."

Kioh nods sagely. "I find it distasteful."

Everyone laughs at this. She feels a fondness in her heart for these people. It's almost startling, how close to family they've become.

"Enough about me, though." Kioh waves a dismissive hand. "What are your crimes and offenses?"

"Directly, I have only ever killed three people," Kabet says. "All were in defense of myself. However, indirectly..." He trails off, then sighs. "I am sure that number is far higher." He pauses. "That is the cost of fighting a war, no matter how you fight, I suppose."

Jaz, surprisingly, pipes up. "It's not about who you kill or how many. It's about the weight of what you've done. Kabet, you're leading a country through a revolution. The good of that far outweighs any misdeeds you may have accidentally caused."

Kabet tries to respond but Rioz cuts him off with quick, sharp words. "Who did you kill, Jaz? What weight do you bear?"

The room grows cold at that. It is silent for a long moment, as sadness seems to pour out of Jaz.

He exhales a long and shaky breath. "My best friend," he says. "It was an accident." He doesn't cry. Kioh has known Jaz for a while, and she can tell, like her, he will not cry easily.

Rioz stares at him. Not harshly, but not softly either. "What happened?"

Jaz is quiet and for a moment Kioh thinks he won't answer. "He tried to leave without me," he whispers. "He tried to leave me there, with *them*. We said we'd leave together and—" He chokes, then continues, calmly. "We were by the cliffs. He was on the edge and I...I forced him to jump off. He did. By the time I realized what I was doing it was too late. He was dead." Jaz looks down at his hands in his lap. His pain is suffocating. "He was my best friend."

"Just your friend?"

Jaz holds his head in his hands. "I don't know. Maybe more. I killed him. I can't know."

The room is quiet with mourning for a moment. The weight of what they've done weighs on all of them. Some more than others.

"I killed some guy," Rioz says, breaking the sacred silence. "I don't feel bad about it."

Jaz snorts and looks up at her with a kind of fondness Kioh has only ever seen between people who've known each other for years. She looks back at him, just as fond.

"Who'd you kill?" Mira asks.

"A nobleman."

"That's hardly a crime. A favor, maybe. Not a crime."

Everyone laughs. Kioh knows there's more that Rioz isn't telling them, that she's just as haunted by her crimes in a different way. Kioh doesn't ask. Some things are better left in darkness; at least until the sun rises.

The conversation moves on. Kioh notices Salem and Bran look especially morose. Salem, she expected, but she wonders what events transpired for Bran to lose his eye. For him to grow quiet and cold.

By the time everyone is ready to go to bed, the streets outside are practically silent, and the lights from neighboring buildings extinguished.

Salem looks at all of them for a moment, the card game they were all playing long forgotten. Kioh was winning, of course. And cheating. Then Salem speaks. "We're burning Atina Parev's house down, tomorrow night."

"Isn't that a little too on the nose?" Kioh japes.

Salem smirks. "Probably. But maybe it will jog her memory." A pause. "I entered the queen's army when i was fourteen. I spent three years gathering intel and preparing myself for whatever she can throw at me. I hated every second of it." She pauses again, considering. "I didn't use my real name when I enlisted. I want to see if she remembers me and the thousands like me who she killed. Burning her house down accomplishes two things. It makes her paranoid. And," she smiles menacingly, "it gives me a feeling of catharsis."

Kioh snorts. Salem continues. "This will be the only job we show our faces during. Kioh, you're not coming."

"Why not?"

"This plan hinges almost entirely on you. If the queen knows your face, which she doesn't at the moment, it will not work." Salem looks grim. "You can do other jobs, we need to get our name out there. But never your face or anything identifying."

"Why not?" Kioh echoes.

"As you all know, we are going to rob Atina Parev." They all nod. "We're going to do it in front of every royal in Shka, with the whole country watching.

Because not only are we robbing her," Salem's face splits into a wide, sadistic smile, "we're doing it on the most important day of the year."

She looks around the room. Mifeng and Moe are the only ones absent. "So get ready, my friends. Because in four months, The Wolf Queen's hide is mine."

CHAPTER TWENTY-SIX

SIX

ATINA

ATINA AWAKES TO THE smell of smoke and the sounds of fighting.

As she jolts upright and pulls a robe on, she has a horrible ominous feeling. Like a guillotine about to drop.

Atina files it away. A person like her does not reach a position like she has by being dismissive of threats. A person like her gets to where they are by crushing and killing anything that stands in their way.

She rushes through her quickly burning house. The estate is large enough that the fire hasn't quite reached her yet. As she runs towards where the fight seems to be coming from, she ignores the fire: she's not afraid of a little heat.

One of the personal guards Atina hired goes down just as she reaches the scene. A small, slight girl stabs him ruthlessly in the throat and bares her teeth in a vicious smile. There are four people behind her. None of them have any sort of disguise.

Confident brats, Atina thinks, as she takes in all of their faces. She will recreate their likenesses later. She recognizes one of them.

No one in the world has an artistic eye like her. No one in the world can do what she does. She is unparalleled in almost every way.

"We have an audience, Truth," the other girl says. She's Talirian, Atina notes by the piercings in her face.

The one called Truth, the one she recognizes, dispatches another guard by stabbing him right in the forehead. Atina hears the wet crunch of bone as Truth's dagger goes right into his brain.

"I'm aware," Truth nods curtly towards the Talirian girl and turns towards Atina. "Remember me?"

Though Atina knows her face, she does not know where it's from. "Should I?" she snarls. Atina is not afraid. She will always be cautious, but never afraid.

"Look at me, Atina." Atina starts slightly at Truth's casual use of her real name. She made sure that name was buried the year she took the throne. She pulled every mention of it. Erased it from history. She hasn't heard that name in almost seventeen years. "I said *look at me*, Atina," she hisses. Atina decides to listen.

She nods. "Good," she says. "Memorize my face. Become intimately familiar with it. Because this face, this burned and ugly face, will be your undoing and your end." She considers something. Then, faster than Atina can think, the girl is clutching her by the collar of her robe.

Truth stares into her eyes. Atina senses something in this girl. Something very, very dangerous. Something worthy of her fear.

Before Atina can act, Truth raises a dagger and crashes it towards her head. A sharp pain flares through the side of her head and she makes a strangled noise just as she hears the wet smack of something hitting the hard floor.

Truth steps quickly away from Atina before she can retaliate. She kneels and picks something up off the ground. It's her ear, Atina realizes.

"I'm keeping this," Truth says. "Maybe I'll cook it and eat it." She laughs, wicked and malicious.

She places the severed ear in her bag and stands back up. "As you know, I am Truth." She points. "That's Howl. That is The Empty One. Our dear friend Dragon." As she points at this boy, his body alights in acid green flame. Atina almost takes a step back. Almost. "And that is The Hare King. We're missing our Grifter, sadly."

"Right now," she says, "you probably don't recognize any of us. Maybe me. Maybe Hare. But either way, we are not important enough for you to even think about. However, you would do well to start. Because the six of us? We're going to ruin you. Deliberately and slowly."

"Atina Parev, I will be your end." Truth pauses and starts walking back away from Atina, out of the burning house. She speaks with her back turned to Atina. "I would use what little time you have left to reflect on the choices and the actions that have led you to this point. I would eat the finest foods and live the greatest life. Because there's not much of your life left. So," she turns back around and the five of them crackle with malevolence, "live the greatest life you can. Take the four months you have left and try to make up for your miserable, pathetic existence. For, in four months, your ugly fucking head will hang on my wall."

"And there it will stay until I get tired of it. And then I will throw it out. You will be absolutely nothing, Parev. Even the maggots won't want you. Isn't that terrifying? I would bet for a person like you that being nothing would be a horrible sensation." She looks down at the knife in her hand. The one she cut Atina's ear off with. She wipes the leftover blood on her pants.

"Every story has a villain, Parev." She throws her head back and laughs. It's cold and empty and confident beyond measure. "You should question what horrible choices you made to have me be yours."

They turn and walk away. And for the first time in seventeen years, Atina is very, very afraid.

ACKNOWLEDGMENTS

I firstly would like to acknowledge myself, because I did most of the work. However, there is no way in hell I could've done it by myself. So without further adieu, thanks to these people:

Junjie, for being one of my biggest fans and the cover art.

Lou, for being one of my biggest fans and the constant stream of fanart she provides.

My editors, Raven and Gabe.

Pepper, for their amazing support and the Salem cannibalism art. (It's a joke, don't worry.)

Xiafei, for his unending support and articulating myself better than I ever could.

Wini, for being my friend and reading this mess when it was still in second person.

All my friends who didn't read it, but supported me anyways.

You, for taking a chance on (what I believe to be) a wonderful book.

About Author

Esmae Shepard is an avid reader and frenetic author. She can either be found working a dead end job or relaxing in her studio apartment. Prismo (her service dog, not the Wish Master) is her best friend and constant companion. *The Domino Children* is her debut novel.

You can find her on her personal Tumblr @corahawes.

You can also find her on her professional (and rarely used) Twitter @ragingmae.

9 781087 936307